OWLS AND OTHER ASSASSINS

OWLS AND OTHER ASSASSINS

A LOVE STORY

MEGAN MOORES

For David

1

GEMMA

On a steamy Tuesday in late August, I woke up sure of several things: I had no job, no love, no family, and no pants. I'd spent the long weekend ordering takeout and watching movies in just a t-shirt and underwear, snuggling up to the only other living thing in my house: a spider plant I'd named Louis. I was spectacularly alone, and that was fine with me.

Exactly one week later, I was surrounded by birds, bugs, and boars. I was also in the company of a Swedish sex god, killer owls, and a stalker gone rogue. And I still wasn't wearing pants.

I'd almost missed Rava's call. My phone chirped and vibrated and I dug through the couch cushions in search of it. I'd fallen asleep on my scratchy too-short sofa and never made it to my bed. I tried to sound chipper when I saw Rava's name on the screen.

"Hello, my dearest and oldest friend."

"Gemma, were you asleep?"

"How's life in The Big Apple?" I cleared my throat mid-sentence. So graceful.

"You were asleep."

"Why would I be sleeping at noon?" I sat up, got a head rush, and flopped back down.

"Make some coffee and pack your bags. I don't know the exact forecast for where you'll be in Sweden but expect mild days and cool nights. Maybe some rain. You leave on Saturday."

"Awesome. I'll brush up on my Swedish and pack my clogs. Why are you *really* calling me?"

Rava was not in the mood for my jokes. "If you don't want the interview assignment of the year, then fine. Stay on your scratchy couch, in your Air Supply t-shirt, with cookie crumbs in your butt crack. Just don't say I never did anything for you."

I waited for the punchline, but Rava remained silent. Also, how did she know about the cookies? "Could you repeat that?"

Rava sighed. "Erik Nillson was set to interview Jonas Hellgren tomorrow here in New York at the *Profile* offices. But Erik had some kind of family emergency involving his brother, a Ferris wheel, and a hot air balloon. Don't ask questions because I don't have answers. I think everyone survived, though some limbs might need to be reattached."

"I heard you say Jonas Hellgren," I said, "but I'm not sure I can move past this tragic State Fair scenario."

"Hellgren has a new movie coming out for the first time in a decade, and I think he has a book that's coming out, too."

"The movie's called *Vanishing Echo*, and the book features his drawings," I said, sitting up again but without the head rush this time. I brushed the crumbs off the front of my Air Supply t-shirt.

"Right. I knew you'd be up on all things Jonas Hellgren, which is why I suggested that you'd be the right person for the job."

My mouth felt arid, and the first prickles of a cold sweat rushed across my skin. "What job is that?" I asked.

"Interviewing Jonas Hellgren, Gemma," she said, obviously irritated. I lay back down and tried to catch my breath. "There's no time for you to prepare for an interview tomorrow, so we're delaying it a few days. Also, Hellgren got cold feet when he heard that Erik had to back out. I think he only initially agreed to do it because Erik is also Swedish."

"Jonas Hellgren doesn't do interviews. He hasn't spoken to the press in seven years . . . and two months and like three days, depending on leap years. In fact—"

"Save it for your prep," Rava said. "He tried to cancel altogether, but his agent wasn't having it—Jonas is required to do press for this movie. So, we're attempting something new. I told Pricilla you'd be perfect. We want to try a more literary profile piece. A combination interview, travel diary, conversational biography type of thing. I don't really know, and I don't think the board does, either. We don't want to lose this piece, so get off your ass, pack your bags, and check your email for flight details."

"Why me?"

"Why *not* you?"

"No, really. Why me?"

"You're a published author. You've proven that you can construct a compelling narrative and that you're not afraid to go off the beaten path."

I felt like there was an ellipsis at the end of her sentence. "And . . . ?"

Rava sighed. "And . . . Pricilla owes me a favor."

I let it sink in. I had a thousand questions, but none of them made the transition from racing thoughts to actual words. Rava waited out my silence.

"Can I bring my Air Supply shirt?" I asked.

"The one with the hot air balloon? Sure. Think of it as a sign from the angels."

"I think it's actually a parasail, because—"

"Whatever. The details are in the email. I'll see you Saturday."

Rava ended the call.

I'D SEEN all of Jonas Hellgren's movies. His more recent American films were easy to stream, but the Swedish films he'd made earlier in his career were harder to get. I'd purchased an all-region DVD player and ordered his movies from Europe, and they'd been worth the wait. His performances were stellar, in my opinion. He infused sharp darkness into his villain parts, showed up with humor and light into the arthouse films, and exuded pure sex appeal in his leading man roles.

I knew a lot about him without having to do an internet search. I got out a notebook and jotted down the information I knew off the top of my head:

Jonas Alexander Hellgren. 48-years old, born in Gothenburg, Sweden on December 16th. Only child. Sagittarius sun, Scorpio moon, Cancer rising. Hobbies include drawing and hiding from the paparazzi. Father is Anders Hellgren, play-

wright and stage director. Mother is Astrid, actor and painter. Wife was Anna Eklund, who died eight years ago at age 33. First Runner-up for Sexiest Man Alive at age 38.

Filmography by age, up until he stopped working:

22 - Runners (Swedish)
26 - The Alchemy of Solitude (Swedish)
30 - Hothouse (Lead Role, Swedish)
32 - Ice Walkers (American)
35 - Grand Gothic (American)
36 - Base Camp (American)
37 - Neon Nightmare (American)
39 - City of Devils (American)
39 - The Stone Path (Play, NYC)

THERE WERE a few things I was unsure about.

First, I didn't know exactly what happened with his wife. Some outlets reported accidental death, others said she died of natural causes. It happened in Spain and there was a brief investigation, but it was concluded that there was no suspicious activity surrounding her passing.

Second, I didn't know what Jonas had been doing for the last eight years. Other than a few public appearances and some paparazzi snaps of him looking sad, bored, or stoned (it was hard to tell which one) on a private boat, there was no information.

Finally, I didn't know how this job had landed in *my* lap.

2

JONAS

Sleep and I were no longer on speaking terms. I didn't remember the last time I'd fallen asleep quickly or smoothly. Or the last time I'd slept more than a few hours at a time.

The dreams had started up again. Nightmares, really. Every summer I hoped they were done—that enough time had passed, and my psyche would give up on the annual torture. No such luck.

In my dreams I always fought against the water. Swimming and pushing through the waves but the tide was relentless, and I got nowhere. I was losing time. Losing my footing. Going under. If I could just make it through the water fast enough, everything would've been different. But I always failed.

I was dreading tomorrow's interview at *Profile*. It was just the beginning of months of publicity tours. As clichéd as it sounded, I was trying to take it a day at a time. That had worked when I was filming *Vanishing Echo* last year. Every day, I'd wake up woozy from a restless night, and confused about where I was. To survive, I broke up my day into hours, minutes, and sometimes, just seconds: *Sit up in bed for sixty seconds. Take a shower for five minutes. Stay on set for one hour.* Eventually I would get through each day. Repeat, repeat, repeat. Make it through.

MY CELL PHONE vibrated against the wooden surface of my nightstand. I felt like ignoring it, but I gave in, rolled over on the bed, and grabbed the phone. The screen read FREDRIK HOLM. My agent of twenty years, Holm was one of a few people who still consistently talked to me. Most of my friendships had disintegrated when I'd fallen away from life, mostly because I didn't return phone calls, respond to texts, or answer emails.

"Hello, Freddi."

"Good evening, Jonas."

"How's Stockholm?"

"About how you left it."

"Has to be better than New York."

"I have good news and not as good news," said Fredrik. "Which would you like first?"

He was always down to business. "I'm feeling lucky. Let's start with the good stuff."

"Erik Nillsen, the writer scheduled to do your interview tomorrow, has a brother who is in a Connecticut hospital after some sort of . . . ." I heard him shuffle some papers around, "roller coaster derailment?"

"If that's the good news, please don't give me the bad news."

"I'm sorry. That's not exactly the good part."

"Have you been drinking?"

"I should've started by saying that your interview tomorrow has been canceled."

"Now *that's* good news."

"But . . ."

"Can't wait to hear what's next. Should I be sitting down?" I was already lying down. I was on the hotel bed, staring at the white ceiling. Flat. Sterile. The room was supposed to be airy and modern, but it felt like a cave closing in on me.

"They've rescheduled it. The interview will take place next week in Sweden."

"I get to go home?" I asked. "Are you sure you don't have the good news and bad news mixed up?" There was silence on Holm's end of the line. "What aren't you telling me?"

Freddi cleared his throat. "They've selected another inter-viewer. An American woman. She'll be accompanying you from New York to—"

"I'm not traveling with anyone. I travel alone," I said, and sat up on the bed. The skin on my neck felt itchy.

"You don't have to travel *with* her, exactly," he said. "You'll just be seat mates on the flight."

I lay back down. "Fine. And she's one of their interview writers?"

"She's more of a freelance professional, from what I under-stand. She was available at short notice. I'm not sure she has any experience in interviews, per se—"

"This keeps getting better."

"But she's a published author. And you'll be spending a week with her in Sweden where you'll—"

"The hell I will!" I hopped up and began pacing, my bare feet slapping across the wood floor.

"You won't have to spend time with her exclusively. You'll be participating in some photography sessions with—"

"Oh, for fuck's sake," I barked into the phone.

"Freja Jansson."

"Freja?"

"Correct," said Fredrik, who sounded like he needed to loosen his collar and have a few shots of whiskey. "She's already scheduled to be in the area for another celebrity client."

"I haven't seen her since—"

"That was several years ago," he said. "I'm sure that's water under the bridge."

"Right," I said. "So, to summarize, I don't do the interview tomorrow but instead I do a week-long interview with an unknown, inexperienced, American writer. And I'll be posing for pictures with a photographer who may or may not have vandalized my apartment because I broke it off with her?"

"Something like that."

"I regret answering this call."

"I'll be emailing you the itinerary, flight details, and contact information from *Profile*."

"Can I say no to this?" My question was met with silence. "Alright. I get it."

We ended the call. My stomach was rolling, and I felt a headache coming on. What had I gotten myself into? I was out of practice with being part of the human race, and I wasn't sure I wanted to be back. I pushed aside the urge to open all the little bottles of alcohol in the room's minibar. I pulled on socks and shoes and left my room, locking the door behind me. Maybe some fresh air would clear my head.

3

GEMMA

On Wednesday, Rava emailed me some initial information about the interview, but promised to supply a bigger packet when we met in person at her office over the weekend. The email included forms to sign, *Profile* guidelines, and contact information for several of the people with whom I'd be working.

There, in the middle of the list, like it was no big deal, was Jonas Hellgren's email address. His phone number wasn't listed on the form, but I HAD JONAS HELLGREN'S EMAIL ADDRESS. Looking more closely, I realized that *Profile* magazine must have provided him with a contact email just for this job because the address was jhellgren@profilemag.com. But still.

Was I supposed to email Jonas? I hadn't gotten much guidance. I sent a text to Rava.

GEMMA: That packet you sent me has an actual email address for JH.

RAVA: Yep.

GEMMA: Am I supposed to use it??

RAVA: If you feel like you need to.

GEMMA: Does telling him I've had a crush on him for 15 years constitute "need?"

RAVA: Probably not.

GEMMA: Should I send him an introductory email before we meet next week?

RAVA: Probably should. Good luck!

"Rava has notifications silenced" popped up on my screen.

I paced my living room floor. My kitchen floor. My bedroom floor. None of the pacing calmed me down or helped me solve the puzzle of whether or not I should email Jonas Hellgren. I caught a glimpse of myself in the full-length mirror propped up in my front hallway.

I tried some affirmations. "You can do this! You're capable, you're smart, and you're not bad looking!" My pep talk wasn't working, and my mirror was no help—my reflection wasn't throwing off a capable, smart, beautiful vibe. My dark auburn hair was tangled and frizzy; I hadn't been tending to my curls properly. If I shifted so my head caught the light coming in from the front window, I saw my red highlights shimmer and glow, but my hair was too long and overdue for a trim. My bare face appeared somewhat fresh for a 40-year-old woman, probably because of my freckles, but also, I looked tired. I was wearing jeans and my *True Blood* t-shirt. Having *Fangtasia: Life Begins at Night* blazing across my chest didn't really scream "professional." I wasn't skinny, but I didn't have killer curves; I fell somewhere in the middle. Sometimes that felt like the problem; I wasn't tall or short, loud or quiet, brilliant or dumb. Always in the middle. Was there anything interesting about me at all?

My phone rang loudly in my pocket, causing me to belt out a strangled squeak and jump like I'd just been electrocuted. Living alone came with the benefit of being able to do ridiculous things without witnesses.

I didn't check the caller ID. No need, really. It was always Rava or a telemarketer.

"Yellooo," I answered.

Silence on the other line. That meant telemarketer. It always took a few seconds before the robocall software computed that a real person had answered the phone.

"Gemma Lane's House of Horrors, how may I help you?" I considered it my duty to spice up the lives of call center employees.

"Gemma Lane?" said the voice on the other line. Male. Deep. Sexy. This telemarketing firm was killing it with their personnel choices.

"The one and only."

"This is Jonas Hellgren. I was given your number by *Profile* Magazine."

I didn't have to imagine what my face looked like because I was staring straight at myself in the mirror. What. The. Hell. My mouth was open, my eyes were wide, and a wave of red was moving up my neck and toward my face at an alarming pace. I'm not sure if my heart started racing or stopped all together, but I did feel it stumbling around in my chest. I finally managed one word—the first one that came to mind: "Howdy!" My greeting got no response.

Did I just say "howdy" to Jonas Hellgren, Swedish heartthrob, award-winning actor, and international movie star? Youbetcha.

"Hello?"

I had to save this, though it probably wasn't salvageable. The "you never get a second chance to make a first impression" thing was most likely shot to hell, but I had to try. "One moment please," I said in my best professional voice. Then I hit mute and took a deep breath. I stood up straight and walked away from the mirror. Unmute. "This is Gemma Lane," I said, attempting an entirely different persona than the deranged cowgirl who'd possessed me moments earlier.

Silence on the other line for a moment. "Howdy," Jonas said dryly.

Shit. Plan C was to plow through and leave this disaster behind as fast as possible. "Hello, how're you?" I hoped that I sounded calm, confident, and sane.

"I'm calling because my agent said you might be emailing me with a list of possible interview topics. I was hoping to get those in advance but hadn't received anything yet."

I guess we were getting right to it. "I just received your contact information earlier today. I'll be getting a list to you later this evening." I had no idea what was going to be on that list, and I hadn't really been planning on sending one, but now I was locked in.

"Alright. Thank you."

"No problem. I look forward to—" but I stopped talking when I realized the line was dead.

I spent the next few days packing, cleaning the house, and making notes about ways to approach the interview with Jonas Hellgren. I sent him a list of possible topics, but it was generic at best. I'd had almost no time to prep, and I went with the things I already knew about him. He did not respond to my email.

The interview wasn't supposed to be a traditional format anyway. The plan was for it to be more like a conversation that ebbed and flowed over a series of sessions. A photographer would be taking photos of Jonas in idyllic Swedish locations, and I'd meet with him at least once each day over the course of the week.

I could do this. I could do this. I could do this.

On Friday morning, my bags were packed. The house was clean. I had a few hours before my flight to New York, and then I'd fly to Sweden Saturday afternoon.

My house was mine, but it didn't always feel like mine. It was my family home—the place I'd grown up. I moved back in after my father's dementia diagnosis so I could care for him. I had a house sitter when I was gone for a year on my walk, and then returned when my journey was over. I couldn't bring myself to sell the property even though I didn't envision it as the place I'd live out my life. It felt familiar, suffocating, comforting, and limiting, all at once.

Nestled into a sweet spot in western Michigan, our house came with around five acres of land, which seemed like an entire universe when I was young. There was a small wooded area to explore, a field that grew long grass and wildflowers, and a creek where I could walk in water up to my ankles, turn over rocks, and see what treasures I might discover.

Inside the house there was rag rug in the living room, woven by my mom, its colors layered in spirals of blues, greens, browns, and pinks. Hanging on the walls were a mix of fine art, family photographs, and portraits of the Madonna that my mother picked up at flea markets. Her Catholic upbringing left her resentful of nuns but nostalgic about images of Mary.

The kitchen was small but bright, with blue and white tiles on the backsplash and wooden floors and countertops. The kitchen table was the same one we'd had as far back as I could remember. It soothed me to know that my mother, father, and I sat at that table together for years. It was where we shared meals, argued, and cried. It was where my mother drew maps for me as a child to help me overcome my childhood fears. I was sure the oils from our fingers must have been pressed into the grain of the wood, leaving behind warm invisible imprints of love.

I watered Louis and checked for any wilted tendrils among his fronds. "Hold down the fort for me," I said as I put him near an east-facing window to catch the morning light while I was gone.

4

JONAS

I'd spent the day reading *Sole Searching: A Yearlong Walk to Self-Rediscovery,* by Gemma Lane. The same Gemma Lane who'd been tasked with interviewing me, and the woman I'd be trying to avoid for the next week or so.

I downloaded the book so I could continue to wallow in my distaste and resentment for this interview, for *Profile* magazine, and for Ms. Lane herself. The only other item on my agenda for my extra day in New York was "HIDE FROM EVERYONE," so there was room on my schedule to add some light reading.

The title was shit, for one. A bad attempt at a pun followed by some self-help mishmash. Not my type of literature, though I wasn't above reading something just for spite, so I loaded the book onto my e-reader and started the first chapter. Then I read the second chapter. And on to the third. I read about Gemma as she lost her father, lost her friends, and lost her way. And then found . . . not herself, maybe, but some kind of peace after walking hundreds of kilometers across her country.

Three hours and three hundred pages later, I looked up. The light outside my window had faded and I was startled to realize that I hadn't thought about my own life or troubles for the entire time that I'd been reading. Three hours was a longer block of time than I usually slept at night. I felt strangely rested, relaxed, and transported. I'd started out in a chair by the window and didn't remember shifting over to the bed where I was stretched out on my stomach with my feet hanging off the end of the mattress. That's how I used to read as a child: sprawled out and clueless to anything else happening in the world.

Gemma had suffered some losses and was possibly unhinged. Why else would someone walk out their front door and not return for a year? With no plan?

I felt unhinged too, and I wondered if our shared madness made me more vulnerable to her words. She was also a wanderer, a listener, and a mapmaker of sorts. She didn't draw out her maps like I did, but she put pins in her stops by talking with the people she encountered. Each story she gathered was crafted into a vignette, and over time she'd created an eclectic album to chart her journey.

The more I'd disappeared from the world over the last eight years, the more ostracized I felt. I knew that I'd done it to myself, but I couldn't help feeling like I was transforming into the madman hermit everyone made me out to be. For a moment I let myself hope that this Gemma Lane—persona non grata— might recognize the lost spirit in me, and I might see it in her. No one had seen me for a long time. Would that make us both feel found?

I gave myself two minutes to do an online search of Gemma Lane. That would be long enough to find her photograph and some basic information. But not long enough for me to obsess or go down a rabbit hole.

I opened my laptop and pulled up the search bar. I set my phone timer for two minutes and pressed START. I typed in GEMMA LANE. Three links for her book, an Instagram page (2200 followers), and a few images. I clicked on a photo.

Not what I expected. What *had* I expected? When Freddi first told me about Gemma, I'd assumed she'd be young, flighty, and banal; a thirty-year-old American party girl with a self-obsessed memoir. Once I started reading, I didn't think she could be young at all. She had too much experience in her voice. Too much perspective. Maybe she was older than I was. Maybe she was weathered and weary and worn out.

She was none of those things. I couldn't take my eyes off her photo. It was a picture of Gemma Lane at a signing event, standing next to a table displaying a stack of her books. She was around forty years old, give or take. She had long, deep brown curls laced with touches of scarlet and copper. Like someone had captured an autumnal fantasy, bottled it as hair color, and let it loose on her head. Her eyes were wide and dark, maybe brown, or maybe midnight blue or slate? I couldn't tell from the photo. She might have freckles dotting her cheeks. God help me if she had freckles. She looked like she'd been caught mid-laugh and her eyes had slight crinkles in the corner. Her lips were full and generous. She was medium height and wearing a red sweater, light jeans, and dark scuffed boots. She was curvy, and the way the sweater hugged her breasts—my alarm went off, making me jump.

No. No.

I slammed my laptop shut. A crush was a waste of time. Attractions were dangerous. Trying to connect with someone wouldn't get me anywhere except alone in the end. My guard was up for a reason. I was insane to consider, even for a moment, that there might be a light at the end of this tunnel.

I needed another walk. I rushed out of my room, skipped the elevator and took the stairs. My hand brushed the iron rail as I went down the switchbacks of staircases. finally springing free out onto the city street, I nearly caused a collision between a bike messenger and a dog walker. After untangling two chihuahuas, a French bulldog, and some kind of terrier with three legs, I kept walking.

I strode block after block until the lingering brightness in the sky fully disappeared and was replaced with streetlights, headlights, and the flashing neon of the cityscape. I hated crowds, but I headed towards Times Square. I needed noise and chaos to crush this little flame that had sparked in my heart. If I let that ember grow into a blaze, I'd put myself at risk of total destruction.

5

GEMMA

Saturday afternoon, inside the quiet and mostly deserted *Profile* headquarters, Rava and I went over some last-minute documents.

"Here's the paper itinerary in case you can't access your email on the plane and want to look things over," said Rava. "It's been revised about ten times, but I think this is the FINAL final draft."

"You *think*?" I asked. I didn't like surprises. I usually tried to manage my anxious feelings by knowing exactly what was going to happen, in what order, and at what time.

"The organizers are Swedish. They're super exact. I'm sure it's correct, down to the minute," Rava answered.

"I'm pretty sure you're thinking of the Swiss."

"Whoops. Well, they'll update you when you land."

Rava handed me a heavy folder. "This is the extra background research. Some inside information on Hellgren. There's also a list of things you can't ask about. Part of the terms of the publicity contract." I opened the folder and started to flip through the papers, looking for the list. I didn't want to accidentally bring up a taboo topic and immediately violate the contract. "It's near the back," she said. "It's mostly obvious stuff. Like his wife and her accident, his sex life, things like that."

"It mentions his sex life?"

"I think it says: "Romantic and intimate relationships.""

"Awesome. A week of trying to avoid any conversations about real things. This'll be great!"

"It's not like you'll be fully together for a whole week. There are several on-location photo shoots with a Swedish photographer. You'll have sporadic access to him for seven days. He might be overwhelmed and grumpy, though, from what I hear. So, good luck with that."

Rava had a taxi waiting on the street to take me to the airport. I thought I should at least get a private car and driver, but she hadn't asked my opinion.

"So, Mr. Hellgren won't be joining me on the ride to the airport?" I asked, trying to sound casual and upbeat.

Rava glanced around the empty office. "*Mr. Hellgren?* I don't know who you're putting on this performance for, but you're going to have to upgrade your acting skills if you want to play in the big leagues. And no, MR. HELLGREN will not be riding in the taxi with you. He has his own driver and all that."

I pulled up my plane ticket on my phone. "I *am* sitting next to him though, right?" I was starting to worry that I'd pass right by him lounging in first class as I made my way to the back of the plane.

"You're sitting with him. We want it to seem like you're on the same level with him. We want him to feel that this is a meeting of the minds, that you're fully capable, professional, and talented—"

I narrowed my eyes. "I know you want to finish off that sentence with "even though you're not.""

Rava handed me my backpack and went in for a hug. She gave me a quick once-over and fixed a piece of my hair. "You're my favorite person in the whole world."

"I'm your favorite person because I'm NOT capable, professional, and talented," I said as I started rolling my suitcase toward the elevator.

Rava walked with me and hit the down button. The elevator doors opened. "Total bullshit. You're perfect. Text me whenever you can. I want all the juicy details." The doors closed and I was on my way. Alone.

I BARELY MADE it to the gate on time. I got to use the first-class check-in line, but I didn't have TSA pre-check, so I waited 45 minutes for security with about 2,000 other people wanting to catch their flights out of New York. I'd barely had time to use the bathroom before rushing to the gate. No time to fix my hair, put on some make-up, or freshen up in general. I knew that the airport bathroom lighting was horrendous, but I didn't think that was the primary reason my reflection in the mirror was so frightful.

My hair had taken on a life of its own. Rava, another member of the curly hair club, always said that curly hair had two modes: "famous" or "homeless." My curls had moved beyond "homeless" and landed firmly in the "imprisoned and abandoned on a humid island for two months" camp. My dark amber waves were tangled, flat, fluffy, and frizzy, all at the same time. My choice to forgo coloring my hair seemed foolish now. I had some sun-bleached brassy spots along with gray sprouts at my temples.

My face was under-moisturized and blotchy. I put on some mascara in the hopes of salvaging some kind of dignity, but I rushed it and ended up with a black splotch under my left eye. I tried to wipe it off, but then I just resembled a raccoon with a drinking problem.

I had tried to dress comfortably and casually, while still somehow coming across like I belonged in first class. Now my black joggers, t-shirt, and sweater looked frumpy and too tight. I usually saw my soft belly and thighs as feminine and strong, but at that moment, I just felt like a mess.

I rushed out of the bathroom and searched for the information board at my gate. The boarding time was five minutes away. Didn't first class passengers board first? That didn't make much sense to me—why wouldn't you want to load the plane from back to front?

There was no time for coffee or a snack, and *definitely* no time to make small talk in the VIP lounge with my favorite international movie star.

Would it make sense to board with Jonas Hellgren? Before him? Wait until he was already seated so we didn't have to stand there and shuffle our carry-ons at the same time? Did he have the window seat, or did I? He was 6'3". Surely, he had an aisle seat. Or did that not matter as much in the bigger seats up front? Did he know I was coming? Would he wait for me? How would he recognize me?

While I'd been torturing myself with endless questions, I'd missed the first boarding announcement. A few people were starting to line up and enter the jetway. I hesitated. Did the passengers look like first class folks? My eyes scanned the crowd for Jonas. Would he be wearing some kind of disguise? He was famous but also kind of not-famous. A-list actor, but his eight-year hiatus from the public eye made him less of a household name. Didn't live in the United States, so had the ability to fly under the radar. Super-recognizable in context, but he might not stand out in the mass of people in an airport.

I saw a taller man disappearing into the jet bridge but couldn't tell if it was Hellgren. I hadn't seen any current photos of him; the latest ones may've been from almost five years ago at a benefit he attended in L.A. He was in his late forties now, so perhaps he looked different. Maybe he was gray and shrunken and tired and unrecognizable. I was a few years younger than Jonas, and I *often* felt gray, shrunken, tired, and unrecognizable.

I heard the final call for first and business class passengers, and the first call for boarding group A, in coach. A mass of people swarmed into a line. So much for early boarding.

6

GEMMA

Ten minutes later, I stepped onto the plane. I followed the other passengers in line as they turned right and started the search for seats. I was assigned seat 3D. The cabin I entered seemed like a first-class cabin. The seats weren't even seats . . . they were more like pods, or suites. They were spacious and private, and each pod had its own screen, reclining seat, counter, cabinet, shelf, and even a sconce light on the wall.

I didn't see anyone who looked like Jonas Hellgren, and I didn't see my seat, either. These numbers started at nine and went up from there. I continued walking. I left the fancy cabin and was now in some sort of premium seating. I would've thought it was first class if I hadn't seen the pod people first. We were in rows 20 through 22 and the numbers were getting higher. Next up were rows 30 through 35. I was stuck in a long line of people, and I was pretty sure I was headed in the wrong direction, unless there was a secret cabin at the rear of the plane. Was I even on the right flight? That cold-sweat feeling hit me, making me feel even more panicky, and my stomach started to flip.

I would have to turn around at some point. I entered the last cabin at the back of the plane. It was clearly coach. The row numbers were 45 and higher, and there were nine seats in each row. There was, however, a wide-open spot in the middle where a flight attendant stood, welcoming passengers in both English and Swedish. His name tag said MIKAEL. I jumped out of line and tried to smile at him, but I felt like crying.

"I think I'm lost."

He glanced at my phone to check my boarding pass. "You got turned around. Let me show you to your seat." He swiftly ducked into the far aisle and efficiently made his way against the tide of bodies. "Coming through! Excuse me!" Mikael said with such authority that everyone jumped out of his way. We were back up at the front of the plane in no time. It turns out I should've immediately turned left when I stepped on board; that was where rows one through eight were tucked away. We made a U-turn at the very front of the plane, headed back down the aisle, and then stopped at 3D. Mikael held his arms out and presented my seat like I'd won a game show prize.

I *had* won a prize. There, in the adjoining pod, wearing blue jeans, a soft black button-down shirt rolled at the cuffs displaying gorgeous wrists (who knew wrists could be so sexy?), was Jonas Hellgren, seemingly lost in a book. And let me just say that he was NOT shrunken, tired, or unrecognizable. His hair was a bit silver along the temples, but in the most spectacular way possible. He was beautiful.

I was frozen in place. My mouth may or may not have been hanging open. Please god, let it not have been hanging open. Mikael needed me to step into my pod so he could go back to his regularly scheduled programming, but I felt suspended in time and couldn't seem to remember how to move my feet.

Mikael waited, arms extended, for me to enter my airplane suite. He looked like the tin man who needed an oil can so he could put his arms down. I had the feeling that it was airline policy to make sure that first class passengers were entirely pampered.

I think Jonas took pity on us. I suspected that he was only pretending to read and was probably hoping that I'd just sit my ass down so he could continue with his book. Jonas made eye contact with Mikael and me and unleashed a disarmingly gorgeous smile.

"Hello," Jonas said, in a voice that was both deep and soft and resonated like a liquid warmth right in my veins. It wasn't just me. That simple "Hello" had gotten to Mikael, too. Now he was frozen for real, just like I was. Mikael and I were both trying to play it cool but were utterly confused about next steps. This probably all took place over a span of three seconds, but it felt like an eternity. Jonas extended his hand over the divider. "Gemma Lane? I'm Jonas Hellgren. It's nice to meet you." He shot an extra smile over to Mikael.

Mikael and I unfroze at the same time; I was reaching for Jonas's hand, and Mikael was trying to shift out of the way of his annoyed colleague, who was attempting to deliver cocktails and coffee to other first-class passengers. We bumped into each other, and for a moment we were both wedged in the entrance to the pod.

If there was a freeze-frame of that moment, it would've looked like a still from a ridiculous sit-com: handsome movie star with his hand outstretched towards two bumbling, starstruck commoners now engaged in an awkward physical comedy sequence. There was no way anyone was getting out of this scene with their grace intact.

I leaned forward to shake Jonas's hand while Mikael leaned back in an attempt to free us from the pod entrance. We were suddenly and sharply unstuck, with me tumbling into my pod and Mikael careening toward seat 3A. The only thing that kept me from ending up in Jonas Hellgren's lap was the low wall between our pods. I fell into my seat like a figure skater who had missed the landing on her jump. Jonas pulled his arm back just in time to escape significant personal injury.

Mikael seemed to have avoided any major mishaps and popped back up at my pod door with a broad smile and a slightly sweaty brow. "Well!" he huffed, trying to catch his breath. "That was exciting! I'm glad you're finally seated, Ms. Lane. Is there anything else I can get you?" The other first-class flight attendants had identified an interloper in their cabin; there was an icily stunning six-foot Swede closing in fast. Mikael was risking life and limb to get a few seconds of face time with Jonas Hellgren; I knew I owed him one.

"I'd love a sparkling water," I said, and that was not a lie. I needed something to drink.

"Excellent!" Mikael squeaked. "Anything for you sir?"

"Nej tack," said Jonas, who already had a drink sitting there on his pod shelf. Mikael shot me a look of thanks, and he disappeared into the galley to retrieve my water.

I was feeling shy, exhausted, and embarrassed, and my butt had only been in my seat for thirty seconds. Jonas had gone back to his book, and I pretended to busy myself with organizing my carry-on and belongings. I stood up to take off my sweater and got a better view of the cabin. The window seats hosted single pods, and in the middle of each row there were a pair of pods. That made four seats total across each row. Some pairs had their dividers up, and others were down. I realized that passengers who appeared to be couples had theirs down, and strangers had the dividers automatically up as everyone boarded. Our divider must have been down because our tickets were purchased together.

I was both thrilled and terrified that our divider was lowered. Over eight hours of unlimited access to Jonas Hellgren! You could learn a lot about a person just by observing how they moved, what they read, how they spoke to others. This could really help me write a nuanced and informed profile of Jonas. I took a deep breath and felt some of my anxiety release its grasp on my stomach. Maybe everything would be ok.

I sat back down as Mikael delivered my water in a beautiful glass. I took a sip and the bubbles fluttered down my throat.

Jonas was still reading his book, or at least holding it. I hadn't seen him turn a page since I'd arrived. He had just the right amount of hair on his forearm, hand, and fingers. He wore a simple and masculine silver watch, but no rings. I couldn't believe that he was so close to me. I wondered if I'd be able to pick up the scent of any cologne if I leaned in a little more.

I saw Jonas glancing my way and I offered a bright smile and looked right into his eyes. They were the color of slate, laced with flecks of blue, green, and brown. The effect was celestial in nature, as if his eyes were mysterious planets sprinkled with stars and blue-gold oceans.

"I'm looking forward to—" I began, but then I stopped short when I noticed that Jonas was not smiling back at me. His face had closed. Shut down. The warmth of his earlier greeting had disappeared. He had put up some kind of energetic wall and his expression was blank and unreadable. His mouth was in a straight line, his eyes suddenly flat and hooded. His countenance was stern, and frankly, cold.

Jonas gave me the tiniest, almost imperceptible nod, and then his beautiful arm reached out again. This time he wasn't offering to shake my hand. He touched the arrow button on his side of the wall and our divider slowly went up.

So much for that.

7

JONAS

I felt like an asshole when I raised the seat partition, but I had no choice.

My first in-person glimpse of Gemma Lane had been in the airport terminal, before we'd boarded. I'd arrived at the airport hours before I needed to. I had no ambition to do anything between checking out of my hotel and getting on the plane. I could've walked the streets of New York, browsed in a bookstore, taken lunch at a cafe, but I felt too exhausted and sluggish to come up with any other plan than waiting in an airport lounge. There may have been a part of me, though I could barely admit it to myself, that held a sliver of hope that Ms. Lane might also be early to the airport and perhaps we would see each other.

She never made an appearance in the lounge where I spent several hours tucked away in a private booth. I stretched my legs out on a soft purple leather couch and worked on my drawing and sipped a club soda and lime. I wanted a beer. Or a gin and tonic. Or anything that would help loosen the knot in my stomach, but I needed a clear head. I couldn't let my guard down.

I walked to the gate almost an hour before the scheduled boarding time. The desk was unstaffed and most of the chairs were available. I took an end seat with its back to the window so I could watch the other passengers as they arrived. I placed my shoulder bag on the chair to my left, knowing that it would prevent someone from sitting next to me, but that it would also keep an extra spot available if my traveling companion wanted to sit with me while we waited for the plane.

Over the next hour, people arrived and the chairs in the waiting area filled up. I held my book in my hands, but my eyes just skimmed the same paragraph over and over. No signs of Gemma Lane. I wasn't sure I even wanted to talk to her before we boarded, but I wanted to see her. I wanted to see if she looked like her photo and if my jolt of feeling was the same when I saw her in person as it was from seeing her on the screen of my laptop. There were ten minutes until boarding would commence and I still hadn't spotted her. But then I did.

A flurry of movement had caught my eye. Gemma Lane, clad all in black and hair flying, dashed into the restroom. I felt something unclench in my stomach. I must've been worried that she wouldn't make the flight. Or that she wasn't real. Or maybe that the photo I'd seen wasn't of her, but someone working at her book launch. But she was real, and she was in the airport bathroom. Our boarding call was minutes away.

I stood up and made my way toward the restroom. I didn't want to stand directly at the door and come off like a stalker, so I stood against the wall to the side of the entrance. I would be in her sightline when she exited. A few minutes passed, and suddenly, there she was. She had bolted out of the door and then stopped short, evidently to look at the information screen and check our boarding time. She was just a meter away from me. She had her back to me, and I didn't want to startle her by approaching her from behind. If she turned her head, she would see me. I wasn't wearing a hat or sunglasses; I felt vulnerable standing openly among the crowd, but I wanted to be recognizable.

I caught a lovely scent as Gemma rushed by. She smelled of sandalwood, rose, vanilla, and some other note that felt ancient and woodsy—frankincense, maybe? I was suddenly struck with a sense of longing and melancholy that I couldn't identify. I'd spent so many years feeling numb that any kind of strong feeling felt alien and unnamable. I was out of practice at feeling things.

Her hair fell in mahogany waves with touches of claret. I wanted to reach out and catch a few strands in my fingers to see if her curls were as soft as they appeared. I took a step closer and moved two paces to the side in the hope that she would catch sight of me in her peripheral vision. No luck. I waited for her to respond to the boarding call for first class passengers, but she remained still. A few minutes passed and I'd gone from feeling shy to feeling ridiculous that I hadn't already tapped her on the shoulder and introduced myself. I'd waited too long. If I did so now, she'd know I'd been standing there all along like a real creep.

The counter attendant made an announcement welcoming boarding group A onto the plane, and Gemma jumped and walked forward. I waited a few beats and then followed her. At least this way we would find our seats at the same time. I was two people behind her in line and we slowly made our way up the jet bridge. When she finally stepped into the plane, Ms. Lane turned right when she should've turned left. She headed toward the back of the plane, and I paused. I considered following her, but instead I went the correct direction and found my seat within seconds.

I was welcomed by a flight attendant who greeted me by name, and in Swedish. She had a drink already poured for me and she placed it on the shelf in my seat vestibule. Fredrik had told me that Gemma would be seated next to me. That seat remained empty, and Gemma had gone toward the coach section of the aircraft. Perhaps we weren't seat mates after all. I opened my book and distractedly tried to read the same paragraph that I'd been working on in the airport.

To my right, a different flight attendant flashed by me, with Gemma Lane following closely behind. They crossed over at the front of the plane and headed down the aisle, arriving at the seat next to mine. I waited a moment and pretended to read my book. Why was I making this so hard? I could feel my heart beating in my throat. I looked up.

"Hello," I said.

The three of us made eye contact and I could tell that they both recognized me. The attendant, who according to his name badge was called Mikael, went red in the face. Gemma's cheeks got a little rosy and her eyes widened. She offered me a shy smile. And dammit, she had freckles.

I introduced myself and held out my hand. There was an awkward moment when they seemed to get wedged in the doorway of Gemma's section, but they soon got themselves unstuck and Gemma plunged breathlessly into her seat. Mikael went to fetch a water for Gemma, and I shifted my eyes back down at my book to give her a moment of privacy while she collected herself.

That luscious sweet and green scent had returned, and I fought against leaning closer to breathe her in fully. I was hit again with an overwhelming nostalgia that I couldn't place. The page of my book blurred before my eyes as feelings washed over me. Those wisps of memory of what it felt like to be drawn to someone. The fluttering of butterflies in the stomach. That excitement when everything is new and unknown, and all your senses are sharper and brighter and stronger. They were dangerous feelings, laced with the possibility of brutal loss. I had to shut them down.

I turned toward Gemma at the exact moment she turned toward me. She offered me an open and generous smile that made her face glow with the radiance of a thousand stars in a black sky. Her eyes were the darkest grey, with sprinklings of amber and aquamarine. I was lost . . . so lost. She started to speak but I was overcome with everything I wanted and everything I could never have. My stomach cramped and I pushed the button to put up the divider. I was mortified, almost heartbroken, and feeling sorry for myself, which was a shift from my normal habit of refusing ever to feel anything at all. I closed my eyes and feigned sleep while I waited for the plane to take me back home.

8

GEMMA

The flight was uneventful and frustrating. There were no heartfelt conversations with Jonas, no connections, and no progress on our interview. Other than slight eye contact and nods of acknowledgment if one of us stood up to stretch or go to the restroom, we didn't engage at all. To add to my annoyance, Jonas was friendly and warm in every interaction with the flight attendants. He spoke Swedish with a few of them and at one point he must've made some kind of joke, because he had two attendants laughing so hard that they were in tears.

Not that I wanted him to be rude to the others on the plane. I just felt envious of the attention he paid to others while he treated me like a stranger. I mean . . . I *was* a stranger to him. But we were supposed to be working together on this interview project. I wasn't sure this piece would even get off the ground.

On the plus side, steaming towels were delivered to our hands with gold tongs before and after meals. Food was served on real plates and with actual utensils. For dinner, I had salmon with sushi rice, braised pineapple, seaweed salad, edamame beans, crispy onions and shoyu dressing, far better than the usual takeout or grilled cheese that I usually had for my evening meal. There was unlimited alcohol available, and while I was tempted to drink myself into a stupor to get through the flight, I only had a glass of white wine (ordered right after Jonas put his divider up) and a beer with dinner.

I did get some sleep. The luxury class perks of a feather pillow, wool blanket, earplugs, eye mask, lavender misting spray, and a fully reclining seat made for a comfortable nesting spot. After a few hours of sleep, the sun shone outside the windows. For breakfast we were served coffee, cinnamon buns, and fruit.

With all of that, it was difficult to complain about my experience on the flight. But I was frustrated about having so little contact with Jonas Hellgren.

For most of the flight, Jonas did one of two things: he rested, or he drew. When I would peek into his pod during stretch breaks or after my trips to the bathroom, I saw him either reclined, with eyes closed and headphones on, or hunched over his little table with a paper in front of him. I couldn't make out what he was drawing, and his posture made it obvious that he wasn't inviting others to see his work.

Jonas was famous for his movie roles, but he was also an accomplished artist. He mostly made pencil and pen drawings. He'd done some portraits, landscapes, and a few street scenes, but his upcoming art book was a collection of hand-drawn maps. They were conceptual and whimsical maps. The only full map I'd seen published before, in a magazine piece about celebrities who were also artists, was a map of his childhood. I recalled that it had floating oceans and hilltops and drawings of a grove of birch trees and various birds. There was a quilt, a bracelet, a swing, and a ball. I remember a woman's hands and the back of a man who was sitting in a small boat. The different elements came together in a way that was magical and ethereal. Softly shaded with colored pencils, it was breathtaking, and it captured the hazy dreamlike memory of a childhood well-lived.

OUR PLANE WAS NEARING its descent into Stockholm, and the voice over the loudspeaker told us to secure our seatbelts and remain seated for the duration of the flight. There were some storms in the area, and we were warned of "choppy air" ahead. Great. I wasn't a particularly nervous flyer, but if I lost my cool, I really lost it. Turbulence seemed like just the thing to jump-start a nice mid-air panic attack.

I quickly grabbed my backpack and started searching for my rose quartz palm stone. I'd had it since I was ten when my mother and I went to an arts and crafts fair. I'd been stung by a bee that was on the rim of my lemonade and I was tired, hurting, and inconsolable. My mother saw a vendor who had a beautiful display of crystals and she quickly picked out and purchased two pink oval stones.

She put one in my hand, and one in hers. "This is a stone of love and comfort," she said. "Hold this in your hand, close your eyes, and breathe in slowly. Now breathe out. I'll hold mine, too. You'll feel better soon." She sat with her arms around me, and we both held our crystals.

A minute later I felt a warm calm wash over me. My lip still hurt, but I wasn't crying. I felt more peaceful and relaxed, and I was pretty sure that my mother was magical. "Told you so," she said. That memory was vivid in my mind because my mother died not long after that day.

Where was it? My hands were shaking as I unzipped pockets. I could feel my heartbeat increasing and my face felt hot.

Had I forgotten it? Did it fall out somewhere? I never went on a trip without it. Tears began to threaten my eyes, and I felt them building up.

The plane had started to dip and lurch. Jonas had been in the restroom when the announcement was made, and he quickly returned to his seat. He glanced at me before he sat down and then he disappeared behind our seat divider.

There it was. The quartz was in a tiny zipper pocket near the bottom of the backpack. I got it out, set it on my armrest, and put my backpack back into the cabinet by my feet. Just as I closed the cabinet, the plane fell out of the sky.

We experienced a fast drop, and then just as quickly, we stopped dropping. Everything that was not secured in the airplane flew up and fell back down. I saw some drinks take off and heard a glass break. One of Jonas's pencils landed at my feet, and my crystal slammed into the ceiling and then shot off into the great yonder. I really hoped that it hadn't hit anyone in the head. A few people cried out, and the plane started to tremble and bounce again.

The divider lowered and I saw Jonas's handsome face peek around the corner.

"Seen my pencil?" he asked. His pencil? We were all about to die a watery AND fiery death in the Baltic Sea and he wanted his pencil?

"Sure, right here," I said, leaning over to retrieve it from the floor. My hands were shaking so badly that I almost stabbed him with it as I tried to give it to him.

"Thank you," he said. "Does this belong to you?" He held out his palm, and resting there was my rose quartz. I was so relieved that the tears burst out of my eyes without my consent. I reached out and gently slid the stone from his hand to mine. "I thought so," he said. "You're going to have to try harder than that if you want to kill me. I recommend a nice chunk of lapis lazuli next time."

I laughed, but it hitched in my throat and came out sounding more like a hiccup. And I still had tears coming out. I'm sure I looked amazing. The plane jerked and dropped again, but this time the pencil and the crystal were secured.

Jonas tapped my right hand, as if asking to see my rock again. I opened my fingers. He removed the stone, reached over and held it above my left hand. I took it from him and held it tightly in my left palm. Jonas then took my empty right hand and squeezed his fingers around mine. The plane wobbled and tilted roughly from side to side. "It's going to be ok," he said quietly. "We should level out soon." He sat back in his seat but kept holding my hand. He held it until I stopped trembling, and until we moved into the calm air below the clouds and could see the land beneath us.

9

JONAS

Gemma's hand was shaking and warm when I took it into mine. I'd never been so glad to be pelted in the head by a flying rock as I was when Gemma's crystal careened into my seat. I'd spent the entire flight trying to figure out a way out of the situation . . . the situation being the fact that I was feeling my feelings for the first time in years, and it was proving to be a painful reawakening.

I tried to sleep, I tried to draw, I tried to read, but I was unsuccessful in all my endeavors. I'd worked myself into an internal frenzy knowing that just over the divider sat someone who apparently had the power to raise the emotionally dead.

I did not want her to interview me. Though I found most interviews tedious and trite, I wasn't worried that my interview with Gemma would be any of those things. I was afraid that I might tell her my secrets, my fears, and my heartbreaks. I wanted to release my demons into her care and watch her slay them one by one. What was wrong with me? If she got to know me, she might see me—the real me—and I might shatter under her gaze.

The turbulence provided an opportunity to speak to Gemma without seeming like a complete fool. She was so eager to grab my hand. My nerve endings seemed to wake up one by one under her touch, and my stomach felt calm and agitated at the same time.

We hit several more pockets of rough air, for which I was eternally grateful. The longer the airplane shook and dipped, the longer I could hold on to her hand, which had stopped trembling. Her skin was predictably soft, and I resisted the urge to rub my thumb across her knuckles. I wanted to interlace my fingers with hers to be as tightly enveloped in her flesh as possible, but I didn't dare shift my hold.

Holding hands was a practice I usually found objectionable unless it was for parent and child. It always felt cumbersome to me, and the hands of others never seemed to fit quite right in my own. If I was sitting with someone, I'd rather put my arm around them. Walking while holding hands was idiotic—it made navigating more difficult, and my pace never seemed to match the other person's. Holding hands made everything a joint venture in discomfort.

But as I sat there holding Gemma's hand, nothing had ever seemed more natural. Her hand, delicate and smooth, nestled into mine like a pearl resting in an oyster.

I wanted to speak to her, but the words racing through my mind refused to form into sentences, so I settled for silence. After ten minutes of calm flying, I didn't feel like I could hold on to her any longer. She was probably pitying me while suffering from a numb arm and sore shoulder.

I gave her hand one squeeze and released my grip. "We seem to be in the clear now."

She left her arm where it was and let her hand sit on the rest between our seats. I was relieved that she hadn't pulled away immediately.

She leaned forward and turned her face to me. Her hair had fallen across her face and a few strands got caught in her long eyelashes. I moved to smooth back her hair but stopped myself at the last second. "Thank you," she said. "I wasn't sure we were going to make it out alive."

I noticed that she was still holding the stone tightly in her left hand. "Does that rock help you with anxiety?" I asked.

She shrugged and a light blush moved across her cheeks. "It's supposed to, though it might be magical thinking on my part." She opened her hand and showed me the crystal again. "My mother gave it to me a long time ago. Maybe it's the invocation of her that calms me down, but whatever it is, it usually seems to work."

She unzipped her bag and slipped the stone into an inside pocket.

Silence fell between us again. I wondered how much of the angst I was feeling was self-inflicted. Maybe it was just that I'd seen a beautiful woman and that led to me torturing myself with these fantasies of feelings. It'd been so long since I'd felt truly drawn to someone—since Anna, really. Poor Gemma may have just been a spark that set off a chain reaction inside me that was part of an inevitable collapse; my heart was a tinderbox, vulnerable to any flame.

As I was thinking about that, Gemma reached her hand over and let her fingertips brush against my forearm. It was a casual and gentle touch, meant only to gain my attention, but its effect on me was anything but gentle.

"You really helped me," she said.

I nodded in response, but again, could make no words come

out. Waves of sensation were radiating out from the nucleus of her touch. Chills shot down my arm, over my chest and neck, and settled in my lap, where my groin began to feel warm.

I was ridiculous and pitiful. I was getting turned on from someone tapping my arm? Well, not just someone. Someone named Gemma Lane, whom I'd known for mere hours. I'd only spoken a few words to her. There was no rational reason for me to have such a strong reaction to her.

I had to keep it professional, not just because it was the right thing to do, but because I was starting to worry about how close I was to losing control of my carefully constructed defenses. What would happen if I let her in at all?

10

GEMMA

We were on the ground, and Jonas was gone. By the time I'd collected my things and stood up to disembark, he'd disappeared from our cabin. How did he do that? It's hard to lose sight of a man that tall and that famous anywhere, let alone on an airplane.

I'd assumed that we would leave the plane together and travel to the Stockholm Profile office, but now I didn't know what to think. I took off my backpack and extracted the agenda that Rava had given me before I left.

<u>Day 1</u>
12:00 – Transport from Airport to Sweden office
13:30 – Lunch buffet and Information meeting
15:00 – Transport to Stockholm Archipelago
18:00 – Dinner with JH, staff, and crew
20:00 – 1-hour interview session with JH

"Transport" was vague. If I couldn't find Jonas after I got off the plane, I'd call Rava for assistance. There were some contact numbers on my info sheet, but I really, really didn't want to start off my time in Sweden by getting lost or calling for help.

I walked off the plane and tried to appear confident as I followed signs pointing toward baggage claim. No Jonas anywhere.

I spotted a young woman, maybe twenty-five years old. She wore a worried expression on her face and held a tablet above her head that read GEMMA LANE. I made my way toward her.

"Hi," I said. "I'm Gemma Lane."

"Oh, hello! Welcome!" she said, in such a bright and cheerful tone that I immediately had trouble staying in my funk. "I wondered where you were! Rava sent me a lot of photos of you, but I didn't recognize you." Her English was perfect, and she had a slight Swedish accent. "I'm Kristina and I'm driving you to the office. Do you have checked luggage? Of course you do. Let's go get it!" Every sentence of Kristina's felt like it ended in an exclamation mark, but somehow, she came across as authentically joyful and not maniacally saccharine like an over-eager cartoon character.

"Do I resemble my photos?" I asked her, as I tried to keep up with her quick stride.

"Well," she said with a laugh, "you currently appear to be sober and not in pajamas, so I'd say you look a bit different."

So much for presenting me as capable, professional, and talented.

WE COLLECTED my suitcase and began the drive to the office. Kristina filled me in on the schedule as I took in the scenery. Stockholm was bustling. Cars and long busses jockeyed for position on the road and pedestrians filled the sidewalks. Cyclists were riding on the streets, walking their bikes near storefronts, or securing their bikes into one of dozens of crowded racks that appeared on every block. Apartment and office buildings lined both sides of the avenue, some with sleek modern exteriors and others older with intricate facades.

"We were supposed to start off at the forest location," Kristina said, "but the owner had some kind of family emergency, so we had to switch up the order of things. We'll go there in a few days after we finish the city and seaside shoots. That makes more sense with the weather, anyway."

"What's at the forest location?" I asked. "Besides a forest?"

"It's a beautiful area," said Kristina. "There are all these amazing cabins and saunas and a lake, I think. I haven't been there before, but I'm really looking forward to assisting the crew out there! It's normally a very rustic getaway. No electricity, no Wi-Fi, no indoor plumbing, but I think they're setting up some extras for us while we're there. We'll stay in a little hotel a few kilometers from the site, so we can have running water and, you know, a lamp or something."

I didn't mind some light camping, but indoor plumbing sounded like a good idea to me.

"Now that you mention it," Kristina said, "I did get an email with 'Itinerary Change' as the subject, but I haven't opened it yet. Maybe they've switched it back."

I was just happy to be on the ground. Both the forest and the city were fine with me. "Have you met Jonas Hellgren before?" I asked her.

"I haven't. The only people here who know him well are the chief and Freja."

"Who's Freja?"

"She's the photographer. Freja Jansson."

"Oh, *that* Freja," I said. I'd seen her work but had never met her. She had a reputation for taking gorgeous portraits and for being more beautiful than her models. She had quite the Instagram following.

"Yes, that Freja."

"What's she like?"

Kristina paused before answering. "She's a bit . . . she's a lot. Just stay watchful. You'll be fine."

I hadn't worried about not being fine, but now I *was* worried about that. I wanted to ask Kristina for more details, but we'd arrived.

KRISTINA WALKED me into the Stockholm office, which was stunning. The large common area had a wall of windows two stories high along the entire length of the space. Through the glass I could see other office buildings in shades of orange, green, and even blue. A river channel sparkled in the distance and the water reflected the bright sky and the architecture that lined its banks.

There was a floating staircase along with an iron and glass elevator shaft that was like a work of modern art. The second-floor offices had walls of glass, giving each inhabitant a full view of the city, the common area, and each other.

Kristina pulled my luggage into a small meeting room that looked out over the city.

"Could I have a minute?" I asked her. "I'd like to make a quick phone call."

"Sure, just come on out when you're ready." Kristina gave me a little wave and left the room, shutting the door behind her.

The room held a long wooden table and twelve chairs. I sat down in a leather and metal swivel chair that looked like it could either be heavenly or hellish when it came to comfort level. My assessment: heavenly. I could've fallen asleep right there. Instead, I dug my phone out of my backpack and called Rava.

She answered on the first ring, "Are you there?"

"I'm here."

"Tell me everything. How was the flight? How was HE?"

I swiveled my chair around so I could put my feet up on the table and look out the window.

"We nearly crashed."

"What?" squeaked Rava.

"Well, maybe not *crashed*."

"Don't give me a heart attack, Gemma."

"Sorry. The turbulence was just so bad, and I thought we might die, and—"

"I don't mean to downplay your suffering, but can we get back to how it was flying with Jonas Hellgren?"

"Pretty much like flying alone. Except higher tension level."

"What does that mean?"

"It means he pretty much ignored me the whole time. You're right that he doesn't seem into this whole interview thing, and he certainly doesn't seem interested in talking to me about it. Or about anything, for that matter."

Rava sighed. "Shit. Well . . . is he sexy?"

"Sexy as hell," I said, right as I heard someone clear their throat behind me. I pulled my feet off the table and spun around in my chair. There was Jonas Hellgren, in the flesh, arms crossed, eyebrow raised. I gawked at him like he was an alien who'd wandered into the conference room.

"Howdy," he said.

"Rava, I gotta go. Call you later." I heard her protests but I disconnected and put my phone in my pocket.

"Hey."

"They've sent me in here to see if you're ready for some food."

I stood up quickly, but a little too quickly, it seemed. The force of my movement sent the chair rolling backward and me falling forward, my face nearly smacking right into Jonas's chest; he reached out and easily caught me. Something about Jonas Hellgren always made me lose my balance.

"Just testing your reflexes," I said, as I tried to straighten myself. I couldn't shake the knowledge of how close I was to Jonas's body. And that his hands were around my waist. "I give you an A+."

"I appreciate the report card," he said. "Ready?"

I put the chair back in place, tucked my bags up against the wall, and straightened my shirt. "Ready."

Jonas led me to the center of a lounge, where an impressive smorgasbord was set out on the table. Kristina appeared out of nowhere with that bright smile still across her face. The food was so beautiful that I was hesitant to touch it. I pulled out my phone and took a covert photo to send to Rava.

"It looks amazing, doesn't it?" asked Kristina. "Let me get you a plate. You must be hungry." I was famished, and I didn't know where to start. I turned to speak to Jonas, but he had disappeared. How did he keep doing that?

I turned my attention back to the table. There were slices of herring and stacks of smoked salmon. I saw jellied eel, piles of cold meats, liver patè, and a roasted chicken. Further down there were cubed cheeses, sliced cheeses, shaved cheeses, and wheels of cheese. Alongside were crackers and rye, sourdough, and Wasa bread. The other end of the table offered meatballs, soup, and a kind of casserole that Kristina said contained potatoes, anchovies, and onions baked in sweet cream. And that didn't include the dessert section, which boasted pastries, cookies, filled pies, and a rainbow of fruit.

"We went all out for the rare Jonas Hellgren appearance!" Kristina said, as she started to put some herring and rye on a plate for me. "Where did he go?" We both turned and surveyed the office, searching for him among the glass walls.

"He has a talent for vanishing into thin air," I said as I added some brie to my plate.

I SPOTTED a man holding court at the end of the table. He was surrounded by several admiring women and was loudly chortling at his own joke. His mouth took up more space on his face than any of his other features; his teeth probably entered a room a few seconds before the rest of him. He was handsome, in an obvious way. Perfect hair without a lock out of place. He looked familiar.

"Is that Derek Drach?" I asked Kristina. Drach was German but had been in several American movies.

She rolled her eyes. "Yep."

"What's he doing here? Is it International Sex Symbols Week?"

"*Profile* is doing a piece on him, too. For the European market, I think. Freja will be doing some photo shoots with him as well."

"You don't like him?"

Kristina shrugged. "He thinks he's god's gift to women *and* men. Too full of himself for my taste." Her eyes widened as something across the room caught her eye. "There he is!" Kristina hissed into my ear. She had spotted Jonas again. Her cheeks were red, and she was suddenly piling about twenty pieces of salmon onto my plate.

"Fish overload!"

Did that man even have a bad angle? He was standing against a wall in the corner of the lobby. He was still in jeans but had changed into a modern white button-down shirt with the cuffs rolled up. I hadn't noticed the outfit change before, which was odd considering I'd nearly had my face pressed up against his chest. He held a small plate in his hand and was in a close conversation with a woman so stunningly attractive that she almost, just almost, overshadowed the beauty of Jonas.

"Freja," Kristina and I said at the same time.

She wasn't as tall as Jonas, but she was in heels and came close. Her blonde hair was cut sharply and cleanly at chin length, leaving ample room for everyone to admire her long, graceful neck. She wore a black jumpsuit that looked casually runway ready.

Why did I not change clothes after the flight? Not that I had the right outfit to compete with the likes of Aphrodite over there. And why did I feel like I should compete anyway? Lots of people told me I was pretty. Or, "cute" was the word more often used.

Freja was the photographer, and I was the writer. This wasn't a contest. Which was good, because surely I would've lost in all categories.

11

GEMMA

"It should be illegal to be that gorgeous," I said to Kristina, but it turned out that I said it not to Kristina, but to a man suddenly standing next to me. He was in his early sixties with wire-rimmed glasses, short white hair, and a very sleek black t-shirt, black blazer, and dark pants. Kristina had abandoned me and was moving down the table with her eye on Jonas and Freja. Was it a Swedish talent to teleport in and out of locations?

"Trying to meet your yearly fish quota?" The man regarded my plate with amusement. I hadn't noticed how much fish Kristina had loaded up for me. To top it off, she left me with the serving tongs as well.

"Needed an Omega-3 boost," I said, putting the plate down on the table.

"You're Gemma Lane," he said, extending his hand. "I'm Carl Berg."

"Editor-in-Chief." I shook his hand.

"I've been a fan of yours for quite a while," he said as he

plucked a piece of fish from my plate. "I found *Sole Searching* quite moving. And inspiring."

"That's kind of you," I said, and felt my cheeks go a little warm.

"Your journey broken down into those unique moments really stayed with me. The smallest act of putting one foot in front of the other, just walking, and ending up with a journey of thousands of kilometers, visiting with such interesting people, and so much solitary time . . . it's a lovely book," said Carl.

"I hadn't planned on writing it," I told him, "but what good is personal desperation if you can't capitalize on it later?"

"I'm assuming that Rava had a hand in pushing you to publish your blog posts in book form?"

"You assumed correctly."

"I like thinking about what it might take for someone to just walk out the door and not look back for a year."

"I didn't have much to lose," I said. Carl grabbed a bottle of mineral water and put it in my hand. "Both of my parents were dead, and I was alone." Was this appropriate Smorgasbord talk? What were the pairing notes on death talk and Swedish meatballs?

Carl seemed completely engaged in our conversation, and so far, he'd consumed herring, some cheese on rye, and I thought he might be considering getting himself a bowl of soup. Why was I still talking?

"I was an emotional orphan," I said.

"And a real orphan!" he said, a little too brightly. "Sorry."

I got myself a cracker and took a bite. "My fiancé and I broke up around that time as well." Apparently, I was going full-on confessional with Carl. "I was always tending to my father and never to our relationship. I think I pretty much starved our love to death."

"Brutal!" Carl seemed to be enjoying this.

I was on a roll. "I also lost contact with most of my friends. The caretaking that I saw as an act of love also became an act of isolation. As my father forgot me, I forgot myself right along with him." I stuffed the rest of the cracker in my mouth. Carl and I stared at each other.

"I need to write that one down. Just a moment." He fished out a little notebook from inside his jacket, and he had a tiny pencil in there, too. He scribbled down a few words. "Continue."

"So, basically, I was thirty-five years old with no love life, no family, no close friends, and no sense of self."

"A real winner," Carl joked.

"So, I started to walk."

"You walked twelve miles to the house of your childhood best friend, the famous Rava."

"I always used to feel so at home at her place. She had a big family, and her house was always chaotic, messy, loud . . . and supremely comfortable."

"You have a strange definition of comfort."

"My house was always so quiet. The noise at Rava's made me feel less lonely."

"And that's when you slept for most of a week, and Rava's family tended to you?"

"Yes, that's right."

I thought back to that morning when I'd decided to leave. I'd walked back home, loaded up a backpack, and then just walked some more. What initially started as an unplanned, unmapped journey became more of a pilgrimage. I averaged 10 to 15 miles a day. I stayed with friends, with distant relatives, and often on my own in campsites or on farms. I began a blog of my travels and started to accumulate followers. Those followers wanted to send me money, which I didn't need much of, so I asked for supplies instead.

My bottle of water made a hissing sound as I unscrewed the cap. "I wouldn't have made it very far without Rava's help." She was the mastermind behind the supply drop-offs, the safety protocols, and the sign-ups for walking buddies.

"I was delighted when Rava suggested you for this job with Jonas Hellgren," said Carl.

"You approved my contract?"

"Guilty as charged. Ever since I read your book, I'd hoped to have a chance to work with you on a project. I think you'll be well-suited to this interview process."

"You might not think that if you knew how little success I've had so far with getting anything out of my subject."

Carl laughed. "No one ever said it would be easy." He walked toward the dessert end of the table, and I followed. He eyed the pie selection as he leaned in closer to me. "Jonas has closed himself off, but I think you might have what it takes to break through those walls."

"You mean because I blindly jump into potentially dangerous situations and make it out alive on pure luck?"

Carl handed me a piece of apple pie and got a slice for himself. "I was thinking more about your patience," Carl took a bite of pie and chewed, "your tenacity," another bite of pie, "your ability to listen," now a sip of coffee for Carl, "and your comfort with silence." We let the words hang between us as he finished his dessert. "And some dumb luck wouldn't hurt either."

"I appreciate your confidence in me," I said. "I'll see if I can break through the ice."

An employee approached Carl with a stack of papers and apologized for the interruption, stating that he had some itinerary questions to go over with the chief. Carl leaned over for a final word as he nodded his head in the direction of Jonas and Freja, who were still in their corner, now chatting with Kristina, "it absolutely *should* be a crime to be that good looking."

12

____

JONAS

*S*exy as hell . . . sexy as hell . . . sexy as hell . . .
Freja was ranting about one of her recent assignments, but I couldn't focus on her words. Echoing in my head was the phrase that Gemma had spoken into the phone in the conference room.

I'd opened the door and had been waiting for her to notice me, not wanting to startle her, when she uttered the "sexy as hell" comment. Could she have been talking about me?

I cleared my throat, so she'd know I was behind her. She'd quickly finished her call, and I escorted her out to the table. I dropped her off with Kristina and slipped away; I felt a little dizzy in Gemma's presence and it felt safer to keep my distance.

I knew that Freja would monopolize me if I gave her the chance, and she did not disappoint. She moved her body close to mine and touched my arm a few times as she told me her story.

I noticed that when Freja touched me, nothing magical happened. No waves of sensation, no nerve endings awaking, no stiffness in my pants, thank God. Freja and I had already dipped our toes into the waters of possible romance, but there was no chemistry there, at least on my end. Freja had not exactly taken kindly to me walking away from our situation, but several years had passed and things seemed settled between us. Freja was extreme—hot one moment, cold the next—which made her interesting and a bit dangerous, but I was generally attracted to sweet over salty when it came to women; Freja wasn't my style. We maintained a mostly professional relationship, though she'd told me that the door was always open if I changed my mind.

I was glad that Freja was in monologue-mode. It gave me the opportunity to let my gaze wander across the room to where Gemma was standing. She was in an animated conversation with the *Profile* Editor-in-Chief. Christ. I was jealous. It had been a while since I felt that particular pull on my solar plexus and with it the urge to claim, occupy, possess the object of my affection—all so stereotypically masculine. Gemma laughed, gestured, listened, and chattered on to Carl, who looked enraptured by Gemma's presence. Couldn't say that I blamed him. Why was it so easy for him to engage her when I could barely manage to string four words together in her presence?

I felt uneasy but couldn't put a finger on why. I wasn't thrilled with the onslaught of feelings that were raining down on me over the last few days. Would it be too much to ask that attraction, fear, nervousness, anxiety, lust, jealousy, and unease take turns and give me a chance to come up for air?

Freja was still talking, her hand now firmly planted on my elbow. I scanned the room. There it was . . . the source of my vague agitation: Derek Drach, pacing around the table like a toothy shark circling his prey. He had his eye on Gemma and was moving in closer and closer as she finished up her conversation with Carl. I didn't like his plastic hair, his ridiculous blinding teeth, or his stupid strong jaw. But what I really hated was his energy. In my previous interactions with him I'd noticed that he was grabby and domineering and seemed to think that anything within his reach was rightfully his to seize.

My jealousy raged again, but this time it was laced with the instinct to protect. My heart pulsed more quickly. Sweat prickled the skin under my arms. I took a deep breath to calm my nervous system.

"Jonas." Freja's voice pulled my attention away from Drach. "What?"

Freja sighed and rolled her eyes. "Where's your head? I asked you how you felt about the schedule for this week."

Derek was getting closer to Gemma. "I'm dreading it," I told Freja, which was truthful. "I'd rather hide away for a few days, all alone. I'm not sure I'm up to it."

"Do you need any help?" she asked.

"With what?"

"What are you staring at?" Freja asked, turning to follow my gaze. "The American?"

"No. Drach."

Freja smiled, but her lips were pulled too tightly across her teeth. She pushed her grin wider, but no warmth reached her eyes. "He's not a complete waste of time."

"You're dating him? Derek Drach?"

"Not that it's any of your business. We're not together, but we've had a few memorable . . . encounters," she said.

"I thought you had better taste than that."

"You had your chance to have a say in the matter," said Freja, dropping the smile and arranging her features into a scowl. "Your loss."

Kristina hopped into my line of vison, her face open and kind. "Hello," she chirped.

I managed a smile but was thoroughly distracted by what was happening across the room. My stomach dropped as I watched Gemma Lane walk right into the arms of Derek Drach.

13

I turned to find a place to put my plate down and almost ran straight into Derek Drach, German Heartthrob. What was it with me face-planting into sexy chests?

"Hey there, pretty lady," said Derek.

Pretty lady? Maybe this guy didn't have the best grasp of English. "Excuse me?"

"I just didn't want you to get away without getting a chance to say hello!" Derek boomed into my face.

"I'm Gemma Lane," I said, backing up several steps and putting my hand out for him to shake.

"I know who you are," he said, ignoring my hand and moving closer to me, putting a meaty paw on my shoulder.

I backed up again and twisted my shoulder out of his grip. "And you are?" I asked him.

Derek's brow creased but then he guffawed. "Not only an amazing writer, but funny, too!"

I saw that Derek's overtures had attracted Jonas's attention. Jonas's brow was furrowed, and he was glaring in our direction.

Derek took another step into my personal space and tried to

put his arm around me. "Tell me more about your book! I find walking fascinating." That guy really needed to work on his pick-up lines.

"Excuse me, Dirk," said Jonas coldly. Where the hell had he come from? Jonas was standing between Derek and me. Jonas was taller than the German. I swore that the volume of the room dropped, and that everyone was looking our way without trying to look like they were looking.

"It's Derek," said Derek, as he backed up a few steps.

"Whatever," said Jonas. "Gemma, I'd like to introduce you to our photographer," Jonas said to me, but he was still in a staring contest with Derek.

"Freja?" said Derek. His gaze darkened and he glanced over to where she stood in the corner. "Don't see why she'd want to talk to you, Hellgren." Derek leaned toward me, his teeth invading my personal space. "I'll catch you later, little lady." He made a gun with his thumb and forefinger and pretended to shoot me and then blew the invisible smoke off the end of the gun barrel. How was this guy an international success?

"Asshole," Jonas muttered under his breath.

JONAS and I approached Kristina and Freja who were heatedly discussing something in Swedish. Kristina switched to English as soon as I neared, but Freja continued speaking in her mother tongue.

Kristina held her arm out towards me, as if she was making a gesture to introduce me; Freja rejected the hint and turned her body toward Jonas, thus turning her back on me, and asked him a question . . . in Swedish.

He was silent for a moment and let her question hang in the

air. Then he said, in English, "Freja, this is Gemma Lane, my interviewer." Freja turned slightly and regarded me out of the corner of her eye. The look on her face made it seem like she'd just been forced to watch someone's toddler poop on the floor.

"I've heard so much about you," I said, a touch too loudly. I wasn't in the mood for this.

"Verkligen," she said.

We all stood and stared at each other for a few seconds. I heard a vibrating sound, and Jonas reached into his pocket and pulled out his phone. "Excuse me. I need to take this." He disappeared around the corner.

"Did you get something to eat?" Kristina asked me.

"A little bit of salmon."

"Whoops." Kristina glanced at the food. "I should go get my own plate. I'll be right back!" And then she abandoned me again, leaving Freja and me in a silent face-off. Maybe it was the jet lag, but wow, these people were odd. Freja threw off the opposite vibes of Derek Drach; she did not want to be close to me or talk to me about my writing or anything else. It was obvious that Freja was not my biggest fan.

I didn't know any Swedish, and Freja was pretending not to know any English, so we stood there in silence. She was about six inches taller than I was, and I stared up at her, my gaze unwavering. Go ahead and try me, Ice Queen.

Freja broke first, which I considered a personal accomplishment. "I suppose I'll see you later this evening," she said with a scowl. I didn't know how I'd managed to offend her already. She knew nothing about me, and we'd never had any interactions before this moment.

"Yep. Either the city hotel or the forest hotel. No one seems to be able to agree on which stop is first."

Freja tilted her head slightly. "What do you mean?"

"You know, do we go to the forest first or the city first? Apparently, there was some kind of family emergency that changed the schedule?"

"Where's your itinerary?" she asked. I dug around in my purse and brought out the first few pages.

"Is this day one?" I asked, holding up one page, "or is this day one?" She snatched the papers out of my hand and one of the sheets sliced the skin on my finger. I winced and she ignored me.

Freja's face shifted as she examined the itinerary. It was brighter. Warmer. She even smiled a little, but I wasn't letting my guard down.

"They haven't given you an updated copy. I'd email you mine, but it's not in English. Let me help you." She took a gentle but firm hold of my elbow and began to lead me to a back hallway. I looked back for Kristina who seemed to be intensely interested in the roasted chicken and some olives. I stopped walking, but Freja held on to my arm.

"I'm sorry," I said. "Do you know where the restroom is?"

"Follow me." Freja led me down the hall.

"I thought I saw one right over there?" I pointed toward the lounge.

"The one back here is more private . . . is that your luggage?" she asked as she walked by the small conference room, "Let me grab that."

I didn't like the feel of this.

"Here's the restroom," she said. "I'll call in a driver. You can get to the hotel to rest before the evening activities. You look like you could use it." Ah, the Ice Queen was back. And apparently Freja had remembered that she did indeed speak English.

She read off my phone number from a document on her phone. "Is that the correct number for you?" she asked.

"That's me."

"Excellent. I'll text you the updated English itinerary once my assistant sends it to me."

She nearly shoved me into the bathroom and slammed the door behind me. Was she out there putting explosives in my suitcase?

I really was exhausted. I wouldn't mind a nap before dinner and my first interview session with Jonas. My body had no idea what time it was.

I washed my hands and splashed some water on my face. Screw it. I could shower and change at the hotel. If I was going to succeed at this job, I needed to pull myself together. A little rest and solitude might be just what I needed to get my bearings.

When I opened the door, Freja was standing there with a man in a black suit. She was placing a stack of bills into his hand. He jumped when he saw me open the door and quickly shoved the wad of money into his pocket. He tipped his hat at me and gestured to the back door of the office.

"Who's this?" I asked.

"Alfred. He doesn't speak much English," Freja said. "But he'll get you safely to your next location. Give me your phone and I'll add my contact number if you need anything in the next few hours."

I unlocked my phone and she put in her name and number.

"Your bag is right there by the door."

There was no one else in the back hall, but I could hear Derek's ridiculous barking laugh echoing back from the gathering area. I didn't feel like facing him again.

Freja took my arm again and walked me to the back door.

"Safe travels." And with that, she turned and quickly disappeared back up the hallway. Alfred and I stared at each other.

"I don't trust her," I said. Alfred just shrugged and reached for my bag.

"Ok?" he asked, gesturing to my bag.

"Ok?"

"Ok!" Alfred pulled up the suitcase handle and wheeled my luggage out to the car, leaving me inside the doorway. He put my bag into the back of the waiting vehicle, which was a large black SUV with tinted windows.

A wave of queasiness washed over me, and I didn't know if it was from fatigue, dehydration, or unease. I pushed open the door; the air outside was breezy and smelled of green leaves and ripe berries.

14

JONAS

I'd been hiding out in the back conference room for several minutes. I was sitting on the floor, my back up against a wall, my legs pulled to my chest, and my head resting on my knees. I could hear the din of voices in the distance but had no desire to re-enter the scene. I needed to go back. The whole event was partially for me, and partially for that asshole, Drach. I'd barely put in an appearance. If Freddi caught wind of me shirking my publicity and marketing duties, I'd be in for a lecture and a reminder of the terms of my contract.

Freddi had called to check on my arrival and I was grateful for the chance to step away from the crowd. I wouldn't leave Gemma alone with Freja, but she seemed safe enough with Kristina. I wanted to get out of this office and clear my head.

I'd impulsively phoned my driver to see if he could pick me up ahead of schedule. He was home with a sick wife and child, and I felt guilty at the idea of pulling him away, so I told him I'd make other arrangements. I could handle the party for another hour or so. I stood up and heard voices outside in the hallway. Two women speaking in English. One of whom sounded like Gemma.

I waited to see if the voices would continue, but it was quiet until I heard the back door swing open. I decided to investigate.

I pushed the conference room door and bumped right into Gemma's shoulder.

"My apologies," I said, holding up my phone as if to explain where I'd been. "My agent called. And then I called my driver. He's unable to pick me up." Why did I tell her that? I felt like an awkward adolescent. I put my phone in my pocket.

Gemma looked up at me with serious eyes. Was she worried? Upset? I glanced down the hall for any sign of Derek hovering in the shadows, but everything was clear and empty.

Gemma pointed toward the back door where I saw a dark SUV waiting in the back driveway. "I was just going—this way —I think."

A uniformed man stood by the driver's side door. "You're going where?" I asked.

"Freja set me up with a driver. Do you want to ride to the hotel with me?"

"Freja Jansson?"

"The one and only. She even put her contact information in here." Gemma showed me her phone where Freja's contact information was displayed on the glowing screen. I didn't remember Freja's number off the top of my head, but it looked right.

Another feeling crept into my gut—this time it was worry. I didn't trust Freja in general, and I certainly didn't trust her to lead Gemma in the right direction.

"You're going alone? Just you and the driver?"

She nodded. "His name is Alfred."

Apprehension cast a gloomy shadow on Gemma's face. Her

eyes were bloodshot, and her sweet lips were turned down in a frown. I wanted to pull her into my arms.

"He's taking you to the hotel?"

"I think so?"

I leaned out the back door. The fresh air felt heavenly. I took a few breaths and felt my anxiety begin to dissipate. In Swedish, I asked the driver where he was headed. He responded in Danish. I didn't fully catch his answer, but I did hear Freja's name.

I leaned back into the hallway. "Shit."

"What is it?"

"I'm not sure about you going alone. I don't know this driver."

"I'm sure I could get Dirk to join me."

The little laugh that erupted from my lungs caught me off guard, and a particle of light bloomed in my chest. "I'll come with you."

I grabbed my suitcase from the conference room and wheeled it out to the back door. Suddenly things didn't feel so bleak. The cold vice that had my guts in its grasp had started to loosen and thaw.

Alfred opened the back door and poked his head inside.

"Ok?" he asked.

"Ok?" Gemma asked me. She reached out with her hand again, lightly touching the skin on my wrist.

"Ok," I said. "Let's go."

THE CAR WAS comfortable and for the first time in several hours I felt like I could breathe. I tried to keep myself turned away from Gemma. I watched the scenery go by as we weaved through the streets and began to move out of the city center.

I tried to think of something to say to her, but came up with nothing that sounded right.

"So–" I began, but I didn't know how to make small talk, and I didn't know how to engage in real talk. I felt like I didn't know how to do anything. I missed having someone to talk to. Someone with whom words came easily. I suddenly missed Anna with a ferocity that ripped my heart to shreds, strip by strip.

My mind was pulled out of the car, out of Sweden, and away from Gemma. I was dropped, like a grenade, right back into that August day on the coast of Spain where Anna was walking into the blue-green Mediterranean waters. We had spent the morning making love, eating, sleeping, and making love again. I closed my eyes for a few moments. I recalled those minutes on the beach. The warm air. My satisfied drowsiness. Closing my eyes and only minutes later, opening them to find my world as I knew it forever destroyed.

My mood had shifted to the blackest black. I needed to drink or sleep or run for ten kilometers until I forgot. Even though it had been almost eight years, I hadn't yet learned a good strategy for coming out of the dark hole created by my memories of Anna's final day.

I heard Gemma speak, but it took me a moment to register her words. I felt like I had a foot in two separate worlds, and I didn't know how to exist in either one.

15

____

GEMMA

Jonas and I settled into the back seat of the car. I had made it to Sweden. I survived the prep, the plane ride, the office, Derek, and even Freja. It felt good to be locked away in the dark safety of that back seat. The SUV was luxurious, and I felt like we were back in the airplane. The interior was fitted with a soft leather the color of Bavarian cream. We each had our own screens, adjustable seats, and even little fold-out footrests.

Jonas was staring out the window. Our ride had started out feeling light and hopeful, but something about the mood in the car had shifted. He'd started to say something to me, but he only got a word out before his body language shifted to "all systems down" mode.

After about ten minutes of silence, I tried a conversation opener. "I could get used to this kind of travel."

Jonas did not acknowledge my statement. Next step: ask a question. "Do you know how far it is to our hotel?"

"Not sure," he answered. He was gazing out of the window and seemed to be in a kind of trance. Maybe he was high.

Perhaps he had a smoke break along with his phone call break. "I'm not even sure exactly where we're going."

Two sentences at once! Had to be a record. I had been this man's traveling partner for almost a full day, and he'd probably said fewer than 100 words to me so far. Remembering what Carl told me about Jonas, I decided to start chipping away at his energetic ice.

"You don't want to do this, do you?" I thought my question would startle him a little. Maybe bring out some kind of professional politeness where he'd reassure me that he did want to do this, or that it was nothing personal.

"No, I don't."

More silence. I waited a minute for a follow-up sentence, but it never came. Carl said I had tenacity. I was going back at Jonas with my ice pick.

"I know you're not a fan of interviews. I'd like to find a way to do this that doesn't feel invasive or superficial," I said, and Jonas scoffed, his body still turned away from me, "but I think together we could build a piece that's impactful and meaningful."

He made a little snuff through his nose, and I think I saw his eyes roll. "You're not a professional journalist, and I don't really want to talk about myself, my life, or my work. Not now, at least," he said.

I wasn't ready to back down. "I'm not a professional journalist, but I'm a writer." There was that annoying nose huff again. "I'm interested in you and your story. And I want to collect and present your narrative in a respectful way." More silence from Jonas, so I kept going. "This isn't supposed to be a quick sit-down where I fire questions at you. It's supposed to be an organic conversation over time. Where I can get to know you and—"

"That's the exact problem," interrupted Jonas. "I don't want you to know me."

Ok, harsh.

"I know I'm contractually obligated to do interviews," he continued, "and I'd submit to the quick basic ones. But I don't want to 'go into the depths' with anyone, let alone someone I don't really know."

"You know me. We nearly died on an airplane together. We're almost best friends."

"The turbulence wasn't that bad."

"Speak for yourself."

"Maybe let's not speak at all," said Jonas. With that, he reclined his sandstone leather throne, crossed his arms, and closed his eyes. I watched the city disappear behind us as the road we were traveling became more rural and wooded. Maybe we were heading to the forest location after all.

IT HAD BEEN ALMOST an hour since Jonas closed his eyes. I think he was feigning sleep for a while, but then he fell asleep for real. His breathing was steady and deep. Feeling secure that he was fully out, I decided to take a good look at him.

His tall body was stretched out and turned toward me. His arms were uncrossed, and his face was soft and relaxed. He had a full head of hair, mostly light brown with slivers of gray showing through. It was longer than I'd seen him wear it in past photographs. A lock fell over his brow on one side. I felt like reaching out to push it aside but caught myself before acting on that impulse.

He'd probably gone a day or two without shaving, and stubble ran along his cheeks, jawline, and neck. His lips were full, a little chapped, and slightly parted. His nose was strong and not perfectly straight. He was striking, but thankfully his eyes were closed. His direct gaze was still enough to make me feel a bit weak. He had the kind of eyes that were laced with intelligence, sadness, drive, and some sparkles of both kindness and darkness. They were a cauldron of sexy mystery, and I did not want to fall under that spell right now.

The sun was still up, but the light was waning in the late August sky. My phone buzzed in my bag. Freja's name showed on the screen, and I opened the text message. It was a PDF itinerary with no attached note. I opened the attachment, and the itinerary was in Swedish. I sighed and typed a reply.

> GEMMA: Thanks for the itinerary. It's in Swedish. Do you have the English copy?

No reply. I reclined my seat and closed my eyes. Maybe when Jonas woke up, he'd be in a better mood.

I MUST'VE BEEN MORE tired than I realized. When I opened my eyes again, it was dark out. Jonas and Alfred were in a heated exchange that involved a lot of gesturing, pointing, and sighing. The sounds of their words and the rhythm of their sentences were different from what I'd been hearing since I arrived in Sweden. Jonas slammed a fist against his armrest.

"Everything ok?" I asked.

"I'm not sure." More silence from Jonas.

"That's ominous. Care to elaborate?"

"We've been driving for almost three hours. The trip should've taken about an hour."

Three hours? How long had I been asleep? "Did he say where he's taking us?"

"We're having some communication difficulties."

"What language were you and Alfred speaking?"

Jonas turned his head and looked directly at me, openly studying my face. "Norwegian," he finally answered.

I thought maybe he was impressed that I was able to tell that he hadn't been speaking Swedish. "So, he's Norwegian?"

Jonas sighed. "No, he's Danish."

Was that sarcasm? I wasn't sure which way to go with it. "Really?"

"Yes, really. Danish is frustrating for me to understand when spoken. And he's useless with Swedish. We've switched to Norwegian in an attempt to communicate with each other."

"That's great," I said, in a way that came out bland and vapid. I felt like someone who had just farted during a sudden silence in a movie theater.

Jonas said nothing. I was realizing that he was not the type of conversationalist who paved the way for an easy exchange. Speaking to him was like rusty gears trying to move together: a lot of resistance and uncomfortable scraping of iron on iron.

"How many languages do you speak?" I asked. He sighed but didn't answer. This probably wasn't the time to start in with stereotypical interview questions, but I spoke without thinking and decided to let the question hang in the air.

"That seems like a question to which you should already know the answer. Did you not do your research?"

I felt the heat rising from my chest and move into my throat and face. It was like someone lit a torch inside me, and the sprinkler system went off at the same time.

Sudden anger or embarrassment usually brought tears to my eyes and turned my face a deep red. Rava always said that I resembled a tomato frog when I got pissed off. The catch in my throat and the wet heat in my eyes made me feel even more embarrassed, and I was sure that I was starting to resemble a boiling lobster.

I turned my head away from him and toward the car window. Alfred was turning onto an unpaved road surrounded by trees. I *did* already know that Jonas spoke several languages. I wasn't sure I was cut out for this job after all. Maybe he was hangry, but he didn't need to be such a dick.

Jonas may have been handsome, but every moment of coldness from him stripped his beauty. To me, no man could be both attractive and mean. Without kindness, a face was uninteresting, at best.

He shifted in his seat and turned slightly away, either to ignore me completely or to give me some privacy while I dried my eyes and tried to get my face back to its normal hue.

After a minute he said, "I'm fluent in Swedish, English, French, German, and Italian. I can communicate in Spanish and Norwegian. I could manage some Finnish and Danish if you held a gun to my head."

Well, shit. That was a lot of languages. I knew that most Europeans were multilingual, but this guy was an overachiever. The SUV was bouncing on the rocky and uneven surface of the road.

"I know some Italian," I offered.

That got a laugh out of Jonas, but it didn't seem cheerful. More like a scoff. "Gli americani pensano di essere il centro dell'universo. Riescono a malapena a prendersi la briga di imparare altre lingue," he said.

Heat rose in my face again, but this time I didn't let it get the better of me. I understood everything he'd just said, and he'd basically insulted me and most Americans. His statement wasn't entirely untrue, but it was rude. "Parlo l'italiano più fluentemente di quanto tu creda. Mia madre è italiana. Stai attento, amico," I replied.

For a few beats he remained motionless, with his back still to me. Then he slowly shifted his body toward mine. I thought I saw the tiniest of smiles dance at the corner of his mouth.

"Mi dispiace, tesoro," he said.

My face felt hot for a different reason.

"Did you just call me a piece of wool?" I asked, though I knew exactly what he had said. Jonas let out a real laugh and his face transformed. Fleetingly, he looked open, unguarded, and delighted.

"Yes, you wooly sheep. That's what I called you." He laughed again, and his face remained soft. Our eyes met, and I knew, that he knew, that I knew . . . that aside from apologizing, he had just affectionately called me a treasure.

16

JONAS

I felt like I'd lived a thousand lives in one car ride. I wanted to push a reset button on my past, my present, and my future.

Gemma had caught me in my dark mood, and I was a dick to her. I was sharp, I was sarcastic, and I was plain old mean. I think I even made her cry. Someone needed to put me out of my misery. If Anna had heard me speak to Gemma the way I had, she would've kicked my ass, and I would have deserved every moment of pain and punishment that rained down upon me.

What was I doing? I absolutely knew better than to behave like this. Even Derek Drach was more polite than I'd been to Gemma over the last few hours. I did mean it when I told her that I didn't want her to know me; I had enough self-loathing to not want to unleash myself on any innocent victims. If she didn't know me or get close to me, she wouldn't have to deal with any more of my bullshit than she already had. She called me out, in perfect Italian, no less. It was glorious and I deserved it.

Our car was bumping along a very remote road. The only light outside came from our headlights and a bright moon above us. Dark branches of trees closed in on us like the walls of a cave, and while I should've felt uneasy, instead I felt pangs of liberty, like the ropes holding me down were being cut one by one.

"I need to get Alfred to pull over so we can try to figure out exactly where we're going and why we're going there," I said to Gemma.

"Ok," she said, still turned towards the window.

"And Freja didn't give you any clue that we'd be heading out this far into the wilderness?"

"I don't think Freja thought this was a 'we' situation," she said. "More like a 'me' situation."

"I'm sorry. Again."

"For what? For assuming that all Americans are stupid, or for just being a jerk in general?"

"Both."

"Apology accepted. I'm not big into grudges," Gemma said with a shrug.

The car began to slow down, but we were nowhere. Completely off-road, off-map, off-grid. Surely Freja wouldn't have hired someone to hurt Gemma. To take her into the woods to dump her . . . or worse? The fear and anger that came from picturing that dark scenario ignited rage in my chest. The car hadn't completely stopped, but I jumped out of the vehicle anyway.

I crossed over to Alfred's side of the car, yanked his door open, and tried to pull him from the front seat. Once he got untangled from his seatbelt, he slid from the car with a worried look on his face. I yelled at him in Swedish and demanded the full story of why we had ended up in the middle of nowhere.

Alfred didn't understand much of what I said, but my mood and tone were crystal clear.

Alfred put both hands up and gently pulsed them, in the international sign for "calm down, please don't hurt me." I was in no mood to come at this peacefully.

"Where are we? Tell me why we're here!" I demanded.

Alfred's eyes went wide, as if he had just remembered something. He started to reach into the inside pocket of his jacket, but I pushed him against the car while grabbing both of his hands. I didn't want him to pull anything unexpected or dangerous out of his pocket.

"Jeg har en note. Et papir," said Alfred in choked Danish. It was closer to English than to Swedish.

"Give me the note. The paper," I demand, backing away from him and holding out my hand. Alfred put his hands up like he was under arrest and nodded toward his jacket pocket. He wasn't taking any chances. I reached into his pocket and pulled out the paper. I unfolded it. It was written in Danish but in a familiar hand. Possibly Freja's handwriting. Danish was easier to understand in writing, and I was able to figure out what the note said.

It *was* written by Freja. She had written down the address of the wilderness retreat and made a note that other staff members would be arriving within hours. In an astounding and ballsy move, she had gone above and beyond to sabotage Gemma. But in doing so had given me the accidental gift of temporary freedom.

17

GEMMA

We all stood on a dark dirt road and the headlights of the car were like fuzzy lasers shining into the unknown void of the looming wilderness. The air was humid and thick and if its fragrance had a color, it would've been green.

Jonas had removed some kind of paper from Alfred's jacket pocket and used his phone flashlight to illuminate the note. Jonas read the note, put his phone light down, and raised his face to the night sky. He filled his lungs with air and then released the air in a string of bright loud laughter. Once he started, he couldn't stop. He doubled over and put his hands on his knees, laughing so hard that he had to wipe away tears. Then he squatted down, balled up the note, and threw it back to Alfred.

"Not OK?" Alfred asked as he shrugged his shoulders and put his palms up.

"Well, that depends on how you look at it," said Jonas, wiping the corners of his eyes on his sleeve.

"What the hell is going on?" I stomped my foot and a tiny cloud of dust puffed up from the dirt road.

"It seems that our friend Freja sent you on, shall we say, a special journey."

I put my hands on my hips. I was starting to sweat. "How special?"

"Special enough to get you out of the way for the night, I suspect."

"This isn't the city hotel."

"This is not," said Jonas.

"This is the forest hotel?"

"Do you see a hotel?" Jonas opened his arms wide and swiveled at the waist. I saw trees. A lot of trees. Also, a lot of stars. And what appeared to be a lake shimmering in the distance.

"I do not."

"This is the location of the forest photo shoot. There are cabins here. Somewhere," he said.

"Can we just go to the forest hotel then? Kristina said it was a few miles from here?"

"From what I understand, that's more of a lodge than a hotel. And it's open by reservation only."

"And these aren't the dates of our reservation," I said.

"You're a pretty quick study."

"It's all that salmon. Powered up my brain."

Alfred gestured to the trees and walked towards them. He gave a little wave and then disappeared into the darkness.

"Did he just abandon us? Are we about to be murdered?" I asked.

"I think he has to take a piss," said Jonas. "And if anyone has a hit out on them, it's you, not me."

"Thanks. That makes me feel a lot better. I've heard that Freja's intense but isn't this a bit much?" I asked him.

"Fair assessment."

"Was her plan for Alfred to drop me off in the wilderness alone, and just leave me here? Like, to die? That's beyond bitchy and moving into criminal mastermind territory."

"I don't know," Jonas said, his face serious. "I assume she just wanted to set you off track for a few hours. I think it's my fault."

"How so?"

"I told her I didn't want to do any interviews tonight or for the next few days. That I was overwhelmed. I think she took matters into her own hands."

"Seems a little more personal than that," I said.

Jonas shrugged. "She *is* possessive. And has a jealous streak."

"Are you two dating?" Screw the 'don't ask about his private life' clause.

He laughed a little. "No. At least, not anymore."

"You *were* dating?" This was unimportant information, except in how it pertained to my attempted murder.

"I wouldn't call it dating, exactly. And it was several years ago."

"You must be amazing in bed if Freja wants to kill off any other women in your vicinity," I barked. A smile played on his lips. "And why the hell would she be jealous of me?"

Jonas turned his back to me and started toward the car. "Because she knows you're talented and attractive," he said. "And completely my type."

Alfred picked that exact moment to appear out of the darkness, right beside me. I hadn't heard his footsteps and he startled me so badly that I screamed out and whacked him in the face with both fists. Jonas jumped in and pulled me back from Alfred who was looking like he might cry. "Easy, tiger."

There was no reason for Jonas's touch to affect me like it did. It was two regular hands grasping my two regular shoulders and gently pulling my body toward his, and away from poor Alfred. But nothing about it felt regular.

As a child, I'd always wondered how storybook characters felt when they drank love potions. The illustrations were of wide eyes, red cheeks, and bubbles and floating hearts fluttering around the heads of those struck by love. But what did their stomachs feel like after drinking the magic elixir? I didn't have to wonder anymore; they probably felt like I did right then. Like someone had poured an effervescent hot wax onto my shoulders that sank into my skin and seeped into and settled in my gut. My stomach roiled, fluttered, and flipped while sending heat waves out to the rest of my body. It was either the best or the worst I had ever felt. I had to get his hands off of me.

"I have to pee," I announced, and I marched blindly toward the black night, feeling bewitched, bothered, and bewildered.

THE GROUND under my feet went from rocky to soft, and trees were all around me. I was disoriented and heard a rustling to my left. Great. I was about to be killed by a Swedish boar or giant fanged owl. Freja would get her wish. But I really did have to pee. Suddenly Jonas was behind me, and he pulled me close again.

"Slow down," he said gently into my ear. "I don't want to lose you out here."

This was ridiculous. He'd gone from *Sir Cold Asshole of*

Dickville to *Sexy Wilderness Prince Charming* in the span of an hour? "I have to pee," I said, trying to wriggle out of his arms.

"You can go, but I'm going to stand here."

"You are NOT going to watch me."

"I'll close my eyes."

I faced him and crossed my arms in defiance, but it was hard to look stoic and fierce when I was hopping from foot to foot, trying not to pee my pants. "Turn around," I said.

"Alright," he said, turning his back to me. "But if I hear you make a run for it, you'll have to hold my hand. Anyone could get lost in a second out here. We have to stay together."

"Fine." I slowly walked a few steps, pulled down my joggers, and squatted above the ground. "Is poison ivy a thing in Sweden?" I asked.

"Nope. Just North America, I think."

That relaxed me a little, but then I was hit with pee stage fright. "Could you sing a song or something?" I heard him laugh.

"That might be more painful than a poison ivy rash," he said.

"Please?"

"Uh . . ." He was quiet for a moment and then he began to hum an upbeat tune. It did the trick. It was a weirdly humiliating but also endearing moment.

"Was that ABBA?"

"Yes," he laughed.

"*Take a Chance on Me?*"

"Ten points for Gryffindor."

"I'm in Ravenclaw."

"Of course you are."

"Slytherin for you?" I asked.

"Let's get out of here before a wild boar finds us."

I pulled my pants up fast; who cared about toilet paper? "Those actually exist?"

"Oh yes," Jonas reached his arm out behind him for me to grab. I took his hand. "They have giant tusks and are very dangerous." I pulled on his hand in an attempt to speed him up. "But they only kill five people a year. Give or take."

"What's with the joke cracking? I couldn't get you to speak a word to me before this, and now you're a regular stand-up comedian."

"I'm not joking. Boars really do kill five people a year." We popped back out into the clearing and Alfred was leaning against the car, smoking a cigarette.

I pinched his arm. "You know what I mean."

He turned to me. He was still holding my hand. He was too close. I could smell him, and I had a weakness for men who smelled good. He smelled like birch, pink pepper, and ginger, with a lemon twist.

"My heart lives in the forest," he told me, and he put his hand on his chest like he was taking an oath. "This is my favorite place." He leaned in closer, and his hair fell across his brow as he bowed his head. He swept it off his forehead with his free hand, and his sparkling eyes gazed at me through long eyelashes. He pursed his lips as if considering something, and then relaxed them into a ghost of a smile.

I thought I might swoon. But no self-respecting independent woman would hit the ground just because Mister Swedish Sexypants was trying to cast a spell on her. I stayed upright.

Jonas broke the trance by saying, "This also means that the interview is off the itinerary for tonight!" He squeezed my hand then let go, and he turned and walked back to the car.

18

JONAS

I had decided that Alfred was not a threat to Gemma and was probably as much a victim of Freja's manipulations as the rest of us. Once we all drank some water and regained our composure, we gathered around the car to formulate a plan.

In a mix of English, Norwegian, and written Danish, we somehow landed on the same page.

None of us wanted to drive all the way back to the city. Gemma and I were jet lagged and hungry. Alfred seemed nervous and exhausted, and Gemma said that she saw him take a slug out of a flask that he pulled from his jacket pocket when I was relieving myself in the woods. One could hope that his drink was non-alcoholic, but considering the intense stress level of the situation, I wasn't so sure.

"Are you sure we shouldn't try to backtrack and find a hotel?" Part of me wanted to go wherever Gemma felt safest, but the other part of me wanted to run straight into the forest and never turn back.

"If you feel like it's the option with which you're most comfortable, we'll do that," I said.

Gemma looked me up and down and scrunched up her face as if she wasn't sure she liked what she saw. "You're gazing out into the woods like you've returned to the mother ship and your people are calling you home," she said. She opened her backpack which lay at her feet. After a few moments of digging around she pulled out a granola bar and a printed information packet.

"Is that the information that *Profile* sent you?" I asked.

"I think there are maps of the property in here, along with cabin descriptions, and codes to coolers and pantries."

"Are you open to staying here?"

"Do you think we'll be safe?" she asked.

I could tell she was worried and unsure, and that she was considering staying out here just for me. "We should be fine. We have maps and resources." I tried to sound even and measured, but excitement was bubbling up through my chest and out in my voice.

Gemma put her hands on her hips and surveyed our surroundings. It wasn't fair to put her in this position. In a place where she didn't feel safe.

"We don't have much food for the night, other than a few energy bars," she said, holding up one to illustrate.

"Oh!" Alfred exclaimed, and he went to the back of the car. Gemma and I followed him.

He lifted the back hatch and opened a built-in compartment. It was a cooler filled with enough travel snacks to satisfy even the most spoiled executive traveler. There were also bottles of water and alcohol.

Apparently in a hurry to get rid of us, Alfred grabbed Gemma's backpack and stuffed it with cheese, nuts, crackers, dried fruit, chocolates, and tiny jars of mustard and caviar. He zipped up the bag and pushed it into Gemma's arms, the weight of it causing her to momentarily stumble.

"Ok," said Gemma, looking like Father Christmas holding his bag of toys. "We can stay."

ALFRED GOT the rest of our things out of the car, and I studied the map using the headlights as a torch. "There are three options for lodging tonight: the Air Castle, the Forest Hut, and the Floating Cabin."

"Which one's closest?" Gemma asked.

"The Forest Hut is about three kilometers away, but I don't know how rugged the trail is. The Air Castle is close, but we'd have to take a boat across the lake to get there."

"What kind of boat?"

"There's a drawing of a canoe here on the map. Maybe there are some on the shore." I pulled my phone out of my pocket. "I still don't have a signal. Is there anyone who will panic if you are unreachable for a while?"

"Rava," Gemma said instantly. Then her face fell.

"What's wrong?"

"Nothing," she said, but her voice sounded thick.

"Tell me."

She pulled her hair off of her face with both hands, holding it back in a ponytail. She lifted her face to the sky, closed her eyes, and took a few breaths. "I just realized that I have no other names. No living parents or grandparents, no siblings, no boyfriend or husband. I just depressed myself."

"If it makes you feel any better, I don't have any names on my list, unless you count my agent."

"Agents count."

"We both have one name then."

19

GEMMA

"Ok? Goodbye?" asked Alfred as he backed up toward the driver's side door of the SUV.

We were really about to let this guy leave us in the middle of the Swedish wilderness. Jonas pulled out some cash from his wallet, gave it to Alfred, and they had a final exchange, which I understood none of. Jonas wrote a few things down on paper and handed that to Alfred as well. Alfred jumped into the car with the speed of a panicked getaway driver and literally left us in his dust.

I coughed as the dusty spray from the tires and gravel hit me in the face. "He's really torn up about having to leave us."

Jonas was studying the map. "I think this is the trail here," he said, walking slowly toward a trail sign.

"You grabbing your bags, or are you leaving them here for the wild boars?"

He doubled back, gathered his belongings, and then resumed his march toward the trail. "It's dark, but the moon is near full, and we should be able to see well enough."

"Or we could use this," I said, turning on my flashlight.

Jonas squinted as the light hit his face. "Never leave home without it. When you spend a year of your life walking, you have a flashlight. And extra batteries."

"What else do you never leave home without when you spend a year of your life walking?"

"Extra socks, first aid kit, a LifeStraw, collapsible water bottle, camera, solar phone charger, and condoms."

Jonas raised his eyebrow. "I'm sure we can use most of those things . . . maybe not the first aid kit."

I rolled my eyes. "What did you tell Alfred before he left?"

Jonas shrugged and continued toward the trail. "I think the shore is this way."

JONAS HAD PICKED the right trail and within five minutes we were standing on the shore of the lake. It was hard to tell how large the body of water was because, according to the map, we were standing in a cove. Luckily, we could easily see across the water to the other shore, and I spotted lanterns marking a path that disappeared into the woods.

"I thought there was no one here? How did they put lights on the path?" I asked.

"Probably permanent solar lights." Jonas walked down the shore, searching for the canoes while I lined up our bags. Two rolling suitcases, mine larger than his, one backpack, and one shoulder bag. "Found it," he called.

I shined my flashlight in his direction. He stood triumphantly beside a small canoe that held two oars and two lifejackets. I held the beam of my flashlight on Jonas. I shifted it to our luggage. Then I swung the light back to illuminate the canoe.

"What do you think?" asked Jonas.

"I think you're gonna need a bigger boat."

"YOU SHOULD PACK LIGHTER," Jonas said.

"I didn't know I was signing up for the inaugural Swedish season of *Alone*. Do you think we can outlast the other contestants in the wilderness and come home with 250 grand?"

Jonas stared at me for a moment, then went back to sizing up the boat. "I think we could put your bag in the middle, mine at my feet, and our smaller bags on our laps."

"I could wear my backpack—"

"Absolutely not," barked Jonas. I jumped, startled by his tone. "You'll wear that life jacket, or we won't take the boat at all. We can walk to the Forest Hut."

"Ok, dad." I saw that Jonas's mouth was drawn up in a grimace and his arms were stiffly at his side, hands balled up into fists. This guy was serious about water safety. "I'll wear it. I was planning to." A white lie, but it seemed to calm him down.

"Good." He handed me the life jacket and he loaded the bags into the canoe. I got settled on the front seat while Jonas grabbed the rear of the boat and shoved it further into the water. Jonas hopped in, causing a precarious wobble. We stabilized and he sat down. "Paddle," he commanded. "Let's get there as quickly as we can." This was not a pleasure cruise.

It *was* pleasurable, though. We found our rhythm and the water was still except for where our paddles broke the surface. The surrounding trees shimmied in the wind and there was the gentle dark chatter of life that awakens in the woods at night. Jonas and I did not speak. We were approaching the shore. It was warmly illuminated by glowing lanterns that outlined the gentle curves of the hillside.

My peace was short-lived. I caught motion out of the corner of my eye, but before I could process what I was seeing, I felt a blast of air and then my hair was pulled, and my head jerked to the side. I ducked to the side to escape whatever was attacking me, which caused the boat to heave to the left.

Jonas quickly shoved his weight to the right for counterbalance and the boat rocked and jerked.

"Oh my god," I said through choked tears.

"Stay down," said Jonas. "We're almost there."

I crouched the best I could, but between my backpack in my lap and the bulky life vest I was wearing, I could only move so far. I laced my fingers over my bowed head like I was in a school tornado drill. My hands touched something warm and wet. Blood, probably. I wasn't willing to sit up to look.

I felt the bottom of the boat scrape against the rocky surface of the shore, and I tried to slow my breathing. My adrenaline ebbed and I started to cry. I stayed in my duck and cover position. Jonas jumped out of the boat and pulled it safely out of the water and then he was by my side. "Are you hurt?"

"I don't know!"

"I think that was an owl. Where's your flashlight?" He picked up our suitcases and tossed them onto the shore.

"An owl? Nowhere in my contract did I agree to reenact a scene from *The Birds.*"

Jonas's voice took on a gentler tone and I felt his touch on my shoulder. That damn hand again. "Is it in your bag?" he asked softly. "Let me see your head." I liked the softer side of Jonas.

My heart rate was slowing, and my tears were drying up. I

sat up. His eyes widened when he saw my face and he winced. "What? What is it?" I started to cry again.

"It's ok, Gemma. Really. Come sit on the shore. Let me get your bag."

I handed him my backpack and he guided me to the shore. I plopped down on the rocky sand, pulled my knees up, and rested my forehead on my legs.

Jonas got the flashlight out of the side pocket and shone it toward my head and face. My hands were bloody. "It's ok. I think it looks worse than it is!" he said brightly, though I could tell he didn't quite believe his own words. I decided to lean into the reassurance and only go with the worst-case scenario if reality called for it. "Head wounds can bleed a lot." He moved his fingers gently through my hair.

Jonas found my collapsible cup in the backpack, filled it up with lake water and returned to my side. "I'm just going to rinse your hair so I can see where the blood is coming from." He placed his hand under my chin and softly lifted it up while he poured water onto my scalp. Water ran down my back. I could feel his warm breath on my cheek. "I see it. Not so bad." He pulled a handkerchief out of his back pocket and pressed it on the top of my head.

"How old *are* you?" I asked him. "I haven't seen anyone with a handkerchief since my grandfather was alive."

"I'm an old soul." He kept steady pressure on the cloth, and I stayed quiet. He checked it after a minute. "I think it's stopped bleeding. Just stay here for a few more minutes."

"I knew the giant fanged owl would get me sooner or later."

Jonas exhaled a tiny laugh. "I guess we'll be needing all your safety gear after all. Where are the bandages?"

"Right next to the condoms. You can't miss them."

Jonas found the first aid kit and cleaned my wound. "You ok to walk?"

"I think so."

We gathered our bags and followed the solar lantern-lined path up into the dark opening of the forest.

"It should only be a few minutes from here," Jonas said. "Still ok?"

Was I ok? I was isolated in an unknown wilderness with a grumpy movie star. I had significant jet lag, was famished, had a head wound from a renegade owl, and was pulling a too-large rolling suitcase up a hiking trail. And I knew that the "movie star" part should've been a bonus, but when you were stuck in the wild with someone, did it matter if they were famous? Not really. But if they were sweet, gentle, and dashingly handsome while bandaging said head wounds, maybe it wasn't all bad.

"I'm ok."

Jonas was ahead of me with my flashlight, though the lanterns lit the path quite well. We were almost to the point where the lights ended. I needed to eat, rinse off the blood, and get some sleep.

We came to the end of the lantern trail, but there was no cabin.

"Can I start crying again?" I asked Jonas.

He checked the map. "It should be here, or very close to here. He took a few more steps. I had to watch my footing so I could steer my suitcase around roots, rocks, and bumps. I ran right into Jonas, who had stopped walking. He was staring up. I followed his gaze.

About twenty-five feet above our heads rested a cabin on

stilts. It was hard to make out in the darkness, but I could see that it had a porch and windows and was tucked into the canopy like it was an extension of the trees themselves. It also had a long wooden suspension bridge leading from the cabin to an even higher wooden deck that overlooked the forest.

"How do we get up there?" I asked.

Jonas shifted the flashlight beam to a wooden spiral staircase. I thought of my suitcase and groaned.

"I think this place is made for the backpacking set," I said. "Not the luxury hotel set. Can we just leave our stuff down here for the night?"

"Sure. If you don't mind the bears taking your things."

"I know you didn't just say BEARS."

"Just brown bears."

I started rolling my suitcase over to the staircase and lugged it onto the first step.

"Here," said Jonas. "You take the backpack and my smaller bag, and I'll get the suitcases." No argument from me.

There were thirty-six stairs. I knew because I counted each grunt as I ascended. Out of breath at the top, I waited for Jonas to catch up, but he seemed to fly up the stairs, carrying a suitcase in each hand.

"This code had better work," I said, as I examined the lock on the door. "337, right?" Jonas shrugged. I punched in the numbers and the lock slid open. "Thank god." We were in.

20

GEMMA

It was dark.

"I guess they were serious about the no electricity part," I said.

"None at all?" asked Jonas.

"Not that I can tell, unless there's some in the Common House for event food storage or something."

There was an oil lamp and half a dozen candles on a small table in the corner. There were matches there as well, and Jonas used one to light the lamp. The warm light flickered in the cabin, and we were able to see the interior more clearly.

It was a one room cabin; a half-wall blocked off a small vestibule by the entry door, and the main area held a small double bed which held two bolster pillows, two sleeping pillows, and two large square pillows. There were separate white duvets folded lengthwise, and two blue and white striped wool blankets at the foot of the bed.

One wall was all glass, floor to ceiling; it was like living in the trees. A wood burning stove was tucked into a corner with a pile of logs on the floor nearby.

"Sooo," I said. "Toilet?"

"I saw a bath house of sorts on the map. I'll go check." Jonas headed back out the door and down the spiral staircase. I heard his feet take the thirty-six steps quickly, and then there was silence. And more silence. And several more minutes of silence. I sat in one of the chairs and waited. I wanted just to fall into the bed but: one, my hair, face, and hands were covered in dried blood. Two, it seemed rude to just take over the bed when there was only one. Maybe sleeping arrangements should be a joint decision? And three, I really had to pee.

I pulled my phone out of my pocket. No signal and 23% battery left. What if Jonas had been attacked by a bear? I didn't hear any screaming. Would he scream if a bear approached? Probably not. He'd just cross his arms and give it a dirty look.

"Gemma! HEYYY GEMMA!" I went out onto the front porch of the tree house. Jonas was below, clearly enjoying himself as he shouted my name.

"I suppose you do resemble a young Marlon Brando," I said.

"I found your toilet. You may descend the stairs."

I held on to the rough railing as I made my way down, stepping carefully. When I got to the bottom, Jonas held out his hand. "The ground is a little bumpy, and I forgot the flashlight." He led me to an outhouse about twenty paces away. Next to that, there was a giant cauldron with wood burning beneath it.

"Will we be burning me at the stake tonight?" I asked him.

"It's a rustic shower fed by a hot spring," Jonas said. This was a different man than I'd encountered on the airplane, in the office, and on the car ride. His features were softened by the dim light and the glow of the fire. He was down to his t-shirt and jeans. His shoulders looked broader. I could see the curves of muscles in his biceps and forearms. There was a gentleness and a playfulness to Jonas that was new to me, and it was becoming. He brushed his hair out of his eyes and left a dark smudge of soot in its place.

"You've got a little something," I said. I moved closer and reached up to wipe off the mark. His eyelids fluttered when I touched him, and I thought I heard his breath catch. He seemed surprised and pleased . . . almost as if the touch of another person was new to him. I pulled my hand back. "Guess I'll brave the outhouse."

When I returned to the fire, Jonas was up on the small ladder, testing the temperature of the water in the cauldron. "I think it's ready," he said. "Would you like a shower or a bath?"

I didn't exactly know how either was possible, but I was too tired to ask questions. "I'd love a shower to get the blood off, but I'd love a bath for the rest of me."

He considered my request. "That might work." He ran his hand along the stubble on his jawline. "But answer this question honestly, because it will inform how we go about it."

I wasn't sure where he was going with this.

"How modest are you?"

"Like on a scale of one to ten?"

"Sure. As it pertains to public bathing."

"Um . . . if one is wearing a snowsuit and ten is full nudity?"

Jonas waited.

"Maybe an eight?" I said. "I don't really care. Not when it's dark and I'm this bloody and tired."

"We can make that work. I found some towels in the top of the outhouse cabinet. I'll hold one up and you get out of your clothes. Step up here into the bowl, but make sure it's not too hot. I can add some cold spring water from the pump if it's overheated. Once you're in, I'll rinse your hair over the side with the shower attachment."

"I think that's the most you've said to me at one time since we met."

"Is it?" Jonas collected the towel and proceeded as promised. He held the towel out like a shield and ducked his head behind it. I thought about staying in my underwear but decided to go full ten out of ten and take everything off. I went up the ladder to the big bath bowl and tested the water. Hot, but not scalding. I put one leg in, and then the other. I lowered myself in, and a moan escaped me.

"That good?" Jonas asked.

"You wouldn't believe it."

"I'll try it when you're out," he said.

"It will be like *Little House on the Prairie* with the sharing of the bath water."

"Are you Laura?

"Of course I'm Laura! You're nice and responsible like Pa."

"I'm not sure I'm comfortable with being your Pa. Better make me Almanzo," said Jonas as he lowered the towel. He climbed up a step of the ladder so he could reach my shoulders and head. He pumped a handle leading to a tube, and soon, hot water was pulling from the cauldron and coming out of the shower head. "Lean back," he said.

I can't really describe the heaven that was Jonas Hellgren washing my hair. I was exhausted and it was so surreal that I couldn't really focus on the fact that JONAS. HELLGREN. WAS. WASHING. MY. HAIR.

He used his left hand to run his fingers through my hair and across my forehead. With his right hand he held the shower nozzle and softly sprayed the water, washing the blood away. He worked in silence as I floated euphorically. "Almost done," he said, as he worked to untangle a few of the ringlets at the nape of my neck.

I opened my eyes and was looking straight up at the stars. The starlight felt like medicine as it shone down on my bare skin that shimmered with droplets of hot spring water.

Speaking of bare skin—in my blissed-out trance, I hadn't realized that I was floating upwards and that my breasts, buoyant and free, were bobbing above the surface of the water. My first instinct was to sink back down and cover them up, but I decided to hell with it. Jonas didn't have to look if he didn't want to.

Gently, Jonas took my head in both of his hands. He leaned in close to my left ear . . . so close, in fact, that I felt his lips brush against my skin. "You're all clean."

I sat up and re-submerged my torso under the water. I ran my fingers through my hair and felt the tender spot where the owl had grazed my scalp, but everything else seemed clean and undamaged.

"Thank you," I said. Jonas was over at the wood pile getting another log to add to the fire under the cauldron. The distance was probably a good idea; for a moment I wanted to turn and grab his head with both of my hands and pull his face to mine. I wanted his mouth on my mouth. I wanted to taste him. I wanted to breathe the air from his lungs into my own.

Which was ridiculous. First of all, Jonas clearly said that he didn't want me to know him. That probably included "knowing" him in the biblical sense. Also, I wasn't here for romance. Or sex. Or any kind of intimate connection other than the one between interviewer and interviewee. Not only would it be unprofessional, but romance wasn't on my list of personal needs at the moment. My life was simple, organized, and predictable, and that's how I liked it. Intimacy was messy, and I wanted to keep things just as they were, thank you very much. Being in love was for emotional daredevils.

WHEN I WAS YOUNG, I was desperately in love with my life—with the sensuality of just existing as a child in a safe world. Things I loved: my mother brushing my hair and the sounds the bristles made as they ran over my scalp and down the ends of my dark waves; when my father would sear steaks on the stove and the meat would hit the hot greased pan and send up plumes of smoke and grease and I'd duck for cover behind his back; the smell of coffee brewing on an early summer morning when the windows were open and there was just enough of a chill in the air, not burned off yet, and I could trick myself into believing that it wouldn't be sweltering later.

I spent a lot of time outside as a kid, especially in the warmer months. I didn't like how the air conditioning would lock out that scent of grass and sweet wind. I had no siblings, so I spent most of my time exploring alone. If the weather was bad, I spent time with books, records, pencil and paper, tape recorders, and a lot of boredom. Delicious, indulgent boredom. The kind where moments stretch out in front of you to infinity. Like swimming in a cloudy lake when you can't touch the bottom and it feels luxurious and risky at the same time.

Then my mother died, and all the water drained out of my lake. All the pages of my books were too thin and easily torn. It was too cold outside, too hot inside. I would hit record on the cassette player but would record nothing but static and silent tears. The absence of my mother felt world-ending. But, at the same time, the routine of life went on exactly as it had the day before. I held on to that pink stone, but it still felt hard to breathe. Everything else in the world felt like a time-lapse photo of stars, spiraling in the night sky, leaving trails of brilliant light. I felt like a black hole, my starlight extinguished.

21

———

JONAS

I told Gemma I was collecting more wood for the fire, but I really needed to get some distance and gather myself.

I tried not to look at her when I was at the side of the tub. I really did. I held up the towel while she got into the water, and the night was dark, and the fire only put out so much light. But as I washed her hair and the blood rinsed away and her body relaxed . . . I couldn't look away.

Gemma's nipples had broken the surface of the water, and at first, I closed my eyes. I kept rubbing her scalp gently with my fingertips, careful not to press along her wound. I figured she would adjust herself to make sure that she was fully covered by the water.

I opened my eyes and saw that she had not hidden her body. She was even more on display as her full breasts breached the water. When Gemma was still, stars and firelight were gently reflected on the bath water like tiny diamonds dancing at the edges of her skin.

She held her position long enough for it to be on purpose, so I took that as permission to take in her body with my eyes.

For just a moment I didn't fight my feelings or my thoughts, and I let my psyche run wild. I let myself imagine everything I wanted to do to her, and with her. Some of it was soft and some of it was filthy. I was glad her eyes were closed and that she couldn't see the way I was staring at her flesh or the way my erection pushed out firmly and obviously against the fabric of my jeans.

If, at that moment, she had turned to me, I would've grabbed her face. I would have kissed her hard enough to let her feel the raw and untethered desire that was surging through me. I would've pulled her from the water and pressed her up against the ladder, pushed myself between her legs and unleashed everything.

But, instead, I was slowly picking up logs and willing my dick to soften just the tiniest bit before I made a fool of myself.

"You ok over there?" she called out.

"Almost done." I probably should've jerked off behind the wood pile to put myself out of my misery. It only would've taken a few seconds to get relief, but now it was too late. I walked back over to the tub and added another log to the fire. *Don't look, don't look, don't look.*

I stepped up on the ladder. Gemma's eyes were closed, and her body was still and floating. I put my mouth close to her ear. "Don't fall asleep in there." She stirred and let out a tiny and beautiful moan of satisfaction.

"Why don't you get in?" she asked. "I can get out now, or you can join me. It doesn't matter to me." She sounded so casual. Could she have any idea of all the outrageous things I'd like to do to her in that bathtub? "What's *your* number on the modesty scale?"

What *was* my number? If I got into that tub naked, my

penis would be the star of the show, and nobody wanted that. "That depends." I stood silently behind her. I wanted to get in so badly. I wanted to run my hands along her wet skin. I wanted to put my fingers between—*No. No. No.*

"Get in. I'll move over here. And I'll close my eyes," said Gemma. She shifted to the other side of the bowl and closed her eyes as promised. She looked so sweet. So peaceful. So relaxed. So perfect. None of the worry, fatigue, or uncertainty that I'd seen pass over her face in the last twenty-four hours. "You coming?"

If only. I hopped back down to the ground and pulled off all of my clothes—with the exception of my underwear. My prayer to the woodland gods was that Gemma would keep her eyes closed and that the fit of my underwear would be tight enough to keep me pressed down.

I climbed back up the ladder. Her eyes were still closed. As quickly as I could manage, I submerged my lower half in the water. It was deliciously hot, and the sensation took my breath away. Every muscle in my body started to loosen and relax. Except one, which was still at full attention. "I'm in. You can open your eyes."

Gemma did so, but politely kept her eyes pointed up at the sky. She probably assumed I was naked, and surely that felt a little weird. To be naked in a tub, alone in the wilderness with a man you'd only known for a day? We stargazed for a while, sharing a soothing and easy silence.

"I see you're not a total ten," Gemma said, breaking the silence. She was pointing at my lap. I hoped she could only see the flash of color from the fabric and not the fact that my cock was still quite hard, though not as painfully full as before.

"About a seven."

"I have a question for you."

"Officially starting the interview?"

She laughed a little. Her smile was lovely. "It's off the record."

"Go ahead."

"It's a small question. So, your name is Jonas—"

"Really starting with the basics, I see."

She rolled her eyes. "I speak English, so I say your name with a hard J. You're Swedish—"

"Your astute observations continue to astound me."

Gemma splashed water in my face. I wiped my eyes.

She continued: "So, I assume when you say your own name, you use the soft J sound called for in Swedish, or Danish, Norwegian, German, and all of those languages."

"If I'm speaking those languages at the time, yes."

"But when you introduced yourself to me on the airplane, you used the hard J. I don't want to mispronounce your name . . . so should I use the hard J or the soft one?"

"In a way, I'm translating my name into English. Most English speakers wouldn't use the soft J even if I insisted. It's just not intuitive, as far as the rules of the language go. So, I just say my name in English, so to speak. My last name would be said with a different accent in Swedish as well, but the letter sounds would be about the same. If my name was David, and I was in Italy, I wouldn't introduce myself as David. I would say 'dah-vee-day'. I think it works like that. Just the tiny translations one makes when language hopping. I don't even think about it anymore."

"So I'm ok with the hard J?"

"You're fine with the hard J," I said.

"One more question," Gemma said.

"Alright."

"What changed?" Gemma lowered herself so the water covered her shoulders. I could hear the fire crackling beneath us. "Up until we got here you . . ." She tried to find the right wording. "You were standoffish. Even a bit of—"

"An asshole?"

"Your words, not mine. But yes. You haven't been that way since we got here. What changed?"

So many things had changed. How could I tell her that the forest was one of the only places I felt like I could breathe? That every time I looked at her, I felt strange pulls in my stomach and chest. And that now that I'd seen her naked, I was going to obsess about nothing else for days.

She waited. No rushing. No expectations.

"I'm naturally reserved and sometimes shy," I said. "And that often comes across as standoffish." I swirled my hands in the warm water. She was watching me now. "I've also been angry and sad. The eighth anniversary of my wife's death is in two days. The anniversary can trigger a lot of darkness for me."

I paused to see if she had anything to say or would let me off the hook with this question. She kept quiet, so I kept talking. "I felt trapped by the events planned this week. The interviews, the photo shoots, all the socializing. It was paralyzing." I stopped again. Her gaze was steady as she watched my face. "This lucky mix-up felt like divine intervention. I love the forest and being outdoors. It fueled a very swift change in my mood."

"I understand that," she said.

"But I'm moody." I felt like I needed to warn her. The dark patches often came out of nowhere for me and I didn't feel like I was an entirely safe person to be around, emotionally. "I can dip into black moods quickly. I'm usually quite an asshole to be around when I'm in that headspace. I'm trying to get better, but I haven't had a lot of practice being around other people for extended periods of time. Not in a while." Well. There went half of my life story. Probably more than she wanted to hear.

"Thanks for answering," she said. She stretched out, and though her torso stayed underwater, her foot rubbed against the skin of my calf. I had just about recovered my dignity as far as my erection was concerned, and with just a touch I was back in trouble.

2 2

GEMMA

I let my foot linger on Jonas's calf for a few seconds. I knew what I was doing, and I shouldn't have done it, but I felt a surge of boldness move through me and I let it take over. I don't think he noticed the touch, but it excited me. I wanted to touch him again but didn't dare.

His answer to my question was generous and thoughtful. I liked his self-awareness, his confidence, and his vulnerability. The mental ideal I'd been holding of Jonas Hellgren was dissolving, and the reality of him was starting to take shape.

"I'm glad you got this escape, but won't it be over soon? Won't they come to get us tomorrow?" I asked.

"Maybe. Maybe not." Jonas was deep in the water, and I could only see his head.

I sat up straighter in the tub. "Why maybe not?"

Jonas went all the way underwater. Good lord, I hoped he had his eyes closed under there. He popped back up and shook the water from his hair like some kind of men's cologne model. He rubbed the water out of his eyes with one hand. "I may have told Freja that I was thinking of skipping out on the next few days. Pulling a disappearing act. I often do that on the anniversary of Anna's death."

"Will they not come looking for *me*?" He didn't answer. "Jonas?"

"Yes, Gemma?"

"Why will they not come looking for me?"

"I may have told Alfred to tell them that he left you at a different spot."

"I see. And you gave him some cash so he wouldn't forget?"

"My Norwegian isn't great. And his is worse. So, it may have gotten lost in translation."

"Is this a kidnapping?"

"Does it feel like a kidnapping?"

"No," I admitted.

The water level had gone down, my breasts were in a "don't fence me in!" kind of mood, and I was getting hungrier. It was time to exit the tub. "Do you want to get out first, Captain Underpants, since you're at a seven and I'm over here at a full ten?" I caught Jonas glancing at my chest.

"Um . . ." Jonas put his hands underwater and rested them across his lap. "Maybe you should go first."

I had an idea of what he might be hiding. I considered making him get out first anyway—that was a sight I'd be interested in seeing—but I took pity on him. "Alright. Close your eyes, though." He did as instructed and I stood up in the water. He shifted to the side to let me pass. I swiveled around and backed down the ladder. I glanced up and saw that Jonas, eyes wide open, was openly watching me exit the bath. "Excuse me!" I said, in mock protest.

"My apologies," said Jonas, but he did not look away. He didn't even blink.

· · ·

I WENT BACK UP to the treehouse cabin while Jonas rinsed out my clothes and "secured the fire," whatever that meant. I put on some clothes, brushed my teeth (spit out the water and toothpaste over the railing of our front porch), and put my hair back in a ponytail. I pulled out what snacks we had and put them on the table and re-lit the lantern and candles. It wasn't very cold, so I didn't mess with the wood stove.

I was feeling mixed up. I'd been attracted to men, of course, over the span of my adult life. I'd been engaged to Adam, but I never felt myself just involuntarily light up at a man's touch, or gaze, like I had experienced with Jonas. I was telling myself that I was just starstruck; that if Jonas was a banker or a professor, I wouldn't feel the same. Maybe it was a lie, maybe it wasn't, but I was holding on to that explanation for dear life.

I brought out the water bottles and the small bottles of alcohol as well. We had some mini bottles of wine, vodka, scotch, and two I'd never heard of, one called *Akvavit* and another named *Swedish punsch*. I started eating without Jonas. There were two stoneware plates in the cabin, two mugs, and two forks, knives, and spoons.

I heard Jonas coming up the stairs and he came through the door wearing just a towel wrapped around his waist. I must've stared a little too long because he said, "All my clothes are up here." He saw my food and beverage set-up. "Open or cash bar tonight?"

"Free all-you-can-drink, while supplies last."

He retrieved some clothes from his suitcase.

"I can go outside while you get dressed," I said.

"And know that you're watching me from the porch? No way."

"I'm not the one with the inappropriate watching habit."

"You sure about that?"

Actually, no, I wasn't sure about that. He took his clothes outside and got dressed and came back wearing soft joggers and a navy V-neck t-shirt. Never had I seen an outfit so simple look so magnificent. I stopped chewing my cracker mid-bite and just stared at him. He checked himself as if to make sure he didn't have a stain on the front of his shirt. "What?" he asked.

"Nothing. Sorry." I busied myself with the crackers. Jonas stood over the bed, which was only a few paces from where I sat.

"So," he began, and then stopped.

"Want some food?"

"I do. But should we talk about this bed?"

"What's there to talk about?"

"There's only one. And by the looks of it, it's barely big enough for two."

"We're not giant people," I said, deciding to play it cool and casual. Jonas scoffed at that. "What? You think I'm fat? I know I'm not the most slender willow, but— "

"You're perfect. But—" Jonas put his hands near the top of his head and then waved them down his body indicating that he was above average in height. Also, he just called me perfect.

"Yes, you're a tall glass of water, but you're not gigantic widthwise. I'm not sure anything would hold you lengthwise."

He smirked at me. "You sure there's nothing you can think of that can take my length?" There went my burning face again.

"In bed, I mean!"

"Oh yeah?"

"The length of your body in a bed!" I gave up. "You know what I mean."

Jonas snickered and grabbed a granola bar. He surveyed the drink selection. "Have you had any water yet?"

"Not yet."

"Please drink a bottle, or two. You don't want to mess with dehydration. We'll find a good supply of fresh water tomorrow when it's light out."

I took a water and a mini bottle of wine. "Want any alcohol?"

"Oh, no thank you. Not tonight."

"You sure?"

He sat down at the table with me and took a bite of the granola bar. Then he had a long sip of water.

"You're the king of the pregnant pause."

"The what?"

"Let's get back to the bed . . . so to speak," I said.

"You want to get back to the bed with me?"

"What are we, fifteen years old?"

"Drinking significantly lowers my inhibitions," said Jonas, "and I think it's best to stay clear headed right now. This is a professional situation, correct?"

"If you call kidnapping professional."

"As for the bed, are you comfortable with both of us sleeping there? I haven't found any other options, and there's not much space for anything else unless I go outside."

"I'm not letting you become a bear's midnight snack."

"I'd sleep on the higher deck on the other side of that suspension bridge."

"Then you'd be an owl appetizer. And what if you fell? No way. Sleep here. I'm fine if you're fine."

"Alright. Maybe tomorrow we can explore the other cabins. They could be more spacious."

I wasn't in a hurry to find a bigger bed. I just nodded and ripped off a piece of fruit leather.

We finished our snacks by candlelight, listening to the murmurs and whisperings of the forest. When we finished, Jonas said he was going for a short walk, and that I could have privacy to get ready for bed. I put on a tank top and boy short underwear and got in on one side of the bed. I don't know if I would've found it comfortable on an average day, but right then it was pure heaven.

23

—————

JONAS

I made sure the fire was mostly out and that no food items were left lying around. I tidied the site, folded the towels, and had some more water. I was on the fence about whether or not I should take care of my sexual frustration down in the dark of the woods before I climbed into bed with Gemma. It could be a long and miserable night for both of us if I was poking her in the back with my dick.

I decided to play it safe. Just a few seconds of thinking about being in bed with her was enough to bring back my raging hard-on. I pulled out my cock and pictured Gemma floating in the tub. It only took a few strokes of my hand to bring the hot rush of climax. I put one hand up on a tree to balance myself and waited for my breath to return to its steady rhythm. I put myself back together and walked slowly up the stairs to the cabin, wondering what the night would bring.

The first thing it brought was Gemma Lane, fast asleep. She had the covers pulled up to her neck and was completely passed out. Her face was angelic in the glow of the candles, and I was relieved that she was asleep. Though I was glad not to be in a city hotel with social engagements lined up, I was unsure about my whole situation. I didn't know when people might show up, be they property owners or the *Profile* security team. I didn't know what the weather might bring, or what food and water we would find in the cabins on-site. With Gemma asleep, I was able to relax and let everything sink in.

I opened a mini bottle of gin and took it to the front porch. The darkness was thick but noisy, as wind and night creatures moved through the trees. I put the bottle to my lips and swigged the gin down in one swallow. With Gemma asleep, I didn't have to worry about unleashing my impure thoughts into action, at least for a few hours, so I was probably safe with the alcohol. The warmth spread down my throat, into my chest, and settled in my belly. I closed my eyes and let my feelings wash over me in warm waves. This time the feeling felt like bliss, which I hadn't been acquainted with for several years.

An hour probably passed before I went back to bed. I stripped down and selected a pair of cotton sleep pants from my bag. It didn't seem polite to wear less than that. Gemma was still on her side, facing away from my side of the bed, sleeping soundly. I stretched out on my back, closed my eyes, and let the sounds of the night forest sing me to sleep.

THE DREAM CAME AGAIN.

Flashes of warm tropical light. Fans and hot sand. Anna's hair, the color of honey, falling across my chest. The swell of her belly. Her mouth on my mouth, my chest, my belly, and between my legs. Her laugh rippling through the air, an ocean of joy. Holding her hand as she pulled me to the beach and the drowsy heavy heat. Luxurious spoiled sleep. Too much quiet. Waves turning dark. A flash of her raft and her skin. Her hair the color of muddy straw. Pulling, dragging, swimming, crying, breathing over and over but no breath returning to me. Screaming to the sky and only heartbreak echoing back.

I woke up sweaty, disheveled, and panting. Gemma was on her back, asleep and breathing quietly. I was jealous of her simple, pure rest. Must be nice. I got out of bed and neatly folded the blankets and straightened the pillows. No use in trying to get more sleep after that nightmare. I checked my watch. A little after 4:00 am. I collected my sketch pad and pencils, a few bags of instant coffee, some water, and a mug. I got dressed and quietly slipped out of the room, leaving Gemma to sleep.

The forest was at its most quiet. The dawn creatures had not yet awakened, and the nocturnal animals were finishing their rounds. It was humbling to feel so alone. I prepared the fire and lost myself in the tasks and rhythms of building, sparking, catching, growing, and tending. It grounded me and helped me shake the dreamscape more quickly than usual. The edges of the sky began to lighten in a subtle quiet way. I heated some water for my coffee and wondered what the day might bring.

24

GEMMA

I must have fallen asleep before Jonas got back from his walk. I awoke feeling groggy and disoriented. There was a faint light in the forest, and I could hear the dawn chorus beginning to start. The other side of the bed was empty. I was alone.

My stomach dropped and my mind started to race. Had Jonas even come back from his walk? Was he injured? Did he abandon me here in a complex plot by the *Profile* Swedes to take me out of the picture?

One pillow rested on Jonas's side of the bed. The other pillows were placed neatly on the floor. His blankets were folded, but in a different way than when we arrived. Maybe he slept there after all? Which, if true, was good news because it meant I probably wasn't a solo forest castaway—but it was bad news because it meant that I'd slept in a bed with Jonas Hellgren and had no memory of it. A once-in-a-lifetime opportunity, squandered.

The definite, non-negotiable bad news was that I really had to use the bathroom. Never again would I take indoor plumbing for granted.

Dawn was coming; rosy tendrils of light broke up the darkness of the sky as if one drop of pink paint was splashed onto a sea of indigo. There was no sign of Jonas from my vantage point at the cabin window, so I decided to go explore. I pulled on shorts and a t-shirt, found my flip flops and a cardigan, and went out onto the front deck. It was glorious. The air was heavy with dew and the faint breeze was a swirl of warm and cool, with the colder air starting to win out. Free of any societal noise, it was fiercely quiet. But it was also a growing symphony of birds, insects, frogs, and the chorus of leaves singing a windsong.

"God morgon," I heard from my left. Up on the higher porch was Jonas, sitting at a table with paper and colored pencils in front of him. Next to him was one of the mugs from the cabin and I could see steam rising from it. Did he find a microwave? I waved, but the outhouse was top priority.

I went to the bathroom as fast as possible and did not study the toilet. What if there were spiders in there? Ignorance was bliss. When I exited the toilet shack, I noticed a fire pit about twenty feet away. A small fire was burning and there was a kettle resting nearby on a rock. I saw Jonas's sandaled feet on the stairs as he headed down to the ground level. Then his legs. And torso. And head. Just as gorgeous as yesterday. Dammit.

"Hello," he said. Something about this time of morning, the dusty darkness of pre-dawn, seemed sacred.

"Good morning."

"Would you like any coffee?"

"Where did you find coffee?"

"Single-serve coffee packets are *my* emergency supplies."

Jonas walked over to the fire, and I followed. He put

another log on the fire and rested the cooking grate across the flames.

"It's really beautiful here," I said.

"It's stunning." Jonas poked at the fire and waited for the flames to grow.

I saw an axe with its blade pushed into a large stump and its handle out and ready to grab. Next to the stump was a pile of large round logs. "Did you split some wood this morning?"

"No. There's a whole stack of split wood back there," he said, pointing toward the bathing area from last night.

"That axe is a little unnerving."

"How so?"

"I don't know. It just looks . . . sharp."

"I should hope so." Jonas placed the kettle on the iron grate. "We can be like Thoreau and use the axe to build a cabin here in our own personal Waldon Pond."

"You have a thing for the transcendentalists?"

"I'm always up for some civil disobedience."

"I can't even begin to tell you how nerdy you are."

"Takes one to know one," said Jonas.

"The axe feels more like Chekhov's gun, to me."

"*Now* who's the nerd?" Jonas checked to see if the water was boiling yet. "Why don't you go sit on the porch by the bridge? I'll bring up your coffee once it's ready."

I studied the 30-foot-long suspension bridge high above us. "Is that thing safe?"

"So far."

•   •   •

I STOOD at the first plank of the suspension bridge and considered my options. The two best options, in my mind, were:

1. Turn and walk away

2. Turn and *run* away.

I breathed in through my nose for five seconds, and out through my mouth for five more. Then I made my way across the planks that were suspended above the forest. Each step made the bridge wiggle and sway, and I held on to the rope railing and tried to keep my eye on the prize. That prize was an elevated deck that was tucked into the forest canopy.

Just. Keep. Breathing.

I made it across and I gave the tree, which came up through the middle of the deck, a big hug. There were two chairs and a table on the platform, but I decided to lie down on the wooden floor until I was feeling less nervous. Just when I felt comfortable enough to sit up, the deck started to rumble and shake. The headline would read:

AMERICAN JOURNALIST DIES IN SWEDEN EARTHQUAKE!

But it turned out that it was only Jonas coming across the bridge, holding a mug of coffee in each hand.

He hopped off the bridge and lowered himself gracefully, without spilling a drop.. He handed me my coffee and then leaned against a support railing and closed his eyes. I closed my eyes as well and waited for my coffee to cool. We sat like that for a while, listening to the sounds of the wilderness.

"Did you sleep at all?" I asked him, after a few minutes.

"A bit. Not as well as you, I suspect." He took a sip of his coffee and placed it down on the deck. "I'll be right back." He walked down the bridge to the treehouse, and a minute later returned with a large folder.

He had brochures for the forest retreat and a packet of information, codes, and combinations, just like I had.

"There are pictures here of the cabins that are available to us, and I think it says where extra food and water is stored." He handed me a pile of papers.

I leafed through the main brochure about the resort. "They take themselves pretty seriously here," I said.

"How so?" Jonas was reading through his information packet from *Profile*.

"Take the FAQ. It says:

Q: DO YOU HAVE WIFI? / A: NO. SURELY YOU CAN HANDLE A BREAK FROM CONSTANT CONNECTION.
Q: WHAT DO I DO IF IT'S COLD? / A: BUILD A FIRE. WRAP A BLANKET AROUND YOURSELF. FIRE UP THE SAUNA. USE YOUR IMAGINATION.
Q: WHAT IF I GET BORED? / A: YOU NEED MORE TIME DISCONNECTED IF A FEW DAYS AWAY FROM TECHNOLOGY CREATES ACHING BOREDOM.
Q: HOW DO I COOK MY FOOD WITH NO ELEC-TRICITY? / A: HUMANS ATE AND THRIVED LONG BEFORE THE INVENTION OF ELECTRICITY. BUILD A FIRE AND FIND OUT HOW.

Do you think they intended to be this snarky, or is something lost in translation?"

"Pretty sure it's intended," he said.

The next brochure was about the owners of the property. It was a family business, run by a man and his two adult children. A photo of the three of them graced the front cover of the booklet.

The patriarch was Bjorn Sandström. He must have been around 70 years old, but he looked more fit than a man half his age. The photo showed him in a dusty short-sleeved t-shirt and olive-green outdoorsy pants. His arm was extended as he held a walking stick out by his side, which gave the viewer a chance to see the intense muscles in Bjorn's arm. Those weren't weightlifting, gym rat muscles. They were the muscles of a man who got them in his everyday life—from lifting heavy things, chopping wood, carrying large loads.

Bjorn did not appear to be overly tall, but he was imposing. He and both of his children had the white-blonde hair that you might first think of when you thought of Swedes. Surely a lot of Bjorn's hair was silver instead of pure blonde, but I couldn't tell from the photo.

His son, Hugo, stood next to him in the photo. He was a Bjorn clone, only a smidge taller and a little leaner. Hugo had shoulder-length hair in that same stark color. He had a strong nose and friendly ice-blue eyes.

The last family member in the photo was Katja, Bjorn's daughter and Hugo's sister. Katja was breathtaking. She wasn't stereotypically gorgeous, but something about her energy was captivating. She was as strong and muscled as the men in her family, maybe even more so, if you took into account that she was a woman. Her bright hair was long, almost past her breasts. She stood with her hands on her hips, and her shoulders were high and strong. She wore a tank top and shorts in the photo, which showed off her physique. She had a smile on her face, but not a posed one. It was like the photographer had made a joke and Katja was just recovering from one of those belly laughs that left tears in your eyes.

"What are you staring at?" Jonas poked my arm.

"I think I just found the world's most perfect woman," I said, showing him the photo of the Sandström family.

"Wow," he said.

"Simmer down, Romeo."

"It's not that. It's just that I think any of them could kick my ass in about five seconds flat." Jonas slid a map onto my lap. "Stop gawking at that family and check this out: here's where we are." He pointed to the treehouse on the page and then dragged his finger along a line on the paper. "Here's the lake, and there's the floating cabin." He stabbed at a drawing of a little cabin right in the middle of the water.

Why had I not noticed before how nice Jonas's hands were? His fingers were long and strong, and the skin on his hands was slightly weathered. I resisted the urge to touch the back of his hand.

"You ok?" he asked me.

"All good."

"Ok. So, that cabin is pretty close. I don't think it would take us that long to paddle out there."

"But why would we want to go there? Things seem fine here."

"They *are* fine for now, but we don't have a lot of water. I *assume* that there's water in the Common House, but I'm not sure. I *am* sure that there's water at the floating cabin. This says that there's a large cooler there and that it's stocked with jugs of water and fresh food in anticipation of our arrival."

"Why would they put it there and not in the land cabins?"

"Maybe it was easier to pre-stock that location because it's more difficult to access. And less likely to be raided by bears."

"You know I don't like it when you use the b-word," I said.

"Sorry." Jonas pointed to another area of the map. "The Forest Hut is way down here. We'd have to go back to where we were dropped off, and then hike about five kilometers or so. That's the most remote cabin. It feels like we should start with something closer, just in case."

"What about the Common House?"

"There are no details in my packet about what's in there. I guess they didn't think any guests would need to access that building because it's for the staff. I also don't know if we'd need a different code to get in there. Does it say anything about it in your packet?"

"I'll have to go get it." I stood up and caught Jonas watching me. When he saw me notice, he turned his attention back to the papers in his hands.

I walked to the edge suspension bridge and paused. I wasn't too excited about crossing it again. I put a hand on each side of the railing and took a tentative step onto the first plank. "Maybe we need to stick to the front porch of the treehouse," I said.

"Here, I've got you," said Jonas. Suddenly he was behind me. Close behind me. He put his hands lightly around my waist. His mouth was right by my ear. "Take it one step at a time. We'll keep it steady."

One plank at a time, we crossed the bridge together. With his hands on me I felt balanced and brave. Which also annoyed me; I didn't want him to get to me like that.

We made it across the bridge, and Jonas released his hold on me, but let his fingers brush across my rib cage as he pulled his arms back.

Flustered, I rushed into the cabin and dove straight for my suitcase. "Those papers are here somewhere." After collecting the papers and myself, I approached him with my information packet. We stood shoulder to shoulder as he flipped through the sheets. He smelled of wood smoke and cedar. He dipped his head closer to mine as he read through the packet. We did not have to be standing this close. It was a deliberate decision on his part, and on mine. I wasn't moving away, was I?

"I'm not seeing a Common House code in here, either. Maybe our codes work on all the doors. But I noticed something." He pointed at the list of door codes on my sheet. "Your codes are different from mine. They must have them programmed to match individuals."

"That's weird. My code worked to open the treehouse door. It was 337. What's your code?"

"I think it's 848. My papers are up on the deck."

"Try your code," I said. "I'll stay inside just in case."

Jonas went outside, shut the door, and hit the lock icon. The door locked. He entered 8-4-8 and pressed the unlock icon. The door unlocked and he pushed it open. "Hi, honey. I'm home."

25

JONAS

Gemma and I shared a protein bar, roasted almonds, and a few squares of chocolate for breakfast. We packed water, Gemma's water filter and cup, spare clothes, and some odds and ends in our backpacks.

"What if we need more clothes?" asked Gemma.

"I don't think we'll stay out there too long."

"What if it gets cold? Or rains? Shouldn't we bring more of our things?"

The sky was clear, but I knew that the weather could shift quickly. I remembered something about storms in the extended forecast, but I hadn't paid attention at the time. "Ok. We can put a few things in my smaller suitcase."

Gemma loaded up the bag with a sweater, nightgown, socks, underwear, a solar charger, and paper and pen. I added some shirts, a sweatshirt, an extra pair of pants and my sketchbook and pencils.

We both paused to admire the view from the treehouse before heading out. Neither of us spoke, but I think we both felt that we were leaving someplace spectacular to which we might not return.

"The next time we see this place it could be crawling with *Profile* crew, photographers, and maybe even a German celebrity or two," Gemma said.

"That sounds awful."

"Nightmare fodder."

Gemma pointed at a megaphone-shaped speaker up on the corner of the treehouse roof. "What's that?"

"A horn loudspeaker, maybe? A way to communicate with guests in case of a storm or emergency."

"I wouldn't want to be up in these trees in a windstorm," she said.

"They're strong and healthy. But I don't think it would be a comfortable experience."

We loaded up our bags and began the hike to the lake.

The path down the hill toward the water was much easier to navigate in the daylight. I led the way as the trail gently curved through the woods. The tips of the trees reached out like a grandmother's fingers, gently brushing our shoulders, telling us it was safe to continue. It made for a peaceful hike, especially since Gemma wasn't bleeding from an owl attack. After ten minutes, the view opened up and the lake was in front of us. It wasn't huge, but parts of it disappeared into the dips and coves of the shoreline. It was a shimmering dark grey and mostly calm with mild ripples when the wind blew.

The boat was right where we left it.

"If another owl tries to kill me, you'll be sailing solo from here on out," Gemma said.

I turned the boat around and put our bags inside. I handed Gemma a life jacket and watched as she dutifully put it on. She was down to a thin t-shirt that accentuated her chest. My mind immediately went to the previous evening in the water.

"Something wrong?" Gemma said, snapping me out of my fantasy trance.

"Just making sure you're securing your vest."

"For our tiny trip on this calm lake? Pretty sure you're over-thinking this." She studied the lake. "Do you know where this cabin is? I don't see it floating out there in the middle anywhere."

I pulled out the map to show her. She came closer and she smelled like lilac and cinnamon this time. How was that possible? I tried to concentrate. "If this map is correct, it's north, then east into that cove. I think it's tucked back there."

The lake water was smooth and quiet. We quickly left the shore behind and aimed for the northeast cove.

"I feel better being on the open water in daylight," said Gemma. "At least if something swoops in on me, I'll see it coming."

"It's always nice to look your predators in the eye before they take you out."

Gemma smacked the water with her paddle and sent a splash back toward my legs. "Owls are nocturnal. We're safe."

Was she attempting flirty banter? "Owls can be crepuscular, too." *Way to keep the banter going, dipshit.*

"No boating at dawn or dusk. Got it." The canoe glided quietly through the water. "Speaking of stealth attackers, why do you think Freja sent me out here alone? I know you said she was trying to help you, or whatever, but . . ."

Gemma had asked a question that was bothering me, as well. What Freja had done was a serious breach of ethics and professionalism.

"It feels like she took it several levels past *helpful* or even *jealous*," said Gemma.

"I've been thinking about that." I stopped paddling, and Gemma stopped as well. I rested the paddle across my lap and water dripped down into the boat. "I've known her for a long time. Since before I knew Anna. She's always been volatile, and has a dark streak . . ." I paused. I just couldn't put my finger on why Freja had done it. "But something about this feels more ominous than her usual fare. I haven't been very connected to people in the last few years . . . maybe something happened with her that I don't know about." I put my paddle back in the water and pushed us forward.

"I'm glad you came with me," Gemma said. "Imagine if I hadn't run into you before I left."

The thought of that made my stomach cramp. The idea was ghastly. "I don't want to think about it."

It didn't take us long to get close to the northeast cove of the lake. If there was no food, water, or access to the floating cabin, at least we wouldn't have wasted too much time.

We rounded the shoreline and started heading east. It was like we'd entered a new world.

"Wow," said Gemma.

The trees on shore seemed taller in this cove because the elevation of the land rose sharply all around us. We were in a valley that felt wild and protected. Ahead of us floated two exquisitely beautiful structures. They were works of art composed of wood and glass.

"Did you know it was like this?" Gemma asked me. "Did the brochures show that it was this glorious?"

"I didn't see a photo of this one. I only knew about it

because my information packet had codes, and it was on the map."

We got closer and saw that there was a place to tie the boat, and a ladder next to that for us to climb onto the deck.

I secured the canoe and Gemma got out first. I handed up the bags to her, and then joined her on the floating platform.

There were two separate wooden structures that were each built upon steel catamaran hulls, but they floated together. One was a cabin and living quarters, and one was a floating sauna.

We explored the cabin first. It was more luxurious than the treehouse, but still spare and minimalist. The bed was hand-made, in the most beautiful sense. Its wooden rails glowed in the morning sun that shone through the windows. The mattress was covered with a soft white nubby linen sheet and two impossibly fluffy feather duvets were folded at the foot. At the head of the bed were huge feather pillows and behind that was a movable wall of glass. We could slide it open, along with the glass wall on the opposite side, essentially creating an open-air bedroom.

A stack of towels rested on a chair, and shelves along the wall held a few spices and cookware, plates, mugs, and utensils.

Gemma opened a door and let out a shriek. I thought maybe she'd found a dead animal, but soon realized it was a happy sound.

"I thought this was a pantry," she said, "but it's a toilet room!" Gemma was doing some kind of celebratory dance.

I peered over her shoulder and into the closet in question. "A dry closet. No more outhouse for you." Her effusive joy over a toilet filled with ash was endearing.

There was an indoor wood-burning stove, an outdoor fire pit, and a table and chairs.

I stepped back outside and took a deep breath. A new feeling was creeping in. I should've been keeping a list of all of them. This one felt a lot like peace.

"Jonas!" Gemma called from the other side of the structure. I headed toward her voice and found her sitting before a long wooden box bench.

She lifted the lid to reveal an old-fashioned icebox, complete with a giant block of ice, and fresh food. There were eggs, apples, carrots, potatoes, butter, cheese, and two steaks. Outside the icebox there was bread, jam, jerky, a package of cookies, and a few tins of fish. In another compartment were some bottles of alcohol, coffee beans, a hand grinder, a French press, and, most importantly, six gallons of fresh water.

We gazed at the contents like we'd discovered a treasure chest filled with gold.

Gemma smiled a wide and easy smile. I leaned forward and realized, just in time, that I meant to kiss her. Without any thought or planning, I almost put my mouth on hers. I was losing it, for sure.

THE CABIN WAS LOVELY, but the sauna was a true work of art. I realized I'd seen photos of it in some Swedish publications. It was designed by a renowned Swedish architect, and it cost a fortune to rent out.

The structure was rectangle shaped with slightly curved lines. There were big windows in the middle of each long side, so you could see straight through. The short end walls were made fully of glass, so it was more like being outside than in, as far as the light and the view.

The exterior was constructed of silky pine and the inside

walls and furniture were red cedar. A wood-fired sauna oven stood gleaming in the middle of the structure, with a pipe that led up through the ceiling to a chimney above.

On one side of the structure was a glassed-in vestibule with a bench for changing clothes and getting away from the heat of the sauna. There was also a ladder there that led up to a hole in the ceiling. Gemma climbed the rungs to check it out.

"There's a table and chairs up here, too!" she called from the rooftop.

Back on the main deck there was an outdoor shower and a ladder off the side in case someone needed to get back on after swimming.

Gemma came back down the ladder and joined me on the deck. "That settles it. We're never going back to civilization." Gemma stretched out her arms, arched her back, and let the sunshine settle on her face.

"Fine by me," I said, wanting so badly to put my arms around her and pull her into an embrace.

26

GEMMA

Jonas got a fire started in the outdoor fire pit and I picked some food out of the cooler. We decided on steak because we figured it would spoil the quickest once the ice melted.

We sat on cedar benches as the flames grew higher and stronger. The cove felt like a secluded haven. We had our little spot on the water, and the trees were high on the banks, protecting us. The lake glimmered to the west and cast off a glow like burning sapphire.

I heated up a cast iron skillet and added butter and then the steaks. The searing and spitting of the hot fat and beef in the pan made me think of my father. The smell of the cooking meat ignited my hunger. Jonas sliced some cheese and passed it to me along with chunks of bread ripped from the loaf.

"We should probably talk about this interview," I said.

"Alright. Let's talk." Jonas popped an entire cookie into his mouth.

"Hey, we didn't agree to open those yet!"

"My bad," he said, reaching out with a cookie in his palm as a peace offering. I accepted.

"How are you feeling about it now? I know you've had some reservations."

"Aren't you keeping it polite."

"Keeping it *professional*," I said.

"I think we may have already burned that bridge."

I flipped the steaks by stabbing them with a knife and quickly turning them over. More sizzling. "How do you like your steak?"

"Medium rare," said Jonas.

"Good to know, but I'm not taking requests."

"Then why did you ask?" Jonas threw a piece of cheese at me.

"Keeping it polite." The steaks were maybe close to being done. I really had no idea. "Can you get me the plates?"

Jonas handed me two dishes and I put a steak on each one. He added more bread and cheese to each, and we sat and used our knees as tables.

"I feel ok about the interview. As ok as I *can* feel," said Jonas. "They told me it might be a different format than usual, but no one seemed to have many details. "

I finished chewing a bite of meat. It was medium-ish, tender, and the best steak of my life. It could've been due to the circumstances, but I wasn't going to question it. "It's not just a one-time sit-down Q & A kind of thing."

"So we have multiple sit downs?"

"In this situation, yes. It's supposed to be like a long-form conversation written down. On paper, it's like I asked you some questions and you smartly and elegantly gave a detailed answer. The interview follows the trail we blaze within the conversation, so while I may have points I want to touch upon, we might end up in unexpected territory."

"What if I'm not smart, elegant, or detailed?"

"That's where the editing comes in. I write up a draft of the interview and you get to review every word. You can change answers, and even write new ones in."

"Isn't that a bit dishonest?"

"I don't think so," I said. "The goal isn't to represent perfectly our exact sit-down, or sit-downs. It's to curate an interesting record of conversations with you, so at the end the reader feels connected and possibly moved by what they've read. It's a deeper dive, so to speak."

Jonas thought this over while sipping water from his cabin mug. "So how do you record what I'm saying? Seems like it could be hard to remember everything I've said, or to write it down. And our phones are kind of toast out here."

"I have a small recording device," I said. "With extra—"

"With extra batteries?" Jonas laughed. "Of course you have the extra batteries."

"I'll always let you know when it's turned on, and we can keep it on even if we are having a casual conversation, in case something interesting comes up. You have full veto power on what will be included in the final piece."

"That should be ok." The wind picked up and blew Jonas's hair across his face. He finished a bite of steak. "How would this interview have worked . . . if we had stayed on our original schedule?"

I thought that over. How *would* it have worked? I was just now getting Jonas to talk to me, and it took extreme circumstances to get him to say more than two sentences at once. I didn't know how I would've gotten him to open up in some conference room, hotel lobby, or cafe. "That may have been one shitty interview."

He stuffed another cookie into his mouth. "Super shitty."

INTERVIEW EXCERPT

(The following is an excerpt from the interview with Jonas Hellgren, conducted by Gemma Lane, published in Profile *Magazine Volume 315)*

INTERVIEWER

Let's start at the very beginning.

HELLGREN

A very good place to start.

INTERVIEWER

This is not Do-Re-Me. Keep your focus.

HELLGREN

Sorry. Carry on.

INTERVIEWER

What is one of your first memories?

HELLGREN

Not to go straight back to *The Sound of Music*, but it's probably a memory of being in Austria with my parents when I was about four years old. My father was directing a play, and my mother was acting in it. We were our own traveling drama troupe when I was young.

INTERVIEWER

Is there something specific that you remember from that trip to Austria?

HELLGREN

Yes, I think so. My mother and I were walking in the streets of Salzburg. I remember the roads were narrow and made of bricks and I would count the bricks as I walked on them. The avenues seemed to spiral around, and I felt lost all the time. My mother bought me a small wooden box with a golden dove on the lid. She said it was for my treasures. I still have the box, which is probably why I remember.

INTERVIEWER

Did you keep treasures in the box?

HELLGREN

It was small, so I usually just kept coins, stones, or shells in the box. I'd have to change them out frequently because it didn't hold very much.

INTERVIEWER

Did you enjoy traveling around Europe with your parents?

HELLGREN

I didn't know any different, and it was our existence most of the time until I was a teenager. Sweden was our home, to which we always returned, but I think from age two until twelve, we spent probably six months of the year on the road.

INTERVIEWER

How do you think that kind of nomadic life impacted you, in the long term?

HELLGREN

It's one of the reasons I have such a fondness for maps. My parents always gave me a map of each town we would visit, and sometimes maps for places we were just passing through. I used to think they were infallible. The maps, I mean. Not my parents. I thought there was one supreme cartographer who perfectly mapped every town in the world. But sometimes I would get two maps for one place, and they were made by different people. I was surprised to see how different the maps were. Neither of them was wrong, really, but they could have totally different points of view. I started drawing my own maps when I was about eight, I think.

INTERVIEWER

What point of view did you take when you drew your maps?

HELLGREN

At first, I tried to draw accurate maps of roads, shops, lakes, and whatnot. But it was frustrating, and I wasn't successful. They were a mess. And I knew what a good map looked like, and those maps weren't good. So, I started mapping memories, or landmarks from places that stuck out to me. My maps were quirky. And limited. But they were personal and more meaningful.

INTERVIEWER

Can you remember one of those early maps you made?

HELLGREN

Yes. It was a series of maps. We lived in Regensburg, Germany for several months when I was about twelve years old. There was this towering cathedral. St. Peter's Cathedral, and you could see it from almost anywhere in the city. And there was a huge river with a beautiful stone bridge. It was the Donau River. Or the Danube in English. I had this collection of maps I made, all from different spots in the town, but each one had the cathedral, and most of them had the river, but from different vantage points. One map was where I broke my wrist after falling from a bicycle. Another was where I found a litter of abandoned kittens in an alleyway. And I really remember the map I made of my first kiss. It was on the bridge over the river at sunset, with the cathedral in the background. Her name was Stefanie and she always wore her hair in one thick braid.

27

GEMMA

"I don't know why you don't do many interviews. You're a generous subject," I said, taking a bowl of potatoes that Jonas had peeled and sliced while talking to me. He'd also kept the fire going, so I put some butter in a pan and threw in the potatoes and salt. A second lunch.

"For now."

"I appreciate it."

"Can we take a break for a bit?"

"No problem," I said.

"There's a drawing I'd like to finish before tomorrow, and I might take a swim."

"Why by tomorrow?" I asked.

Jonas paused, and then turned away slightly. "It's the anniversary."

"Oh, yes, of course. I'm sorry. That's tomorrow."

Jonas kept his back turned and started to walk away. "I'm going to get some more cheese from the ice box. Want anything else?"

"An apple?"

Jonas nodded and crossed to the back side of the cabin deck toward the cooler.

I stirred the potatoes and wondered what tomorrow would bring for Jonas, and for me. From what I gathered, he preferred solitude on the anniversary of Anna's death. There were only two of us out on the lake, so he wouldn't have to worry about masses of people. But that also meant that it would be difficult to get away from each other if he needed to be alone.

"Apple." Jonas was back and held out the fruit. I took it from his hand, and he went back into the cabin. He came out a minute later with his sketchpad and pencils. "I'm going up on the roof for a few." He disappeared into the sauna, and I could see him climb the ladder. Once on the roof he settled in at a table, his back to me.

When the food was ready, I passed a plate to Jonas up the ladder. "Thank you," he said, reaching down to grab it.

I ate the potatoes while sitting on the edge of the deck, my legs hanging over the side and my toes just barely skimming the water. The sky was overcast but the breeze was calm. Sometimes I could see fish swim past my feet and under the hull. I felt drowsy.

I made my way back to the bedroom and stretched out on the bed. The gentle swaying of the cabin quickly rocked me to sleep, and I fell into the kind of daytime slumber where your dreams are oversaturated with color and sound and feel like they exist somewhere between reality and your subconscious.

When I woke up, the light in the cabin had a pink-orange hue, and things were quiet. I sat up and untangled myself from the duvet, which was puffed up around me like a marshmallow. Through the glass wall I could only see water and trees. It was so peaceful it was almost unnerving. When everything outside quiets down, you're left with the cacophony of your own thoughts.

The air felt a little cooler, so I changed into jeans and a long-sleeved t-shirt. I walked barefoot onto the deck outside and the wood was cool on my feet. No Jonas. He wasn't in the sauna or on the roof deck, either.

"Hellooooo," called Jonas from out in the water. I saw him swimming about 30 feet away from the boat. He waved. I waved back and then took the opportunity to climb the ladder and sit on the roof deck by myself for a few minutes. I stretched out on a lounge chair and took the time to wake up slowly. The nap had pulled me under and left me disoriented.

I heard Jonas call my name after a few minutes. "Gemma, do you want to swim?"

I stood up so I could see him in the water. "No thanks," I answered. I generally liked the water, but I didn't bring a swim-suit and I didn't feel like getting cold and wet. My mood was a little cloudy. Still needed to wake up.

"I'll be a few more minutes," he shouted. I waved to let him know that I heard and went back to my chair. Three days ago, what would I have thought if I knew that Jonas Hellgren asked me to swim with him, alone and possibly naked, in an isolated lake in the Swedish wilderness . . . and that I turned him down? What *was* Jonas wearing out there, anyway?

I never found out. I missed his climb out of the lake, and when I saw him again, he was tending to the outdoor fire, hair wet but fully clothed, which was still a nice feast for the eyes.

"I'll be making dinner tonight," he said.

"What's on the menu?"

"A surprise."

"Seems like it might be difficult to keep a secret for very long in this environment."

"Maybe. But it's still a surprise."

"I feel like we just ate."

"That was hours ago." Jonas had some food items lined up on the table. I went over to examine them.

"Nope. Back away. Don't you have some work to do or something?"

It was hard to think of working and meeting deadlines when it felt like I had stepped out of the real world. I sat back down and shifted my chair so my back was to the fire, and I stretched out my legs and closed my eyes. "How was your swim today?" I asked him.

"A little cold. But fine." I heard a squeaking noise and then a light pop. "Would you like a glass of wine?"

"You're having wine?"

"These bottles are impressive. Figured, why not."

"The 'why not' could be that you said something about staying clear headed."

"Maybe I could use a little haze right now."

"Deal me in."

Jonas poured some into a mug and brought it to me. Red wine. The first taste filled my mouth with a silky bouquet of flavor and warmed my throat as I swallowed. "Ok, that's nice." I sipped my wine, listened to the fire, and watched the colors of the lake change as the sun began to set. I felt like the day had just begun and now it was ending. "How long did I sleep, anyway?"

"I'm not sure. Quite a while. Long enough for me to catch this," Jonas said. He placed a cleaned fish onto the cooking grate. "You caught a fish? What the hell. Was I asleep for the entire day?"

He shrugged. "Lucky break. For me, not the fish."

JONAS COOKED dinner and I tried to remain neutral and professional as I watched him bend over the fire, flip the fish, and roast the vegetables. I wasn't very successful. As the alcohol settled into my system, I let my attraction to Jonas breathe, much like the bottle of wine on the table. I set the butterflies free in my stomach, I allowed my heart to flutter, and felt my chest start to buzz. My body was a botanical garden of blooming desire.

Jonas wore light pants and a midnight-blue shirt that was fully unbuttoned. The long sleeves of his shirt were rolled up, nicely displaying his wrists and forearms. He was graceful and strong, and even the simple light lifting of a pan or a log show-cased his chest. I didn't think that having his skin exposed was the best fire-safety option, but he didn't seem to care, so neither did I.

Truly, I'd seen men before. Even attractive men. Even very attractive men. But the way I was staring at Jonas, you'd think this was my first time laying eyes on the male form. Maybe it wasn't his physicality, as lovely as it was, that was drawing me in. I was discovering that he was cerebral, sensitive, pensive, obser-vant, and thoughtful. He got my dry sense of humor, and he made me laugh. All of that elevated his beauty.

"Enjoying the show?" he asked without looking up from the fish, which he was examining for doneness.

I guess I was more obvious than I thought. Fueled by a liquid confidence, I decided to be direct. "Very much."

"I aim to please." Jonas refilled my cup and went to get some plates from the cabin. I openly watched him walk away and he caught my gaze. He stopped for a moment and slipped his shirt off his shoulders, letting it drop to the deck. "How's that?" he asked, his beautiful back turned to me.

"Perfection."

Jonas nodded and continued his walk to the cabin to collect the plates.

We ate near the warmth of the fire and Jonas refilled our glasses. Something about the setting intensified the flavors of the food. It was as if every item was its best, simple self. Each bite was a delicacy, though there were no unusual ingredients. Our bodies took to the nutrients, as did our moods.

As Jonas ate and drank, he began to unfold. The lake, the forest, the solitude, and the food had a softening effect on Jonas, but also brought him into focus—like he relaxed enough to allow himself to be seen. It may have been the wine, though, that sealed the deal on Jonas unfurling that evening. It was like watching a moonflower bloom under the night sky. His movements and sentences became more playful and drawn out. He smiled and even laughed a few times as we talked. We both felt bolder as some of our inhibitions fell away. To my immense pleasure, he kept his shirt off for the duration of the meal.

2 8

—

JONAS

Gemma was a lovely companion. My head was swimming because of the wine, in a soft and cushioned way that made me want to reach out, connect, and feel. I wasn't scared to let my guard down. I knew the feeling might only last as long as the buzz did, but I was glad for the temporary relief from feeling dark and anxious.

"I'd say you're a pretty good interviewer so far," I said to Gemma, who had her legs stretched out from her chair to the railing.

"How so?"

"Your questions generally follow a conversational line, and that makes it easier to offer you meaningful answers."

"Thank you, though I think you might deserve more credit there. I'm following your lead. Interesting answers make for better follow-up questions."

Mutual compliments. Mine were a little awkward, but I was getting warmed up at least.

"My turn," I said.

"Your turn with what?"

"Asking questions."

Gemma took another sip of wine. "Alright, but if I can't ask about your sex life, you can't ask about mine."

"I'm sorry, but we haven't signed a contract on that. I can ask whatever I want." There was that heat in my groin again. I got up and went to the cabinet to find something sweet and to hopefully send a message to my dick to stay down. "I found shortbread," I said as I walked back toward Gemma. I held out a piece for her and she took it from my hand, her fingers brushing against mine.

I sat back down, and some hair fell into my eyes. I brushed it away and caught Gemma checking me out. "What?"

She shrugged. "I just like it when you do that."

"Do what?"

"Push your hair out of your face in that sexy way."

"Was that sexy?"

"Immensely." She took another sip of wine. "Did I say that out loud?"

"You did."

She laughed. "Ok, you said you had questions?"

Yes, I had questions. I was having trouble concentrating, though. The sky was shifting from light blue to midnight blue. Soon we would be able to see the light of stars against the darkness. "Your mother and father are no longer living, correct?"

"Correct."

"I'm sorry to hear that."

"Thank you."

"Your father was Arthur Lane, the author?" That had come up in my 2-minute internet search.

"Yep. That's him."

"And your mother's name was Laura?"

"Lorna," she said.

"Lorna Lane?"

"She didn't change her last name. Lorna Piediscalzi."

"Your mother was Lorna Piediscalzi?"

"The one and only."

"Oh shit. Wow." I should've done more googling. Lorna Piediscalzi was a model and actress. She had memorable roles in some art house films and her beauty was legendary. She was also known for her tragic and somewhat mysterious death. "She died in Italy, wasn't it?"

Gemma's face got darker. Why had I started this line of questioning? "Yes, she died when she was visiting family in Italy. She and four companions had gone hiking in the Dolomites. They were all killed."

"In that avalanche?" I asked her.

"Yes. She and my father were married when she died, but they were having trouble in their marriage. I never got the full story from my father and that history died when he did."

"That's heavy," I said. My processing speed had decreased quite a bit since we'd started with the wine, and I couldn't find any other words.

"It can be."

Gemma and I sat quietly for a minute. I started this so it was up to me to shift it. "Can we revisit that later? It seems complicated, and I don't want to dismiss it. But maybe it's not right for tonight."

"Yes, please," she said. "New topic!"

"Let me think." I figured I'd try to change the mood completely. "Tell me about the last time you were madly in love with someone."

"That's an abrupt shift."

"Have a little more wine. It'll help." I opened a second bottle and held it up for her inspection. My question felt somewhat ridiculous, but I was feeling brave, and I wanted to see where the topic might go with Gemma.

"I'm not sure anything can help the historic disaster that is my love life."

"Let me make it more specific," I said. "Tell me about a time, an exact moment, where you felt deeply in love." I'd really gone off the deep end now. I hoped to God she was as tipsy as I was, or I was about to make a complete fool of myself.

"Madly in love, or deeply in love? Which is it, Hellgren?"

"Either. Both." I watched her face. Her eyes were clear, and her lips were fuller and darker than usual. Her movements were slow, graceful, deliberate.

Gemma took a deep breath. "Well, I had a fiancé. Adam. He was very lovely. We just couldn't—"

"No, no, no!" I banged a spoon on the edge of the fire pit, and the clanging echoed out over the lake. "Don't tell me about a situation. Tell me how you felt. In a moment. In your body. I want to know what it felt like to you. I want to feel it."

"Why do you want to know that?"

I shrugged. "The heart wants what it wants—or else it does not care." I'd forgotten how much I liked quoting poetry once I was in giddy drunk territory.

She rolled her eyes. "Alright. Let me think. Can I have a minute?"

"Things take the time they take. Don't worry."

"I can't concentrate if you keep quoting Dickinson and Mary Oliver at me."

"Mi dispiace, tesoro."

Gemma had taken the question very seriously. She put her

chin in her hands and furrowed her brow. She squinted and stared into space. "I can't tell you that," she said, finally.

"Why not?"

"Because I've never felt that way before. Not really. Maybe I never met the right person . . . or maybe I never let myself . . ." her voice trailed off and I thought she might burst into tears at any moment. "This is really embarrassing," she said, and she hid her face in her hands.

I was horrified. I had meant the conversation to be playful, but I should've known better. These were serious topics. I had to make it better. "Ok. That's ok. We'll fix it," I said, standing up and holding out my hand to her.

"We'll fix it?" She asked. She stood up and swayed the tiniest bit before finding her balance. "How? Should I fall madly and deeply in love with you right now?" She slapped her hand over her mouth and then laughed. "Shit. Said that part out loud again, didn't I?"

"I take that back. There's nothing to fix. You aren't broken. But maybe I can help you feel better about it." We stood close together and her breath smelled sweetly of wine and sugar. I wanted to know what her lips tasted like. How warm would they be? "Let's get started."

29

GEMMA

Jonas led me to an open area on the cabin deck. He squared his body with mine as he held both of my hands. It was almost like he planned to give me a dance lesson.

"You're too in your head. I know you can find some of that feeling in your body. Either in a memory or in the present moment. Close your eyes," he told me.

I closed my eyes.

"I want you to stand here. But keep your knees a little loose. Let yourself sway if you need to. Imagine that you're a birch tree planted into this wood under your feet." Jonas let go of my hands but stayed close. He ran his fingertips lightly up my arms. "Your roots go down into the water. Into the sand. And down into the layers of the earth. You are strong but let yourself move if the wind blows you."

"Is this a somatic therapy session?" I asked.

"Not that formal. Learned some of this in theater. No talking." Jonas stepped closer to me, and gently placed his hands on the small of my back. He moved his lips closer to my ear, and gave me more instructions, his breath hot on my cheek and neck. "Keep your eyes closed. Let your hands go where they want to go." He moved his hands to my hips and swayed a little with me to the left. And to the right. And to the left again. We kept up the rhythm together. It really *was* like dancing.

"Notice your breath," he said quietly. "Is it shallow? Deep? Fast? Slow?"

It was a little shallow. I slowed it down and took deeper breaths.

With gentle pressure on my hips, Jonas rocked my pelvis around in a circle. I felt like Baby in *Dirty Dancing*. After a few moments, I let go of my self-consciousness and allowed my body to find its own rhythm. Jonas noticed that I had taken the lead and he switched from guiding me with his hands to just holding on for the ride. I softly swayed and rocked, keeping my feet planted but the rest of my body fluid and soft.

"That's it," he said.

I lifted my hands from my side and put them both on his bare chest. He did not startle or pull away. He pushed into my hands, and I felt him put his head back to open his neck to me. I slid my fingers up the warm skin of his chest, then shoulders, then neck, and up to his face. I weaved my fingers into his hair and my right hand stayed near his mouth, one of my fingers outlining his lips.

He moaned a little when I touched his mouth and his lips closed around my finger. I felt the warmth of his tongue as he sucked on the tip of my finger and pulled it into his mouth. He groaned again and his hands moved lower on my hips, and he closed them tightly on my skin, kneading my hips and then lower, on my ass.

Then I felt it. I might not have been madly and deeply in love, but I was madly and deeply in some kind of feelings for

Jonas. Many of them sprang from my body, but some also from my heart.

"I feel it," I said to him. My voice came out deep and breathless.

He let my finger drop from his mouth. "Keep your eyes closed. Tell me. Tell me how it feels."

"I feel like a fire is growing from my belly. Low. It's red orange and it's spreading, and the heat is rolling in waves."

"Yes." He gently bit my ear.

"My hips want to move. They want to push into you."

Jonas moaned and pulled my pelvis close to his.

"I want to consume you."

"Tell me how that feels," he said. "Describe it."

"I want to breathe the air out of your lungs. I want my tongue in your mouth. I want to find the edges and the depths of your body until I get right into your heart, and I want to hear the sounds you make when I take you in. I want your noises to vibrate in my chest."

I pulled his hair, bringing his head back again, exposing his neck. I opened my mouth on his neck and took his skin into my mouth, sucking gently.

"Oh fuck, Gemma," he moaned, and then his mouth was on mine.

My feet were no longer planted. Jonas had picked me up and brought my face to his and we were tasting each other. My legs wrapped around his waist and our lips, tongues, teeth were all in a perfect rhythm of searching, discovering, opening. It was more than a kiss; it was an unveiling. He tasted like sweet cherries, black grapes, salted chocolate, and whiskey.

"Ok, ok," he uttered in a breathless mantra. "I should stop.

We should stop." He pulled his face back, put his hands into my hair, and groaned. "We have to stop."

I didn't want to stop. "I don't want to."

"I don't want to, either. But we have to." He placed me down gently on the deck and put his arms around me in a tight hug. "I've had a lot to drink. If we do this, we need to do it clearly. It's too hazy."

Hazy was fine by me. My whole life had been clear and stark and all rough edges. I finally found this soft foggy space that felt like heaven, and I didn't want to let it go.

I think he felt bad, and by the hardness I felt in his pants as he pressed up against me, I could tell that *he* didn't really want to stop either. But there was this little part of my brain that pinged at the words Jonas had said. He wanted me. But he wanted to be clear headed when he had me. Was that what he said? What he meant? The fact that I couldn't quite remember probably meant that I'd had too much to drink as well.

"Ok," I said. "Alright. It's ok."

Jonas pulled back from me and put his hands on either side of my face. He studied me intensely. "You're so goddamned lovely," he said. And before I'd even had time to feel the blush heat up my face, he turned, ran, and dove, pants and all, into the dark lake and out of sight.

"If you ruin this moment by drowning, I'm going to kick your ass!" I yelled out into the darkness. I heard some faint splashing in the water, but nothing else.

"SOUNDS A LITTLE REDUNDANT," Jonas called, from somewhere in the water.

I noticed that I'd been holding my breath ever since he went into the water, and I felt relief rush through me. "Get back up here!"

"IN A MINUTE," came his voice again.

I went to the cabin and grabbed a towel and came back out and stood by the ladder. "I'M PUTTING THIS TOWEL BY THE LADDER FOR YOU!" I shouted into the night.

"No need to yell. I'm right here," came a voice by my feet, scaring me so badly that I screamed.

"Screaming attracts owls. I'd be careful if I were you," said Jonas.

I was still recovering from being badly startled. "You're such a little asshole!" I said, catching my breath.

Soon he was back on deck, shivering, and dripping water everywhere. He kissed me softly on my lips and then pulled away. "I'm going to grab some dry clothes and then I'll change in the sauna. I'll clean up out here."

Jonas was gently trying to steer this night in a more wholesome direction. I didn't have the energy to fight against his tide. "Alright. I'll start the clean-up until you get back."

Jonas wrapped the towel around his waist and went to find some clothes. I collected our plates and mugs.

He returned a minute later with an armful of clothes and the towel wrapped around his head. "The bedroom's all yours. I'm going to stay up for a while."

I wasn't that tired after my epic nap, but I decided to go to the cabin anyway. It seemed like Jonas was asking for space, and some distance between us was probably a good idea if we were going to lower the temperature on our evening.

"Thanks. See you in a bit." I felt a little wistful and maybe slightly rejected, but I was still riding the high from our contact. The combination of the high and the low, the closeness and the distance, the push and pull, left me emotionally disoriented. Maybe sleep *was* the best option for the moment.

. . .

IN THE CABIN, I opened the sliding glass walls halfway so the night breeze could move freely through the room. I lit two candles on the table by the bed so I could see what I was doing. It was dark, and without the light of the outdoor fire, it was difficult to see.

I brushed my teeth using some bottled water and spit the toothpaste into my beloved dry toilet. The mirror there dimly revealed my hair as wild and tangled, but I didn't feel like dealing with it. I returned to the bedroom and found a night-gown in my suitcase. It was more like a long t-shirt than a gown, but it was what I found most comfortable. I hated any kind of waistband grabbing at me while I slept and preferred to move freely.

I unzipped my jeans and sat on the bed. I'd had enough wine that it felt safer to take my pants off from a sitting position. I pulled the denim off one leg at a time. I had started to remove my shirt when I noticed Jonas. He was standing at the glass wall toward the foot of the bed. He was only ten feet from me, but he was behind the glass instead of in the open-air portion.

He was staring at me. He was watching me undress. He had changed into soft dark pants and a black t-shirt. He leaned forward and put his palms on the glass. He did not break eye contact.

I stood up slowly and held his gaze. I was barefoot and wearing my shirt, a bra, and my underwear. I waited to see if he would move or turn away. He was very still and my skin tingled under his watch as if I could physically sense the weight of his gaze.

I raised my shirt over my head and removed it. I dropped it to the floor and stood motionless, clad only in my undergarments.

Jonas remained at the glass with his hands pressed into the pane. He could've moved three feet to his left and entered the room, but he stayed where he was.

I reached my hands behind my back to unclasp my bra. I waited again to see if he would leave. He did not leave.

I unhooked the clasps and slid one arm out of a strap, and then the other, but I held the fabric against my chest.

Jonas watched.

I dropped my hands to my side and the bra fell to the floor and joined my shirt in a little heap by my feet.

Jonas stared at my breasts and then lowered his head for a moment and made a soft growling noise. He pushed back from the glass but then leaned in again and resumed the same position. He gave me a subtle nod, as if instructing me to continue.

I hooked my thumbs into the waistband at my hips and I paused. Had I known I'd be performing an impromptu striptease, I might've chosen a prettier pair. But the black and white striped boy shorts were what I had on . . . and they were coming off.

I turned my back to Jonas. I slowly pushed my underwear down my hips, an inch at a time. I glanced to see if he was still there—it would be just my luck to give a show to no audience. He had not moved. I bent at the waist to pull my underwear all the way down and then stepped out. I tossed them over to the pile with my other clothes. I turned back to face Jonas.

I was naked. His eyes took in all of me. There was enough candlelight that I was sure he could see me fully, but maybe in softer lines than if there'd been an overhead light. I waited to see if he would leave now that I was fully undressed. He nodded at me again. He was waiting for more. What more could I give him?

Jonas slowly lowered himself to a squat as he kept his hands on the glass. His palms rubbed lightly on the surface as they slid down the pane. He leaned in closer, still watching me.

I backed up a step and sat gingerly on the edge of the bed, my legs closed. He nodded again. This was what he wanted. My heart was beating quickly, and my mouth was dry. I felt both exposed and revealed.

I leaned back on the bed and rested on my forearms. I let my head fall back so my hair spread out on the bed in tangled waves. Slowly . . . so slowly, I opened my legs.

I did not have the courage to watch Jonas watch me at that moment, but I could feel the heat of his gaze, and the sharp fire of my own desire. I remained still for ten seconds or so, and then looked up to see what Jonas was doing.

He had stood back up and his hands were balled into fists against the glass. His face was flushed and his lips slightly parted.

I crossed my legs and sat up.

Jonas regarded me through the glass. He took his right hand and placed it over his heart. He gave a small bow before walking away, back into the blackness of the Swedish night.

30

JONAS

I was reeling. Aching. Desperate. Desperate to touch Gemma. To taste her, to feel her, to go right into that bedroom and her open legs and push myself between them. I wanted to kiss her. To be inside her. To . . . love her?

No. That's why I had to stop. I didn't want to love her. I didn't even know her. It had to be alcohol and lust mixing a toxic spell and I couldn't let myself give in.

I grabbed my sketchbook and pencils. I flipped past the map I'd been working on for months. It'd become an obsessive habit —every day my hands would itch and shake until I held a pencil and added something to the paper. Shading, details, lines, and shadows. I kept going and going but I had to stop. Each pencil stroke put me right back in that day. I needed to stop constantly reliving it. I couldn't change the past. Going back there, day after day in my drawings, and night after night in my dreams, was ruining me.

On a fresh page, I started to draw something else. Something from what I'd just seen. A mixture of darkness and light, slow curves, and rounded edges. I didn't have a plan but I followed the feeling of my memory. The mystery picture unfolded before me as my pencil moved across the page. It was beautiful.

I couldn't join Gemma in the bedroom. There was no way my body could be in close proximity to hers. I'd either torture myself all night as I tried not to touch her, or I'd go ahead and touch her and maybe regret it later. Eight years ago, at this very hour I was probably in bed with Anna. I didn't know how to make a bridge from my heart in the past to where my heart could be in my future. I was stuck on an island of loss and regret, surrounded by an ocean of sadness.

I walked quietly into the cabin to see if I could get some bedding to take outside. Gemma was lying on her stomach, sprawled out on the bed. Her body was positioned diagonally across the mattress, and I couldn't have gotten in bed if I'd wanted to. She'd put out the candles, so the room was dark. I moved closer to the bed and pulled off one duvet near Gemma's feet. There was an extra pillow, but I had to walk around the bed to reach it. I almost had it when Gemma flopped onto her back and flung her arms out wide. That woman could take up some real space. She was like a starfish. And, I noticed, as she proceeded to kick off the duvet in her sleep, she was totally nude.

It was the last thing I needed in my mind—that image of Gemma. I also didn't want to be the creepy night stalker who watched naked women while they slept. I grabbed the pillow and quickly made my way to the door. I turned to slide the glass wall closed and let myself look at her for just a few seconds.

Unlike my dreams and nightmares, which were dark, sharp, frightening, and ugly, Gemma was a light, soft, peaceful beauty. Also, she was real.

I took the bedding to the upper deck, moved the chairs and tables to one side, and made a bed for myself. The night was cool, but not uncomfortable. I stretched out on the blanket and gazed up at the sky. So much better than a ceiling. Something about the endless space above my head made me hopeful that my nightmares would stay at bay for a night. With so much room to roam, maybe they'd settle deep in the trees instead of in the confines of my tired mind.

The beach again. Anna buries my feet in the sand and teases me for being lazy. She enters the water. I hear waves crashing. It sounds like the tide is coming in and the water sounds louder and closer. But I can't wake up. I can't open my eyes. I can feel the water rush over my feet where they are buried in the sand. It drips through the grains and sand collapses heavy on my legs. I can't get up. I can't get out. Sleep holds me down like a suffocating blanket.

Finally, my eyes open. I scan the shore and the water. The water is like glass and the sun is directly overhead making the scene garish and hot. I see a flash of color in the waves. I'm back to swimming, swimming, swimming against the tide but I never make progress. I see Anna sunbathing on the rocks. She is safe. She sits up and waves and closes her eyes and reclines again. Something rubs against my leg. That flash of color again. Red and brown. I reach down into the water and pull. I bring up a body. It's Gemma this time. Her hair is tangled and wet and plastered against her face. I move it aside and her face is as pale as marble. Blood covers her forehead and runs from her nose. Her eyes are open and glazed over. I hold her body to mine. She is cold. A wave comes and covers us. I can't breathe and all I can see is dark water—

I WOKE up with a scream caught in my throat. The sun was beginning to rise. Today was the day. Another year without Anna. Another year alone. With the memory of that dream sticking to me like the residue of a caustic glue, I got up to start my day.

31

GEMMA

I awoke to a bright and warm cabin. Sun was streaming through the glass in rays of white-gold light like a spotlight highlighting that, once again, I was alone in bed. I thought I remembered seeing Jonas by the side of the bed in the middle of the night, but maybe that had been a dream. The glass walls had been pushed back to the mostly closed position. One of them was cracked open a few inches to let in some fresh air.

I got out of bed and put on sweatpants and a sweater. And then socks—the floor was cold. I went out to look for Jonas.

I found him by the fire pit. His back was to me.

"Good morning," I said.

He glanced over his shoulder and nodded in greeting and took a sip from the mug in his hands. As I got closer, he pointed to the table. "Thermos there with coffee if you'd like some."

I poured myself a cup and sat by the fire. He was still facing away.

"Let me know when you're hungry. I'll make you a few eggs," he said. He stood up and offered me a tight smile. He set a slice of bread on the arm of my chair. "Need to use the restroom." And off he went.

I knew that Jonas. I knew the tight face and forced smile. That was airplane Jonas. I felt a pain in my chest and a twinge in my stomach as a sense of dread trickled down my spine.

I felt like a fool. Last night had been a mistake. It had felt amazing in the moment, but in the light of day I felt stupid and exposed. I held out a shred of hope that Jonas had kept drinking after I fell asleep and got to a blackout level. Maybe he didn't remember a thing. I, however, recalled every second.

Jonas returned from the bathroom, and I couldn't make eye contact with him. He walked behind me, and I kept my head down. As he passed by, he caught one of my curls between his fingers, pulled softly to straighten it out, and then let it go, allowing it to bounce back into position.

He crossed to the edge of the deck and looked out over the water. His shoulders were tense and tight and he opened and closed his fingers into fists.

After a few minutes, I decided to risk conversation. "Did you sleep at all?" I asked him.

He shrugged. "A little."

More silence.

I decided to face the situation head-on. I took a deep breath. "How are you feeling today? I know this is a hard day."

He swung around to face me. Shit. His face was contorted, and he looked like a different man. His eyes were narrow, his nostrils flared, and his mouth was set in a sneer. "How do you think I'm feeling?"

Playing it safe, I decided his question was a rhetorical one. I felt like crying as I watched the fire. I could feel the weight of Jonas's mood fall on me.

I couldn't decide what to do. Go back into the cabin? Stay there as silent support? Go to the roof deck? I remained in my chair and waited. I felt like emotional prey to Jonas's predator. *Don't move too quickly. Don't speak too loudly. Don't draw attention.* Feeling unsafe pissed me off.

"Do you need some space?" I asked.

Jonas scoffed and raised his hands, gesturing to our location. I concentrated on the mug in my hands and the now cold and bitter coffee. We were silent for a few more minutes. Occasionally Jonas would poke the fire. His face was still dark.

"Grief never loses its sharp edges," I said. "When I lost my mom, I—"

"This isn't like losing a mother, Gemma," Jonas snapped. "This isn't about you at all." His angry words rang out across the water and the trees.

Like a slap to the face. My throat flooded with a sob, and the tears that filled my eyes were born out of a mix of anger and surprise.

I waited for him to apologize or make the next move. He did neither. Jonas slumped in his chair and held his head in his hands.

After a minute, my heart rate began to slow, and the tears stopped threatening to fall from my eyes. I tried one last time.

"You're right," I said softly. "I know what you experienced was—"

"You have no idea what I experienced." Jonas's voice was choked and ragged. His words dripped with desperation. "You don't know me, *or* my story. And like I said, I don't *want* you to know me!" His face was twisted up in fury and sadness. "Fuck this." He stormed into the cabin.

My hands shook as I set my mug on the ground. The breath in my lungs rattled like a frantic bird beating its wings on a cage.

A FEW MINUTES LATER, Jonas returned wearing dark gray pants with pockets, a faded long-sleeved green shirt that clung to his chest, and scuffed chestnut boots. "I need space," he said gruffly.

It was my turn to gesture to our location. "I mean, go for it."

Jonas turned around, took a few steps, and then swung back around to face me. I could tell it was killing him to have to speak to me, but I wasn't going to make it any easier on him. He put his hands on my shoulders and pulled me to his chest, enclosing me in a rough hug. "I have nightmares," he said, the words muffled as he spoke into my hair. "I'm a nightmare. I'm sorry." He let go of me and walked quickly to the edge of the platform. "Can I . . . are you . . ." he stammered, "I'd like to take the boat."

Well, shit. Jonas and I had gone from cool to warm to hot and were now at frigid. I felt like kicking him in the shin. Now *I* needed space. "Fine by me," I said, though I wasn't sure if it really *was* fine by me to be left alone out on the water.

I rushed into the cabin and shut myself in the dry closet. Sitting on the lid of the toilet with my feet on the wall and my head on my knees, I started to cry. I cried for myself, shut away in a stupid bathroom, abandoned on a lake in Sweden. I cried for ten-year-old me, who had no mother. I cried because I missed my father. I cried tears of loneliness, frustration, anger, and rage. Tears of weariness came next, and then I stopped crying.

I blew my nose on some toilet paper and caught my reflection in the mirror; a sight terrifying enough that I hoped Jonas was long gone on the boat. I looked anything but "goddamned lovely." Then I reconsidered. Real things were lovely. I was still lovely, even with a red blotchy face.

Back on the deck, I confirmed that the boat was gone. I scanned the shore for the boat or for Jonas. Not too far from the floating cabin, maybe a quarter mile away, the boat was up on the shore. And I saw the back of Jonas right before he disappeared up the trail and into the dense woods.

My only companion on the floating platform was a rotund silver bird with an espresso-colored cap, who had just landed on the table. "Hello, friend," I said. The bird blinked at me and then explored the table, searching for crumbs.

I sat back down in my chair by the fire where the sad slice of bread still sat. I tore off a piece and tossed it to the bird. We were joined by a smaller gray bird with a black cap. They accepted my offerings and turned their heads with jerky movements and pecked up crumb after crumb. The three of us shared a meal and silence, none of us knowing what the day might bring next.

32

GEMMA

I fed the fire and then fed myself. I heated the iron skillet over
the fire until it was too hot to touch. I broke two eggs into
the pan and stirred them with a fork, mixing the white and yolk.
I cut a corner off the cheese wedge and melted it onto the eggs
and then flipped it all onto a plate. Two small oranges served as
my dessert, and I finished off the coffee in the thermos. Clouds
had started to form overhead, but the air was still laced with
warmth.

I loaded up the sauna stove with wood and followed the
instructions printed on the side for lighting the fire and
adjusting the vents. A hot sauna was a cure for almost everything, right?

I was still in my nightshirt, sweater, and socks, and headed
to the cabin to change clothes. As I got closer to my bag, I saw
that Jonas's sketchbook was open and resting on top of his suitcase. He'd never shown me his drawings; he hadn't even let me
peek over his shoulder or glance at any pages he was working on.

The night before, Jonas's bag had been across the room by

the other side of the bed. He must've purposely placed it there that morning. A torn piece of paper lay on top of the sketchpad. Scribbled on the paper were the words "MI DISPIACE." *I'm sorry.* No "treasure" this time, though.

Underneath the apology was a pencil sketch. I moved the scrap of paper and felt like I'd had the wind knocked out of me again.

It was a rough, fast drawing, but there was no doubt about what it was. It was a sketch of me, leaning back on the bed. The drawing was shaded with pencil and created the effect of the dimly lit room from the night before. Much of my body was in shadow, so it was not too revealing. In the drawing, I was transformed into someone soft, strong, exotic, erotic, and beautiful. Or maybe that's who I'd been all along? Was that how he saw me? Behind the woman in the drawing was a night sky filled with stars that swirled in a spiral. The effect was magical.

I sat with that drawing for a while and tried to get used to the idea of someone finding me that beautiful. I also settled into the idea that the magic of last night may have been an isolated moment in time and space where the stars just happened to align. Jonas and I would likely never experience that chemistry again. It felt like a loss but also like a wonder.

I went outside to check on the sauna. Smoke was coming out of the chimney and the air inside the sauna was clear. I wondered if Jonas would smell the smoke and come back to check on me. I scanned the shoreline, but it was empty. I had a prickly, uneasy feeling, like I was being watched. Was Jonas out there watching me from the trees? I was desperate for him to return, but I was equally desperate never to see his face again. I was angry. I was worried. I was confused.

I opened the door to the sauna and a wavy wall of heat enveloped me. The temperature was perfect, according to the thermometer. I took off my socks, sweater, and nightgown and lay down on the hot cedar bench. I let myself bake and breathe and brought the hot air into my lungs.

After about fifteen minutes I went outside, and the air felt cool in contrast. I turned on the outdoor shower and jumped under the stream, not quite prepared for the shock of it. Goosebumps covered my body, and I was fascinated to watch them spread over my skin. I was proudly a full ten in the public bathing category. Maybe I'd found my calling as a nudist.

I went back into the sauna to warm up after the shower, but only stayed in for five minutes. When I was finished, I put my sweater back on and wrapped a towel around my waist. It felt dangerous to spend too much time in the sauna while I was still alone out on the lake.

I made sure to drink water and had a handful of nuts and dried fruit as a snack. I sat on the edge of the platform. I put my feet in the water and considered the rest of my day. What if Jonas didn't come back? I could swim to shore, but I'd be soaked. And I couldn't swim without my phone getting ruined. What would I do once I got to shore? Maybe I could follow the road we drove in on. Surely a car would come by at some point. And were there really any bears out there?

I gave up on running rescue scenarios and went inside the cabin. I crawled back into the bed and stretched my limbs out to the edges of the mattress. If Jonas was going to ditch me, then I got the whole bed to myself.

.   .   .

I DIDN'T LET myself sleep for too long, which meant that I woke up refreshed instead of woozy. I also woke up with an intense desire to swim. I needed to move and to be weightless and free.

I scanned the beach to see if the boat was still there. It sat on the shore, unmoved. The sun was lower in the sky, and the lake was lovely in the light. The surface shimmered darkly, and the sky and treetops were reflected in the water like a blurry film playing on a rippled screen.

I approached the ladder near the sauna, which was on the far side of the platforms. I stripped off my clothing and slowly lowered into the lake. It was cold, but not unbearable. The coolness moved up my calves, my thighs, my belly, my breasts, and my neck as I moved further into the depths. How different it was to swim like this with nothing between my skin and the water.

The wind had picked up and I heard it whistle through the trees. It passed along the shoreline like a ghost as it swirled and spiraled. Small gusts would come and chill my skin, and whatever parts of me were underwater were warmer than those at the surface.

I went between floating on my back and turning over and floating on my stomach. It felt like the water became a part of me and that I'd been baptized into the earth's church. It was a holy homecoming.

I was most relaxed when I was doing my "dead man's float," which I had learned in swimming lessons as a kid. The instructor told us that if we were ever stranded at sea (though why any of us Midwesterners were at risk of being lost at sea was a total mystery), we could use this type of maneuver to conserve our energy. It was blissful. I floated effortlessly, and I let my limbs relax below me. I would lift my head to breathe when needed, and then go back to floating. If I didn't have to keep up the pesky "getting oxygen" thing, I could've fallen asleep there.

I felt so at peace and powerful and fluid—until something wrapped around me and pulled me under.

33

JONAS

Feeling your feelings was overrated. The last eight years of numbness may have been painful and heavy, but the intensity and clarity of my feelings over the past few days was hard to bear.

I'd stormed off in a tantrum, though it was hard to have a real anger moment when you had to ask permission to use the boat and then paddle to shore. You can slam doors, squeal tires, and even break glass to let the world know how upset you are. Canoeing is not the right sport for performative rage.

Not that I was faking my anger. It was real and it was shaking through my whole body. I wasn't angry at Gemma. I was mad at Anna for dying. Mad at myself for not saving her. I was enraged at the world in general. But even as I was lashing out at Gemma, grabbing my things, untying the boat, and heading to shore, I knew that anger wasn't the emotion at the core of my outrage—anger was just a costume worn by fear.

My loss was still sharp, all these years later, but fear had overtaken the sadness. Fear that I might not be able to move on. Fear that I was using my grief as a suit of armor to ward off love, growth, and a new life. Fear that I was a total dumbass; that one was a solid fact.

After I left the cabin and pulled the boat up onto the rocky shore, I looked back, hoping to see Gemma on the cabin deck. But doing what? Waving a white handkerchief as she wept at my departure? Passed out from sadness and angst over my absence?

I didn't see her at all. Was that any surprise? I'd been an asshole, once again.

I'd secured the boat on shore, gathered my bag, and followed the trail into the woods.

BY THE TIME I reached the Common House, I was calm again. The hike helped clear my head and steady my emotions. Maybe I didn't have to be at the mercy of sudden despair. I had a spot of warmth in my belly that was telling me there was a chance that Sad Sack Jonas didn't have to be my persona forever.

I entered my code into the door lock of the cabin and hoped that it would work. It did. I let myself in. I didn't want to stay long; I was ready to get back to Gemma and to apologize. Maybe I could make things right and this day could end better than it started. I took a quick inventory of the place but didn't spend much time exploring. There were basic camping supplies, blankets, towels, and some tools. I checked the coolers along the back wall and found a few things I thought Gemma might like.

The walk back to the lakeshore was smooth and I didn't even need to use the map. The trails had become familiar to me, and I felt more and more at home. I needed to figure out how to bring this peace and clarity back with me into my everyday life. I floated the idea past myself that maybe I just needed to move out to the woods and never return to society . . . and then I tested it to see how it felt in my gut. It didn't strike me as true. I might be able to return to the world of the living. Maybe.

BACK AT THE BOAT, I loaded up my things and launched into the water. The lake was almost purple in the low light of the afternoon. My stomach felt like tangled strands of Christmas lights neglected in the attic for many seasons, and now plugged in and starting to warm up and blink erratically.

I was getting closer to the floating cabin and could see into the sauna and the living quarters, and I still didn't see Gemma. She wasn't on the upper or lower decks. The only place she could've been that I couldn't see was the dry closet. I tried to reassure myself that she was in there. I approached the platform and tied up the boat. I left my belongings behind and quickly climbed to the deck. I was so stupid for leaving. Why did I abandon her here?

My feet pounded against the wooden planks as I jogged to the dry closet. The door was slightly open. I knocked and pushed on the door. Empty. No Gemma. There was nowhere else she could be.

Except the water.

I felt like I might vomit. My ears started to ring, and my vision tunneled. I ran back outside and scanned the lake. Nothing by the boat. Nothing to the north or the south. Only the western side of the float remained to be inspected. I rushed to the other side of the sauna.

Oh god. Oh shit oh shit oh shit. A flash of color in the water. Just like the nightmare. Red and brown. Gemma's hair. The skin of her back. She was facedown.

Everything went dark.

34

GEMMA

When shocking things happen in the blink of an eye, time really does slow down. What must have taken five seconds in real time felt like an hour in my panicking mind.

When I first felt something smooth and strong wrap around me in the darkness of the lake I thought, "If there's a killer Swedish Sea Lion nobody told me about, I'm going to be really pissed." Then more realistically I thought it must be a snake, or an eel, and truly, I was probably dead. I was already in the afterlife.

While spending microseconds pondering which lake creature could be consuming me, I realized I couldn't breathe.

I had inhaled to scream, but unfortunately my head was under water, so I sucked a good amount of the lake straight into my lungs.

I kicked and scratched but I was still being pulled—but not pulled under, as I first thought. I was being pulled *in* to the deck. By the one and only, lost and now found, Jonas Hellgren.

How dare he? How fucking *dare* he. I had finally found peace in my body, mind, and in whatever part of my spirit that now permanently worshiped the lake gods, and he was dragging me out of the water like a man possessed.

He had the determination of a sailor dragging an injured shipmate to safety and he was so damn strong that I gave up struggling against his pull.

Jonas had me in some sort of lifesaving grip, and he was closing in on the ladder. With near-superhuman strength, he held me with one arm as he climbed the ladder and then he tossed me onto the warm boards of the deck.

I had too much water in my lungs to yell or scream or make my feelings known. That only made me angrier, which made me cough harder. I felt vulnerable and betrayed. He'd left me, and I was fine without him. Then he came back and shattered my calm, halfway drowning me in the process.

Splayed out on the deck of the floating platform, I spent the first minute or so coughing up water. I was going to give him an earful as soon as I could use my voice again. As my coughing subsided, I realized that Jonas seemed . . . altered.

He was fully clothed, down to those chestnut boots. He was mumbling and running his hands all over my body. My whole naked body. Like, every inch of skin, above and below the waist. I kicked out at him once or twice. I made contact with his stomach and shoulders, but he didn't seem to notice. I kicked him again. Hard. He still had his hands on me. His fingers were probing and prowling, and I wanted to get away.

Jonas was crying.

"It's ok, you're ok, are you ok?" he was repeating as he searched my body to reassure himself that I was undamaged. Then he moved up to my face, his strong fingers pressing against the bridge of my nose, my eyebrows, my lips, ears, cheeks, and even my teeth. "Gemma, you're breathing, oh my god you're breathing, you're ok, you're not hurt, does your leg hurt, you're breathing, you're ok, Gemma, you're ok," he said, his voice cracking.

"Of course I'm ok, no thanks to YOU!" I yelled at him while shoving him off me. "You're the one who nearly killed me!"

Jonas seemed utterly despondent and confused, his face crumpled. "I saved you! I brought you in and you're ok. You're breathing."

"I was breathing way better before you made me suck up all that water! And I don't need you to save me from anything. Save yourself, asshole!"

Jonas stopped. He stopped touching me, he stopped talking, he stopped crying. He froze there in his wet shirt, drenched pants, and heavy water-logged boots.

And then he tipped over.

He completely collapsed onto the deck outside the cabin. And he wept. He cried so loudly that the birds seemed to stop singing, the insects stopped buzzing, and the wind stopped blowing. For a moment, the whole forest seemed to hold its breath to make space for the keening of Jonas's broken heart.

In a terrible, awful, horrifying flash of clarity, I thought I understood what had happened. Not bothering to waste time with covering up, I crawled over to Jonas and touched his arm. "Jonas . . ." No reaction from him. His shoulders and back were heaving. I thought he might throw up from the violence of it all. "Jonas," I said, right next to his ear, "I'm not Anna."

"I KNOW you're not Anna!" he cried out. "You're Gemma."

I kept my hand on his arm to try to keep his attention with me; I was worried that he might lose himself in his despair.

"Jonas," I said, "did Anna drown?" His sobs abated, but he kept his head down. He was breathing quickly and heavily. "Did Anna drown?" I asked him again.

"No—" he said weakly, his voice cracking. "I mean, no. Not really."

"Jonas," I said again, and I pushed his shoulder a little so he rolled onto his side, and I could see his face. "How did Anna die?"

He lifted his head. He was wrecked. His eyes were red and wet. His face was covered with tears and snot. His lips quivered. He looked a bit like I had earlier in the bathroom mirror: terrible, but still lovely.

"How did Anna die?" I shook his shoulder a little. "It's ok. I'm ok."

Jonas took a deep breath. His voice was raspy and weak. "She died of a pulmonary embolism." He closed his eyes and took another breath. "She was in the water. Floating near some rocks. I think maybe she died and then fell off her raft into the water, but I don't know." He pinched the bridge of his nose and closed his eyes. "I'd fallen asleep on the beach. When I woke up, I saw her empty raft—"

"Oh, Jonas. Oh no," I said, and I wrapped my arms around him.

What we must've looked like from afar. A soaking wet, fully clothed, giant, sobbing Swede, and a naked and bedraggled American with her whole body wrapped around him and rocking him back and forth.

I kissed his head and his ears. "It's ok. It's ok."

"Gemma?" Jonas raised his head.

"Yes?"

"She was pregnant."

"Anna was?"

"Yes," his voice choked up, but he continued, "Anna was pregnant. I lost them both. I lost everything." He buried his head in my lap, and I held on as tightly as I could. I heard a bird sing a sad note, and the wind picked up and blew across our skin, kissing us with its presence.

35

GEMMA

After a while, Jonas grew calm and still in my arms. I released my hold on him and pulled my limbs out from underneath his body. He shifted to help me free myself. My legs were cramping from holding that position for so long and I stretched my calves, quads, and hips slowly to loosen them up and alleviate the ache. I swung my arms up over my head and tried to work out the kinks in my shoulders and back. Jonas kept his head tucked down, which was a good thing, because I probably resembled a nudist trying Tai Chi for the first time.

The sky had gone from blue to purple gold, and the birdsong was beginning to fade. Goosebumps sprinkled my forearms. Jonas, soaking wet, also had to be chilly. I grabbed the towel I'd left out for myself on the deck and wrapped it around my torso.

"Let's go inside. You need some dry clothes," I said. He remained still. I knelt and put my hand on the back of his head and spoke quietly but firmly just inches away from his ear, "It's getting dark. We need to dry off. *Now.*"

Jonas took a slow and giant breath. His chest and back

inflated, and inflated, and inflated. I worried for a moment that he might hold his breath and just pass out. But then he exhaled.

He had no tears, no trembling, no clouded eyes; his storm had passed. He nodded and stood up to his full height. I had to crane my neck to watch his face.

He turned to look out at the lake, put his hands on his hips, and stretched his torso. I waited. Jonas turned back and held out his hand to me. I took hold of it, and we walked the few steps to the cabin. I lit a lantern and some candles, and the lights flickered warmly against the wood walls of the cabin and reflected back on us through the glass.

Inside the cabin, we did not speak, but we took care of each other, and took care *with* each other. I helped Jonas strip off his cold and wet clothing. I hung it outside on the railing while he selected dry clothes. I changed into a long cotton dress and a sweater. We were not shy or modest. We were mostly tired. Any bodily embarrassment had been wrung out of us.

There was a new chill in the air. Jonas sat on the bed, and I placed a towel on his head and softly rubbed his hair and then dried behind and inside his ears. I brushed his hair slowly and gently with my brush, like my mother used to do for me. He made little sighing sounds as the bristles moved across his scalp.

"Would you like me to brush yours?" he asked after a few minutes.

"Thank you," I said, "but it's probably too dry to brush now. If you do that, my curls will frizz, and my hair will take up the entire room. Nobody wants that. Trust me."

"Then here," he said, patting the spot next to him on the bed. I perched on the edge of the mattress, and he sat, cross-legged, behind me. He softly buried his fingertips in my hair and worked his way up my scalp. With gentle pressure he rubbed and massaged my head. Then he slowly drew out his hands and untangled my curls. He did it again and again until my wavy hair was calm, and I was so relaxed I could've passed out right there.

Still behind me, Jonas placed all ten of his fingers on my neck and ever so lightly ran them up and down my skin. He gathered the length of my hair and twisted it around his fist and held it up so my neck was fully exposed. He leaned in closer, and I felt his breath, hot and humid, on my skin. And then I felt his lips. Wet, warm, open, searching. He tasted my neck and held his tongue on my pulse, as if taking in the measure of my life force with his mouth. His lips lingered on my neck and then he let down my hair.

He gently moved off the bed. "I have something to show you." He took my hand and led me to the door. I really would've rather he led me straight back to that bed. My legs were so rubbery that I felt I might stumble.

We went to the canoe, which was tied to its mooring. He got on his belly and reached down into the boat. With a grunt of effort, he pulled out two jugs of water, a bottle of scotch, and a large soft-sided backpack cooler. He unzipped the cooler and produced a sweet potato, several sausage links, salad greens, and—

"Are those cupcakes?" I asked. Jonas was proudly holding up two small chocolate cakes with pink frosting.

"I think so."

"Where did you get all of this?"

"The Common House. This was all I could carry in this cooler. We can go back together tomorrow and get more if you want."

"Do they have a full kitchen there?"

"It's very primitive. There's a sink and a hot plate. I think they're committed to open fire cooking here."

I picked up the food and carried it to the table by the fire pit and Jonas followed.

I kept my eyes on the food. Never had I been so interested in a sweet potato. I felt shy about standing close to Jonas, and about looking him in the eye. My feelings were all over the place, and I wasn't sure that I fully trusted him, or myself. I wanted to take him back to the bed and return to that moment where his open mouth was on my neck. At the same time, I wanted to tell him to piss off and to put his ass in that canoe and paddle right back to the woods.

"Gemma, could I talk to you?" He put his hands on my waist and lightly pulled me toward him. He shifted my body to face his, and he moved his hands to my arms. I kept my eyes down. He let go of me and took a step back.

"I'm so sorry," he began. "I'm so very sorry . . . I'm sorry for this morning. I'm sorry for the lake. I'd rather die than hurt you or scare you, and I'm afraid I've done both of those things."

His face was serious and searching. His eyes seemed wet. "You did scare me. And you upset me." I felt tears sting my eyes, but I held them back. "I know this was a really hard day for—"

"It doesn't matter if it was a hard day for me. It was the worst day, honestly. Not just because of the anniversary of losing Anna, but because I spread that pain over you. There's no excuse for that." He stepped closer to me and reached out his right hand. He softly placed the pad of his middle finger on my collar bone and drew an invisible line on my skin. He cleared his throat. "I promise to be more careful. With you. I can't promise that I won't ever—"

"Go dark?" I offered.

He smiled a little. One of his canines was slightly crooked. Why was that so sexy? "Yes, go dark. I might—no, I'm sure I will—*go dark* again." He put both hands on my waist again. "I've isolated myself for years now. My social graces and interpersonal skills are shit. Please bear with me. Because . . ." He pulled me even closer. My cheek was against his chest. He slid his arms around my back. I heard the little inhale that comes before spoken words. "I *do* want you to know me. I want it so much."

36

JONAS

We went about making dinner quietly. We found a peaceful rhythm with building the fire, peeling and chopping the vegetables, and cooking the meat. A warm-colored glow caught my eye from inside the sauna. "Did you use the sauna while I was gone?" I asked Gemma.

"I did," she said.

"How was it?"

"Heavenly. But not as heavenly as this cupcake." She'd insisted on having her dessert first.

There was that pang in my stomach again. I didn't want her to use the word heavenly about something other than me. I also wanted to be in that sauna *with* her. "I'll be right back."

I walked into the sauna and felt the residual heat from her earlier session. "Are you ok if I heat it back up?" I called out. "And also, is the temperature dropping or is it just me?"

"No, I felt that earlier. It's cooler. And windier. Go ahead with the sauna."

The sky was dense and inky and the clouds covered the stars

and moon. I gathered some wood and carried it back to the sauna stove. I loaded it up and lit the fire. Back on the deck, I opened the bottle of Scotch and held it close to my nose. The woody scent warmed me before I'd even taken a sip. It smelled like old leather, steep cliffs, and like an ancient elixir that held promises of magic, for the right price. "Would you like any? I'm having a small glass tonight. Not much."

Gemma raised her eyebrows. We both knew where too much alcohol would lead us. "Sure. A small one." I poured some for her and put it on the table by her side.

"I'm sorry I don't have ice for that. Would you like to add some water—"

Too late. She'd downed the drink in one big gulp. "Wow. That really burns, all the way down."

"Shit, Gemma. That was for sipping."

"It's been a long day," she said. "I was attacked by Sweden's version of the Loch Ness monster."

I refilled her glass.

I felt like my map was burning a hole in my pocket. I had it folded in there and had been waiting for the right moment to bring it out. There most likely wasn't going to be a right moment, so, now or never. "May I show you something?" I asked Gemma. I pulled my chair closer to hers and sat down. She leaned forward as I brought out my drawing and began to unfold it.

"What's this?"

"It's what I've been working on. For a long time." I took a sip of my drink. "For too long." I gave it to her, my hands shaking as I passed it over. The glow of the fire illuminated the page. I tried to picture it as she might be seeing it, with fresh eyes. I had every detail memorized. It was a map of my life with Anna. There were the Scandies that blended into the Øresund which bridged over to a sketch of our flat in Gothenburg. Lilies of the valley were scattered on the page and across a drawing of Anna, pregnant, sunning herself on the beach. There were other moments and mementos of our time together mapped on the page, and the only legend was locked away in my heart.

"It's beautiful, Jonas."

"I need to burn it."

Gemma half-laughed, as if waiting for me to reveal the punchline of my dark joke.

"Really. Like, in the fire," I said.

"I don't understand," she said. "It's a piece of art. It's exquisite. And it's . . . Anna."

"It's not Anna. Anna's gone. It's my obsession with her memory that you're seeing there."

"You don't want to keep it?"

"I want to keep my memories. But not this drawing. I keep adding things to it and I can't stop. It's moved beyond memorial into a demented dirge. I think I need help with this."

Gemma stretched out her arm and tried to give the map back to me, but I kept my fingers laced around my glass and shook my head. She brought the drawing back to her lap and her gaze moved over its surface. The reflection of the flames in her eyes revealed tears that sparkled on the edges but did not spill over.

"I'll help you," she said. "But you're the one who needs to put it in the fire. And I need another drink."

She finished her next drink in one swallow, stood, and paced on the deck. She wore a long black dress with a velvety mocha-colored sweater over it. Her hair was long and loose over her shoulders. She was softness personified.

"We need some type of ceremony. We can't just dump this in the fire pit," she said.

"Any ideas?"

"Do you know any poems or songs Anna liked?"

I used to know the answer. But now the details were fuzzy. "Not that I can recite by memory."

"Was she religious?"

"She was raised Catholic but didn't practice."

"But she wasn't offended by the church or anything like that?"

"I don't think so."

"Is there anything you'd like to say? For Anna?"

"There's nothing left unsaid."

Gemma continued to pace. "Ok, I know a prayer that will work, and I have a few poems memorized. I don't think we need a Shakespearean sonnet or Shel Silverstein, so we're going to have to go with Rabindranath Tagore."

"I don't know who that is," I said.

"A poet my mother loved, and I have one memorized that should be ok for this." She held her hand out to me. "Come stand with me. And you hold the map."

Gemma stood in front of the fire, and I stood next to her, our arms touching. She slipped the paper between my fingers. I had the urge to add another line, another memory. But I knew it was time for it to go.

"You're sure?" she asked.

"I'm sure."

Gemma cleared her throat and then began to speak the lines of a poem, her voice soft and strong.

"Peace, my heart, let the time for the parting be
   sweet.
Let it not be a death but completeness.
Let love melt into memory and pain into songs.
Let the flight through the sky end in the folding
   of the wings over the nest.
Let the last touch of your hands be gentle like
   the flower of the night.
Stand still, O beautiful end, for a moment, and
   say your last words in silence.
I bow to you and hold up my lamp to light your
   way."

I dropped the map into the flames. The corners caught fire first and began to roll inward. The paper turned black and shades of orange danced on the drawings as heat overtook it.

"I'll say the Hail Mary now," whispered Gemma.

"Ave Maria, piena di grazia
il Signore è con te;
tu sei benedetta fra le donne,
e Benedetto è il frutto del tuo senso, Gesù.
Santa Maria, Madre di Dio,
prega per noi peccatori
adesso e nell'ora della nostra morte. Amen."

I felt sad, but also calm and renewed. The burning of my drawing felt like it had also incinerated the last of the confusion, guilt, and rage I had over Anna's death. What was left behind felt like love, pure and simple.

"May I have a moment alone?" I asked.

She brushed her fingers along my arm and walked toward the sauna platform. I closed my eyes and listened to the night sounds as the forest groaned in the wind.

37

GEMMA

I got a bottle of water and checked on the temperature of the sauna. It was heating up nicely. I climbed up to the roof deck and stretched out on a chair. I was worn out and weary. The stars were still hidden in the hazy sky. I closed my eyes. The wind had picked up. The sound it made as it rushed through branches and leaves made an urgent humming that ebbed and flowed. Birds cackled from time to time and foxes cried out to each other.

Suddenly, a heavy silence landed, like someone had hit pause on the forest soundtrack. Something was wrong.

I opened my eyes and sat up. That moment of silence felt laced with threat. The air had shifted. I saw a light flash on and off among the trees. "Jonas!" I yelled, panic rising in my throat.

"Gemma?" he immediately called back. He must have sensed the fear in my voice because I heard him running on the deck and quickly scale the ladder. "What's wrong?" He was out of breath.

"I'm not sure. Come here. Get down."

Jonas squatted by my side. "What is it? What happened?"

"Something just feels wrong. And I saw a light flickering in the trees for a second."

"Where?"

I pointed to where I'd seen the light. The woods remained dark. A few moments later, a light flickered again, but to the right of where I'd seen it before.

"Did you see that?"

"I saw it."

"Is someone out there?"

"I don't know. Maybe the owners? I left a note in the Common House today, in case they came."

"I don't like this."

"It's ok. We're safe out here," Jonas said, but his voice was tight and tense. "And if it's not the owners, whoever it is can't get to us unless they have a boat or want to go for a night swim. And we'd hear them coming."

"I'm not sure how comforted I am by that."

"Let's just watch and listen for another minute."

We sat in silence and scanned the woods for light or movement. There was nothing.

"Tomorrow we'll head back to the Common House and get this straightened out," he said.

I had no idea how we'd accomplish that, but I liked the idea of having a plan.

"Ready to try the sauna again?" Jonas asked.

I was ready at least to get off the observation deck—instead of me observing nature, I felt like the one being watched.

Jonas went down the ladder first, and he waited for me to safely descend.

The effect of the glow in the sauna at night was spectacular. Because most of the walls were glass, the light from the fire in the sauna oven reflected again and again and again in the glass of the room. And those reflections bounced out toward the dark water, and it looked like fire was dancing on the waves.

"Let's go in," he said. Jonas had towels laid out for us on the cedar benches along with two bottles of water. We opened the door and were hit with a surge of heat. He peeled off his shirt and pants which left him in a pair of blue boxer briefs.

It was too hot to wear clothes in there. I took off my dress and sweater but kept my bra and underwear on.

Jonas and I stretched out on separate benches. He chose a bench up high, where it was hotter, and I picked a lower one for the slightly cooler temperature.

We baked and basked in silence, other than the occasional groan and sigh. The heat settled into my limbs, and so did the reality of the last few days.

My entire life had shifted in a very short time. I was also dreading returning to my normal world. How could I go back to my little house that felt like a time capsule of my life with my parents? Once I started breathing the air of this forest, I began to realize how I might have been slowly suffocating at home.

The last few days seemed like a fever dream. For a moment, I wondered if I had just imagined it all. But no. It was real. Jonas was real, in the most confusing ways. He put me on edge but also calmed me. He made me feel like there was an undiscovered universe of yearning inside me. Did I even know myself?

How could such intense feelings spring up for someone I'd only known for a few days? Even more troubling, was there any way that Jonas could have real feelings for *me* in such a short period of time? I wasn't famous. Or gorgeous. Or rich, successful, tall, thin, or young. I was a wild-haired, middle-aged, scattered, searching woman.

I thought about the reality shows where strangers were stranded on an island and within days they proclaimed life-long alliances. There was an instant intimacy when people were abandoned together. Maybe Jonas and I had Forest Fever, and as soon as we hit the city streets again, the spell would be broken.

Then, with the added trauma of Anna . . . what if Jonas's interest in me was a grief anniversary rebound?

My internal dialogue was a real shit show. I sat up and drank my entire bottle of water. "I shouldn't stay in here much longer," I said. "It's pretty hot."

"So hot," said Jonas, who also sat up and slugged his water. He slid off his upper bench and came down to mine. He offered me his hand and we stood up. Jonas opened the door and cool air rushed in. The temperature dipped and was more comfortable with a mixing of the hot and the cold. I wrapped a towel around myself and started to walk out into the night, but Jonas pulled me back.

"Wait." He placed his hands on either side of my face. He tilted my chin up and he leaned down. He kissed me so softly that my heart nearly broke into pieces.

With that kiss, the reality of everything rained down on me. There was no hiding from my feelings. From any of them. Dozens of realizations hit me at once, and my knees almost buckled. Jonas had a hold of me and kept me from falling. "Gemma? You alright? It's too hot in here. Let's go out."

I realized that not only was I not alright—I was in serious

trouble. I had intense and real feelings for Jonas Hellgren, and I was petrified about what that might mean.

"I'm *not* okay," I said.

GEMMA

"What's wrong?" The sincere concern on his face nearly destroyed me.

I felt a tsunami of emotion build up in my belly, and then my chest, to my throat, and up through my head. I burst into tears. "You left me!" I cried out.

"I—"

"You left me on this floating thing in the middle of nowhere. I didn't know if you hated me or wanted to hurt me or if you were ever coming back." The feelings that I'd been pushing away all day, all week, all year, all this decade—shit, almost all my life—came rushing out.

"I was alone! If you hadn't come back, I would've had to swim to the goddamn shore."

"I'm so sorry, Gemma. I—"

"Don't apologize to me." My tears were falling and I rammed my fists up against his chest. "My mother left me." Those words surprised me. What did my mom have to do with this? I let the words tumble out. "She left me with a father who had no idea what to do with me. We were lost without her." I sat down on the bench and started to cry harder. Jonas sat next to me and put his hand on my arm.

"And my father left me, before he even died. In his last year he didn't even remember he had a daughter. Some days he thought I was my mother and he'd get angry if I didn't answer when he called me Lorna." I wiped my face with the corner of my towel. "When someone forgets that they ever loved you, part of you disappears."

Jonas knelt in front of me and put his hands on both of my legs. It was no mystery why I was falling for him; he was stripped down and ragged, tired and grieving, but he looked at me with an intensity and vulnerability that lit me up on the inside.

My words continued to bubble out. "I lost my mom, I lost my dad, I lost Adam, I lost myself. And today I lost you and I didn't know if you'd ever come back. I'm—"

Jonas waited for me to finish my sentence, but I wasn't brave enough to do it. I tried again. "I'm—"

"You're . . . ?"

Screw it. I'd gone this far. "I'm falling for you."

"Oh!" Jonas gasped a little and his face went slightly white.

I covered my face with my hands. "It's awful and obvious and embarrassing."

"It's not awful—"

I put my hand over Jonas's mouth. I couldn't bear to hear what he might say. I stood up and he stood up with me. He tried to put his arms around me. "Gemma—"

"Don't say it, Jonas. I already know it's ridiculous."

"It's not ridiculous—" he started to say, but I muffled his words by trying to cover his mouth again. "Stop that!" he demanded. He pushed my hands off his face and held my arms tightly by my side. We stood there staring at each other for what felt like an eternity. Jonas looked like he was trying to find some words, but I was too scared to hear what they might be.

"Don't say anything. Please," I said.

He let go of my arms and waited. I bent over at the waist and rested my hands on my knees like I was trying to catch my breath after an especially grueling marathon.

I collected myself, stood up straight, and was face to face with Jonas. His eyes flashed like green golden fire as they reflected the flames. I noticed wisps of gray peeking out along his temple as he held his hair back from his face and waited for my next move. His lips were chapped from the heat and his earlier tears. Sweat ran down the skin of his torso, mimicking winding roads on a dark map and settled on his hips, where his boxer briefs rested. Muscles tensed in his thighs, calves, and feet as he shifted his weight from one foot to the other, and back again.

I felt like I could breathe again. I'd released those words, and along with them I released some of my fears, anger, and insecurities. I felt powerful. And beautiful. Everything was fleeting. Impermanent. I wanted to take what I wanted, no more hiding, no more waiting.

"Back up." I told him.

"Back up?"

"Back up against that wall." I pointed to the cedar wall behind him.

Jonas walked backwards until his shoulders were up against the wood.

I moved toward him and stopped when I got a foot away from him. "Put your hands behind your head," I said.

"What?"

"You heard me. Put your hands behind your head."

Jonas held my gaze for a moment. Then he lifted his hands and laced his fingers behind his head.

"Move your foot a little," I said, gently kicking the inside of his left foot. "Make some space here." I pushed my knee between his legs to indicate where I wanted him to open.

He moved his foot.

"Now don't move until I say you can move."

"Alright."

"No matter what. You can't move from this wall or put your hands down until I say you can."

"I understand," he said.

Jonas was beautifully on display for me. It was only fair. I was exposed to him the night before. Now it was his turn. There was one difference, though . . . I wasn't behind glass.

I ran my fingernails softly up his torso starting at the waistband of his briefs and ending at his neck. He started to move his hands to put them around me. "Gemma—"

I didn't know what had overcome me. The wave of power had me in its swell and I intended to ride it until I made it to shore or until I crashed and burned.

"Do NOT move your hands."

"Bossy," he said.

"May I touch you?"

I heard his breath catch in his throat. "Yes, you may."

"Then no moving." I stood on my tiptoes and kissed him roughly on the mouth. He met my pressure with his own mouth and kissed me back. He started to move his hands until I caught him. "No," I said, pushing his arms back into position. He retaliated by biting my lip. It surprised me, and it hurt a little. But it didn't break the rules. "That will cost you," I told him.

The fire in the sauna was dying down, and the door was still open. I was grateful for that cool air. Otherwise, we both would've passed out by now. The shadows and reflections of the flames danced across Jonas's skin. He was a work of art.

I put my face close to his and looked up into his eyes. At the same time, I slid my hands into the sides of his underwear, along his hips.

"Gemma . . ." he said, in a warning tone.

"Shhh," I said. "I'm in charge." I grabbed hold of the fabric and pushed it down past his knees.

"Oh god."

I knelt in front of Jonas and took him in with my eyes. He kept his hands behind his head, but he started to whimper. I wrapped my hands around the back of his thighs and moved my mouth closer to his groin.

"God," he moaned again. I glanced up. He was watching my every move. His eyes were half closed and his lips were parted. His face was a picture of vulnerable, raw lust. It was perfection.

I opened my mouth and extended my tongue. He was so hard, and I could feel the waves of heat coming off his body. His legs started to tremble. He tilted his pelvis forward a little.

"Keep your back against the wall," I ordered. He did as he was told.

With the tip of my tongue, I flicked the skin of his engorged head. He cried out when I made contact. I approached again and slid my tongue up and down his shaft. His moan turned into an open groan and then into a growl that came straight from his chest.

In one quick move I jerked his body closer to me and took

his entire length into my mouth. He shouted and his hands came down onto my head. I was in no position to audibly correct him, so I let him pull my hair.

"Gemma," he choked out. "I can't last . . . I'm going to . . . you need to—"

I swirled my tongue around him and moved my lips from base to tip and back again. My hands held tight to his ass, holding him firmly in my mouth as he tried to buck and move.

He held out for a few seconds but then he lost control, and his wet warmth flooded my mouth. Jonas was making animal sounds and digging his fingers into my curls.

I held on to his body with my hands, my mouth, my lips, and my tongue and rode the full wave of his pleasure.

When he had stilled, I moved my mouth away and held him in my hands. "You're free to move as you wish."

Jonas slouched backwards and used the wall to hold up his body. He was panting and his eyes were closed. Then he bent forward and swept me up into his arms. He kissed me all over my face and neck and then collapsed with me onto a bench.

"Christ, Gemma," he said into my neck, where his face was pressed.

I moved my hands to his face and kissed him softly on the mouth. His face suddenly appeared more familiar, and I felt like there was a Fourth of July sparkler burning in my chest. "Jonas . . . you're so goddamned lovely."

39

JONAS

I'd only had one glass of Scotch, but you would've thought I'd had ten. It had been the worst day, the longest day, the best day, I'd had in a long time. I was both exhausted and wired and thoughts were shooting off in my brain like flares on a dark night, only to be extinguished in the water of my fatigue. My body felt languid and boneless. If I couldn't get a few hours of sleep on this night, there was no hope for me.

Gemma and I got into bed and under the covers. It was the first time we'd both been awake in bed together at the same time.

"Hello," I said. The room was dark, and Gemma's features were shaded in the low light.

"Hi there."

I wanted to touch her. To really touch her, but my hands and mind weren't communicating well. My eyelids kept falling even though I was willing them to stay open. She deserved my full attention, and I wasn't sure I could offer that. Under the blankets, I reached my hand out and ran it along her arm and onto her hip. I circled my fingers toward her belly.

"I want to touch you," I told her.

"Soon, but not now," she said. "Let's sleep."

Too tired to fight off sleep any longer, I put my arm over her body and let myself fall away from consciousness.

IT FELT LIKE A MINUTE LATER, but it must have been hours. It wasn't daybreak yet, but the room was lighter. My body was rolling, and my bones felt like they were rumbling. Was this what real sleep felt like?

"Jonas, wake up!" Gemma was shaking my shoulder and things *were* rumbling, though it wasn't my bones, it was the entire platform. What had been a gentle swaying of the cabin when we fell asleep had changed into a violent lurching.

A crash jolted me fully awake and the cabin lit up as if the universe had just taken a flash photograph. I sat straight up, disoriented and dizzy. I raised my arm as if to fight off an invisible intruder.

Gemma started laughing and fell back onto her pillow in a fit of giggles.

"What is it? Why are you laughing?" The lightning was creating a strobe effect and our cabin felt like a disco from hell.

"I'm sorry," she said, between laughs, and then hiccups. "Your hair has all these spikes going in different directions. And your face . . . you look like a cross between a baby owl and the statue of liberty."

I flopped back down on the bed. "I'm glad I can provide you with amusement. I was sound asleep, you know."

She was still laughing and wiping tears from her eyes. "Give me your tired, your poor, your huddled masses."

"I'm going to lift my lamp beside your golden door if you don't hush up," I said.

This made her laugh even harder. I put my pillow over my head.

"I guess even movie stars have bad hair days—" she was saying until a cataclysmic combination of thunder and lightning made us both yelp.

"*Skit också!*" I jumped out of bed and took a moment to find my balance. I didn't have a plan, but I felt like I had to do something. I slid open the glass wall to the cabin. A gust of wind burst inside like a freight train, and I heaved the door shut again. The platform wobbled erratically on the water.

"Are we safe here?"

I had no idea. Probably not. "I think we're safe. For now," I said. "But I'd rather not be out here for an extended storm."

"I don't want to be in the treehouse, either."

We were silent as we both went over the options in our heads. I should've planned for a storm or had an escape plan ready.

"Canoeing doesn't sound super fun . . . maybe we need to just stay here?" Gemma said, her voice timid.

"*Fan!*" I pounded my fist on the wall.

"Did you just say the f-word in Swedish?"

"Fucking right I did." Rain started to hit the glass and the lightning and thunder were coming quickly. "We can't leave now. It's dark and not safe at all to be on the open water. I'm going to get wood for the stove in here before it's too wet to burn."

"Might want to put on some clothes first."

I realized that I was clad only in underwear. I quickly pulled on pants, a jacket, and my boots that were still wet from yesterday's plunge in the lake. I slid the door open and pushed my way out into the storm.

It was dark, except for when lightning gave me a glimpse of the landscape. I should've stayed in the cabin. It was treacherous on the deck, and I felt like a walking target. How many people got struck by lightning each year? Surely more than were killed by wild boars.

I grabbed some firewood and ran back to the bedroom with it. Rain pounded the platform and pummeled the lake. The little collisions of water on water made a deafening racket.

Gemma was waiting by the door. I dropped the wood on the floor and had to pull her back before she got out onto the deck.

"We don't both need to be struck by lightning," I yelled, trying to raise my voice over the noise of the storm. "Get back in bed. Under the covers and away from the glass."

"It's not like a tree's going to fall out here and crash through our window on the lake," she shouted.

"No, but there's a fire pit, tables, chairs, logs, and SO MUCH GLASS."

That was enough for her to reconsider stepping out in the storm. She removed her jacket and sat on the bed. "Be careful."

I brought in more wood and grabbed a jug of water. I stripped out of my clothes right by the door so I wouldn't drench the entire cabin. Rain had blown in anyway, and the floor was slippery. Gemma hopped out of bed and picked up a stack of towels. She gave me one and put a few others on the floor. I dried off the best I could.

"Come back to bed," she said, as another crack of thunder seemed to shake the whole earth.

"I'm still damp."

"Doesn't matter." She pulled back the blanket for me and I got in, shivering and very much awake.

40

GEMMA

We huddled under the blankets in the bed, lying on our sides, facing each other. The storm made it sound like the world was ending and neither of us closed our eyes.

He reached out to touch me, but I gently pushed his hand away.

His face fell.

I *did* want Jonas to touch me. I wanted it badly. But I knew that the moment I let him touch me intimately—if I let him see me at my most vulnerable and let him take me to the places I knew I'd go under his touch—then my feelings for him would be set in stone. I'd be a goner. And I wasn't quite brave enough to be fully gone. Not yet.

Something rattled on the deck and collided with the door of our cabin. The glass held, but my pulse was jumpy and racing.

Jonas's eyes were open, but his gaze was low. His mouth was downturned and worry lines creased out from his eyes. I thought about how I would feel if Jonas had refused my touch. I would've felt awful. And embarrassed.

"May I touch your arm?" he asked. I nodded and he lightly ran his fingertips up and down my skin, leaving a wave of raised flesh in his wake. We listened to the raindrops smash into the glass like wet pebbles.

Jonas cleared his throat and asked, "Have you ever made a sound at the exact moment that there's a sudden silence?" A bolt of lightning fractured the sky and lit up the cabin. "And that noise rings out into the void and echoes again and again in your head? You feel like a fool and wish that someone would say something or make another sound to erase yours, which is lingering in the air?"

I pulled the blankets up higher. "I have."

"I'm living with that echo right now, and I hate it."

"What did you say that you want to erase?"

"It's not what I said. It's what I did." Jonas's eyes were closed.

"I don't understand."

"My touches," Jonas's voice broke a little. "The last time I really had my hands on you was when I pulled you from the water . . ."

"Oh . . ." The rain was driving down so hard that I could barely hear him. It seemed to be coming from all directions. We had front row seats to a spectacularly frightening light show.

"I was too rough."

"You were panicking. You weren't even in your right mind."

"Which makes it worse that I put my hands on you when my mind wasn't right." Jonas reached out and tucked a curl behind my ear as we faced each other. "It's a terrible echo. I'm sorry, Gemma." He pulled his arm away from me and hid his face under his pillow.

I rolled over onto my back and I took his hand in mine. He let me hold his fingers, but he kept his face hidden.

This was too risky. I couldn't allow myself to have real feelings for Jonas Hellgren. He was out of my league, not to mention out of my world . . . maybe even my universe. I was a self-employed (and that was being generous) American, bordering on spinster. He was a Swedish movie star with international appeal. Even though I was younger than Jonas, why would he even consider me as a lover when surely he had endless options of women from which to choose.

But, Jonas had let me touch him. And he had tried, repeatedly, to touch me in return. He didn't seem like the type of man who did anything he didn't want to. In fact, he seemed like someone who might stop himself from doing something despite wanting to do it very, very much.

I slowly stretched out his arm and placed his hand on my breast. He peeked out from under his pillow.

Jonas let me guide his hand. I held his finger over my nipple and made circles on my skin. Then I slowly let go but he kept his hand in place.

While the sky unloaded torrents of water, cracks of thunder, and raucous lightning down upon us, Jonas caressed, stroked, teased, pinched, and pulled my breasts, heating me up and cracking me open.

His contact with my skin was so slight that I could barely feel it, but it made every nerve ending in my body hypersensitive to his touch.

His fingers made a light tapping dance down my ribcage, past my belly button, and landed gently between my legs.

I had no thoughts of falling in love or being vulnerable or of my fragile emotional state. Jonas's touch had unleashed a desire so raw and fierce that I barely felt tethered to planet Earth. My mind was shooting in a million directions at once and the only thing keeping me from entering the astral plane forever was my body's intense need for more. More touch. More pleasure. More pressure. More Jonas.

But Jonas didn't give me more. He gave me less.

It was delicious torture. I arched my back and pushed my hips toward his hand, but his fingers just hovered between my legs. I could only tell they were there because I could feel the heat radiating off his fingertips and I could sense the slight tickle and movement as he swirled his fingers between my legs without making full contact.

"Please, Jonas?" I barely recognized my voice. It seemed to come out of some part of me that was undiscovered until that very moment. I opened my legs wider, and I could feel the cool air contrasting with the hot moisture that soaked my skin.

Jonas slid a finger into me and then pulled it right back out. He continued to tease me. I felt like I couldn't breathe. I thought I might hyperventilate. A purr rose up in my throat and crescendoed into a hungry whine. I wanted him.

"You sure?" Jonas whispered in my ear.

I managed a 'yes', but it came out sounding like a low hiss.

Jonas took one finger and gently placed it right on the tip of my most sensitive spot. He swirled his finger in circles, his touch smooth and slippery. "You're so wet. I want to devour you."

I lost it. I lost my breath, my mind, my control, and my connection to the Milky Way, I think. My climax felt unending and almost unbearable. I cried out as a clap of thunder shook the platform and a violent wind sent some wooden furniture flying outside.

Minutes later, when I came back to my body and to full

consciousness, Jonas was in the exact same position as when he started touching me, but his eyes were closed and a smug little smile danced across his mouth. "Now *that's* an echo I can live with."

INTERVIEW EXCERPT

(The following is an excerpt from the interview with Jonas Hellgren, conducted by Gemma Lane, published in Profile *Magazine Volume 315)*

INTERVIEWER

So, you were riding that high. Your film career was taking off, your personal life was flourishing. And then a series of personal setbacks derailed a lot of that. We don't need to talk about the details of that time, but how is your outlook for the future, eight years later?

HELLGREN

We can talk about the details.

INTERVIEWER

I know it was a brutal period. Do you feel like your upcoming movie and book will offer a fresh start?

HELLGREN

I understand that you're not supposed to ask me about the details. But I mean it. We can talk about it.

INTERVIEWER

Alright. Eight years ago, you disappeared from public life. What happened?

HELLGREN

My wife, Anna, died unexpectedly.

INTERVIEWER

In Sweden?

HELLGREN

No, we were vacationing in Spain. It was a late summer holiday. Usually, the beaches are overwhelmingly crowded but we'd rented a home that had a private beach.

INTERVIEWER

Just the two of you?

HELLGREN

Yes. I was set to start promoting *City of Devils*, and we wanted a little time together before I had to start the tour.

INTERVIEWER

Had you just arrived?

HELLGREN

No, it was our fifth day there. We had planned to spend a full week. We had a great few days. Anna had a newfound energy . . . she was about four months pregnant and had just recently gotten over the sick and exhausted stage.

The morning she died, the weather was perfect.

She wanted to swim. I was worn out from drinking too much the night before. She wasn't drinking at that time, of course. So she woke up much more motivated than I. I'm a *sjusovare*. It means a late sleeper, or "seven sleeper" is the direct translation. Anna was an early bird.

I remember that her leg was hurting her. She was limping on our walk down to the beach. I carried her for the last fifty meters. We didn't think much of it. Pregnancy was causing her all kinds of random ailments. It was new to us. So—she—I'm sorry, this is difficult.

INTERVIEWER

Take your time.

HELLGREN

So, she thought the water might relieve some of her aches and pains. She took a raft out and was just floating in the sunshine near a sand bar.

INTERVIEWER

That sounds like it was a lovely day.

HELLGREN

It was. It was lovely. She was content. I fell asleep on the beach. I don't think for very long. Maybe ten minutes? I'm not sure. When I woke up, I saw the raft, but I didn't see Anna. Then I saw her floating near the raft. I swam to her and brought her back to shore. I tried to resuscitate her. But she was already gone. I called for help, but there was nothing anyone could do.

INTERVIEWER

I don't know what to say. I'm so sorry.

HELLGREN

Thank you. What is there to say? It was determined, later, that she suffered a pulmonary embolism. I don't think there was anything I could have done even if I'd been right next to her. It can be so fast. So sudden. It was a terrible and heartbreaking loss. And I had trouble figuring out how to continue without her. Everything changed in a matter of minutes.

INTERVIEWER

Would you like to take a break?

HELLGREN

I *have* taken a break. For eight years. I'm ok to keep talking.

INTERVIEWER

How did you figure out how to continue without Anna?

HELLGREN

I don't know. Maybe I didn't figure it out at all. Maybe I just figured out how to bear the weight of it.

INTERVIEWER

What were some of your coping techniques?

HELLGREN

That's a good question. I mean . . . I think people say "that's a good question" just to buy themselves time when they don't know what the hell to say. That's what I'm doing now. Is it working?

INTERVIEWER

Let me phrase that differently. Did anything specific help you get through that hard time?

HELLGREN

I can list some of the things that I tried that didn't work: isolation, alcohol, avoidance of friends and family, risky behaviors, rage, lashing out, and procrastination. I think it's been helpful to realize that there are still people around who can move me and inspire me. And that's made me think that maybe I still have something to offer to other people. Maybe. So I'm trying.

INTERVIEWER

And one of those things you're trying is being in films again. What made you decide to work on *Vanishing Echo?*

HELLGREN

I'd like to go back to the prior question. I need to mention that I worked with a therapist for several years. It was a literal life saver for me. That is absolutely how I got through that hard time. I still struggled, greatly, but therapy kept me from going under. Now, what was your question again?

INTERVIEWER

I think that's an important addendum. Many people think they should power through hard times on their own. That it's a weakness to reach out for help.

HELLGREN

I haven't always sought help when I've needed it. Even recently. I end up hurting myself and those around me. People I love. We're totally off-track now, aren't we?

INTERVIEWER

We're just on a few different tracks at once. Getting back to track A, why did you return to acting for your most recent project?

HELLGREN

Well, if I'm being honest, the financial benefit was a primary motivation. And I've always dreamed of working with the director, Clara Dewitt. But I was feeling restless. That feeling you get if you've slept for too long and instead of feeling refreshed you feel groggy or sick. I was tired of living in a haze. I knew that acting used to give me a lot of joy and drive, and I was curious to see if I could reignite that part of myself.

INTERVIEWER

Did it work?

HELLGREN

It did and it didn't. It was like the focus of my personal lens had been adjusted. My camera of pleasure . . . that's a funny phrase. I like that. I'm going to go with that.

INTERVIEWER

What do you mean by that?

HELLGREN

My camera of pleasure . . . the focus on what made me happy about acting and performing—it used to be a close-up shot. Of myself. I liked the power of being a star and being in the spotlight. In a performing sense, that is. I liked becoming the characters and discovering what feelings and personalities I could pull out of myself. It felt like being the god of a new world, where you could rule for the months that you were shooting the film. It's an intense form of self-focus, and it was very intoxicating for me.

When I returned to acting for *Vanishing Echo*, I discovered that my camera of pleasure—

INTERVIEWER

There's that phrase again.

HELLGREN

It's my new tagline. Anyway, it's a wide shot. It was about my surroundings, my fellow actors, the crew, the locals . . . that's where the magic was. It was so much more interesting, and satisfying, to watch all those people come together to make art. I felt plugged in to the world again, which was a relief from being trapped in my own head. I did have to hide out for a few months after filming, though. My social endurance is weak, but I'm building it back up.

INTERVIEWER

Does this mean we might get to see you in more projects in the future?

HELLGREN

I hope so. I've had a few meetings about some possibilities. But *that*, I can't talk about yet.

41

JONAS

Gemma and I managed to sleep in short bursts while the storm raged around us. As daylight came, the downpour dissipated and left behind damage with a threat of more to come. No glass was broken, but the outdoor furniture was overturned and scattered, and a chair floated nearby in the bloated lake. I could see some toppled trees near the shore, but nothing catastrophic.

The sky overhead was cloudy and calm, but the western horizon looked moody and dark.

"There are more storms on the way," Gemma said.

"We'll need to leave during this dry window."

"Where are we going?"

"The Common House. It will be safe to shelter there if we need to."

"Do you think we should try to get help?" she asked.

"We'll be fine for a few more days." I put a jug of water into a backpack. "We have supplies, shelter, firewood. It's ideal, really. Storms are normal and we should have no trouble coping."

Gemma raised her eyebrows and tilted her head.

"What?"

"*Somebody* doesn't want to leave the forest yet," she said.

Guilty as charged. "Do you?"

She shrugged. "It's not *terrible* here. Though there's one thing I'm looking forward to upon our return to civilization."

"What's that?"

"Finding Freja Jansson and letting her know what a piece of shit she is for trying to abandon me in the wilderness."

"Or we could thank her. That might be the greatest punishment of all, for her, if she thinks we've enjoyed ourselves out here."

"Which parts have you enjoyed?" Gemma asked, poking me in the arm.

"Mostly the canoeing." She kicked me lightly in the shin. "And the sauna isn't half bad, though the attendants are somewhat domineering." She moved to punch me playfully, but I grabbed both of her arms and held them by her side. I stooped down and put my mouth on her neck, taking small bites and making her squeal. "What about you? Have you found any enjoyment out here?"

She squirmed and tried to escape my mouth, but I pressed my lips to her pulse and sucked on her neck.

"Don't give me a hickey!"

"Then you'd better answer quickly. I see a red spot on your skin. What have *you* enjoyed, Gemma?"

She leaned into my body and stretched out her neck. "I'd have to say the birdwatching."

. . .

WE WERE GETTING the hang of maneuvering the canoe without too many problems. The sky was dark and swirling, but there was no thunder, lighting, or rain.

"This bruise on my neck is ridiculous," she said, touching her skin where I'd sucked too long and too hard.

"I gave you ample warning."

She smacked the water with her paddle and sent a sprinkle of water back my way.

"Missed me."

"Don't make me stop this boat, Jonas Alexander Hellgren."

"Full name? I'm in trouble." Gusts moved over the water and pushed us off course. Gemma had tried to tie her hair back, but curls escaped and danced about in the wind. "We need to get off the water."

After five minutes of intense effort, we reached the shore. I pulled the boat all the way to the tree line and secured it to the trunk of a pine.

"It may just get more difficult from here," I said.

"It's a long hike?"

"I didn't take a direct route the other day, but I think we could get there in a half hour if the trails are good. But I can guarantee that they aren't good."

"Washed out?"

"Probably. Or at best, very muddy."

MUDDY WAS AN UNDERSTATEMENT. Some of the trails were slippery, sloppy, wet, flooded, or just not passable. Several times we had to walk off-trail in the woods where there was more ground cover to help us keep our footing. We also had a rolling suitcase, which would not roll under these conditions. I carried it across my back and refused Gemma's offers to help. I wanted to get to shelter as soon as possible. My sense of unease was growing with each step.

"Why do you keep stopping?" Gemma said.

"I'm listening."

"For what?"

"I'm not sure. I thought I heard something. Or felt something. I feel like we're being watched."

"Are you serious?" said Gemma, her dark eyes flashing as she glanced around at the forest that towered above us.

"Yes. It's felt like this since we started walking. But I'm not sure what it would be. Boars would just barrel through. A bear would be an accidental confrontation, I think. A lynx, maybe, but she'd be smaller and less ominous . . . I guess it could be . . . no, surely not."

"Don't end that sentence there, Hellgren. It could be what?"

"I don't think it's very likely. There aren't that many of them, and they're elusive."

"Out with it. At least let me know what kind of beast I should be looking out for. Killer moose?"

"I was wondering about wolves."

"Wolves? Shit." she said. "New fear unlocked."

"There are only a few hundred in Sweden. I just feel . . ."

"You feel what?" Gemma shifted her weight from foot to foot, seemingly impatient for me to finish my sentence.

"Like we're being hunted."

Her hands flew to her neck, as if to press down a chill that had overcome her. "I don't like that."

"Me either. Let's get to the shelter."

Covered in mud and slogging through dirt and slush, we continued up the trail.

"I recently read an article about the world's top nine deadliest mammals. And wolves weren't even on the list," Gemma said. "Though dogs were number nine."

"Dogs? Like domesticated pet dogs?"

"In North America alone, dogs killed, like, 500 people last year and maimed over 2000."

"*Balders balle!* What kind of dogs are you breeding over there?"

"Labradoodles."

42

———

GEMMA

"Shouldn't we be coming up with some kind of master plan?" I asked.

Jonas pushed branches out of the way as we walked. Thunder quietly rumbled in the distance. "As it pertains to . . .?"

"As it pertains to everything?" I tripped on a root that jutted from the path and Jonas spun around with his arms out to help me. I didn't need the assistance, but it was charming. I gained my footing and resumed walking. "Also, I have questions: When will the owners be returning to the site? When do you think *Profile* will send people out to find us? What's our game plan? While we're at it, exactly how much did you pay Alfred to throw them off our scent, and was it more than Freja paid him to 'lose' me in the first place?"

Jonas stopped walking. "Freja paid him?"

"Yep."

"How do you know that?"

"I saw her pay him at the *Profile* office right before I bumped into you." My feet were starting to sink into the mud.

"Electronic payment?"

"No, cash," I said.

"Paper money?"

Tiny bugs were starting to gather around my head and face. "Can we keep walking?" I asked as I swatted them away.

Jonas started moving again but was walking backwards. Seemed risky. "How much money?"

"I'm not really up on the latest Krona to dollar exchange rates."

"Do you remember what the money looked like? What color, or whose face was on it?"

"Why does it matter how much she gave him?"

Jonas stopped walking and waited for my answer.

"It was a bunch of bills. I saw a 1 and a 0, so either 100 or 1000. I can't remember."

"Were they blue with a woman's face, or brown with a man's face?"

"Orange-ish brown. Definitely a man. Friendly face and bore a resemblance to my grandfather."

"Shit," said Jonas.

"What?"

"That's the 1000 note."

"You have a woman on the 100? Sweden is better than America."

Jonas turned around and started back up the trail. "Astrid Lindgren on the 20, Greta Garbo on the 100, Birgit Nilsson on the 500."

"Wow. Sweden is WAY better than the US. And that dude was absolutely not Greta Garbo."

. . .

"I THINK we should be there soon," said Jonas.

"Do they have a shower? This mud is everywhere."

"I'm not sure. I didn't investigate that closely when I was there before." We walked another few minutes and I was on constant lookout for wolves or other dangerous creatures. "Why nine?" asked Jonas.

"Why nine what?"

"Why just nine dangerous mammals on that list? Isn't it usually the 'top ten'? Would it kill them to round out the list?"

"The good news is that other than dogs, only four of the mammals on that list could be in this forest right now."

"So, by your count, *five* of the most dangerous mammals on Earth could be within kilometers of us at this very moment?"

"When you put it that way—"

"Don't tell me. Let me guess," said Jonas. "We've identified dogs, so that leaves eight."

"Correct."

"Hippos. They must be on there."

"Number six."

"Lions and tigers."

"Eight and five, respectively."

"Polar bears," guessed Jonas.

"Bears are number seven."

"We have five through nine. How have I missed the top four?"

"Well, some of them are kind of surprising or obscure."

"Hamsters?"

"No, but I'm sure they made the top twenty," I said. "I'll tell you four and three, because they're weird, and don't really count for us in our current situation. Number four is horses, but mostly in riding accidents."

"I'd love a horse right about now," Jonas said as he pushed more branches out of the way to continue up the trail.

"And three is deer. But that's because of car accidents."

"Makes sense. So, two and one. And one of those is in this forest?"

"Yes."

"Elephants!"

"Number two," I said.

Jonas stopped to scrape some mud off his boots. "No wild elephants in Sweden. I give up. What's number one?"

"Human beings."

Fifteen minutes later, the Common House came into view. I'd expected to see some kind of headquarters, where the staff lounged in modern comfort while the wealthy guests paid handsomely to live out their off-grid fantasies. But nope. Rustic as shit.

It was a nondescript log cabin with two front windows and a modest front porch. It was about 20 feet wide by 30 feet long. The roof was pitched, and trees closely surrounded all four corners of the building. The only visible modernity was the electric coded lock on the hefty wooden front door.

"We can't go in there like this," I said, motioning to our muddy bodies.

"Let me look for a shower. Stay on the porch."

I felt safer on the porch than I had on the trail, but I was still uneasy. Sometimes a tree limb would make an awkward movement in the distance. It was probably wind, or a (non-killer) moose. But Jonas had me worried about becoming prey to some mysterious hunter.

"I found the outdoor shower," called Jonas.

"Is it going to be brutally cold?" I called back as I walked toward his voice.

He popped around the corner of the house. "It's hooked up to a propane tank."

"Hot shower!" I forgot all about wolves. Back on the porch, we stripped down to our underwear. "We're becoming experts at this."

The shower was short, but heavenly. It was so hot that our skin turned pink. Jonas ran his hands up and down my body to help wash off the mud, and I did the same for him. I stayed as long as I could in the stream of water.

We turned it off and stood shivering in the damp air. "Maybe we should've found some towels *before* we showered," I said.

"There are some inside," said Jonas, heading back to the front of the building.

Back at the front door, Jonas entered the combination.

Stepping inside, I saw that this building did have electricity, but you could tell they were resentful about having to use it. There was no overhead lighting. Candles and lanterns sat on large wooden tables and one lonely electric lamp lay unplugged and abandoned in a corner.

Odds and ends were scattered and stacked throughout the room: a tall pile of camping mats, shovels, hammers, buckets, blankets, and an inviting tower of clean fluffy towels. I quickly stripped out of my wet underwear and wrapped one towel around my head and one around my torso. I got a blanket from the bedding pile and wrapped that around myself as well.

The back wall sported a row of floor-to-ceiling cabinets, working chest freezers, and two refrigerators.

"This would be a fine place to wait out a storm," I said.

Jonas frowned. "Yes. But not very comfortable. No bed, for starters."

"Come on, mountain man. There's a whole pile of sleeping mats!"

Jonas ignored me and continued to sift through a crate of canned goods.

"You're a wilderness snob! Are you into *glamping*?"

"Use that word again and you'll regret it!" Jonas said, wagging a candle stick at me.

I wandered over to the freezers to inspect what kind of food they had. I felt like a queen examining her kingdom with my towel crown and blanket train.

Jonas was rifling through some cabinets that held backpacks and other gear. I was almost to the back of the room when something caught my eye. It was a table, off to the left in a small vestibule. I could only see the legs of the table because a thin curtain hung down from the ceiling. Why would there be a curtain in front of a table?

I changed course and walked toward the mystery vestibule. Maybe this was where they kept the good stuff! I was reaching out to move the curtain aside when I heard Jonas call out, "Gemma! Wait!" His tone apparently triggered my rebellious and reckless nature. Instead of waiting, I did the exact opposite, which was to rip the curtain aside with such vigor and flair that I felt like a magician revealing her most spectacular trick.

Behind the curtain *was* the good stuff. Or the bad stuff, depending on how you looked at it. Behind the curtain was a telephone. A working telephone, connected to the outside world.

43

GEMMA

"What the hell, Jonas."

Jonas's face was ruddy and flushed, and beads of perspiration dotted his temples.

"Did you know this was here?" I asked.

Jonas's mouth opened, but no words came out.

"Cat got your tongue?" I picked up the receiver and heard a dial tone. "Just hoping I wouldn't see this?"

"No!" Jonas said. "Just let me explain."

"How could you not tell me there was a phone here?" I slammed the receiver down. "I *know* this didn't just slip your mind!"

"Actually, Gemma, it *did* slip my mind. I planned on telling you when I came back yesterday, but then I thought you were dead in the water, and I basically *lost* my mind. Not to mention the monsoon and the best blow job of my life. So, yeah. I fucking forgot the phone for a few hours."

The best of his life? I glared at Jonas, though I could feel the anger leaking out of my body.

"It's hard to take you seriously with that towel wrapped around your head," he said.

"I'm not projecting power and grace in my terrycloth crown?"

Jonas grabbled the towel on my head and pulled. My body rammed into his. My head wrap came undone in his hands and he slid it off my hair and threw it to the ground. He pushed his hands into my wet hair and pulled my face to his.

"Geeze, Jonas, you—" But before I could finish my sentence, his mouth was covering mine and his tongue moved past my lips, pushing and probing. His hands tore at the blanket around me, and he flung that off as well. The towel that had been wrapped around my body came undone with all that manhandling, and fell to the ground, landing at our feet. I didn't have time to think about my nakedness because Jonas, still kissing me, had wrapped his arms around me, picked me up, carried me to a large pine table in the middle of the room, and laid me gently down on my back.

He pushed my thighs open and wedged his body between my legs. He bent down over me and pressed his torso to mine.

Somewhere in there I realized that I had very few defenses when it came to Jonas's touch. His skin on mine, whether the slightest, like his hand on my shoulder, or the most intimate, like the table adventure, made me melt and unfurl like a wax flower to an open flame. I still wasn't letting myself believe that Jonas really, *really* liked me. But it was apparent that he was attracted to me. And that we had intense chemistry.

Also clear? Jonas and I were both impulsive. I wasn't sure yet if that would work in our favor or to our detriment.

There were two things that saved me from instantly taking it to the next level with Jonas in that moment:

One: Jonas's towel. Like some kind of bath soap commercial model, Jonas had his towel so perfectly and securely wrapped around his waist that it would've taken a grizzled sailor to undo the complicated knot Jonas had wrought. Great if you were a Scotsman who needed his makeshift kilt to stay on, but not so hot for a Swede trying to get busy with his possible love interest.

Two: karma. Nothing ever came easy for me in the romance department and that moment was no exception. I always appreciated a good dramatic twist, and I got one. While I was pulling Jonas to me and he was reaching to lift his towel, (he couldn't get the knot undone either, especially not amid the lusty haste in which he attempted the feat) we were interrupted by a sound almost impossible to ignore: a ringing telephone.

"EXPECTING A CALL?" I asked, pushing Jonas off of me.

"Ja," he said, sprinting to the phone with his towel still intact. He picked up the phone on its third ring. "Jonas hos Allmänt Hus."

He obviously knew the person on the other end of the line. He rushed into a conversation of which I didn't understand a word. I waited to see if he'd relay any of the information to me, but he did not.

I grabbed my blanket from the floor and wrapped it back around myself and I watched Jonas as he spoke on the phone. Because I couldn't understand what he was saying, I was able to take in how, well, *sexy* he was. His voice was deeply resonant and took on an entirely different timbre in Swedish than it did in English.

I wondered if he presented a different personality in

Swedish than he did in English. My mother taught me Italian, but I was not fluent, and I probably sounded a little childlike in my vocabulary choices. Jonas was fully fluent in English, but the way a language was structured could change the way a speaker thought and presented themselves. It made me feel melancholy to realize that I would probably never fully know Swedish Jonas.

"Yes, she's here. Hold on," Jonas said. When did he switch over to English? "Gemma." Jonas beckoned me to come closer to the phone and then hit a button, sending the call to speaker. "This is my agent, Fredrik. Fredrik, Gemma can hear you."

"Hello, Gemma," said Fredrik.

"Hi."

"Are you doing alright?"

"Yes, I'm fine. Thank you."

"Let me update you on where we are with things today."

I felt like I'd missed a few steps here. Last I knew—back when I was naked on a stranger's kitchen table—Jonas and I were stranded in the wilderness, and no one knew where we were or if we were safe. How much was Jonas not telling me? I felt my anger start to bubble up again.

Jonas could probably see that my temper was flaring. "I found this phone yesterday and immediately called Fredrik," said Jonas. "I only got his voicemail, so I left a message asking him to have his phone on him until I was able to call again. I let him know where we were."

"I was able to contact the owners of the property and I also got the number for their main phone, which we are on now," said Fredrik. They called me a few minutes ago to let me know that your code had been used to access the door lock, so I called in, hoping to speak to Jonas." Jonas went to get his own blanket while Fredrik continued. "Gemma, I have spoken to Carl Berg about the situation, and he assured me that he would let your contact in the United States know that you are safe."

"Did the owners have any instructions for us?" Jonas asked.

"Yes," Fredrik said, "but they would like to speak to you directly. I will text Hugo Sandström when our call is finished and then he'll call you on this line."

"I feel like we're about to get in trouble with the principal," I said.

"The Sandströms are not angry," said Fredrik. "They were relieved to hear from me. They knew that lock codes were being used but were not able to get back to the property to assess the situation. And Jonas," he continued, "I assured them that you would pay for any items that were used that were not covered under the *Profile* fees. Carl also said that he would be fine to cover extra expenses. He seemed quite pleased about the situation once he realized that everyone was safe and accounted for."

"Has anyone spoken to Freja Jansson?" Jonas asked.

"Not that I know of," Fredrik answered. "I'll check with Carl later today to see if he has made contact with Ms. Jansson."

"Thank you, Freddi," said Jonas.

"Yes, thank you," I said.

"You're welcome. When we hang up, I'll send the text to Hugo, so wait there for his phone call. Jonas, you will have to take the call. Hugo's English is limited."

"I'll be back in contact as soon as I can," said Jonas.

We ended the call and then waited for Hugo to ring in. "I'm sorry," said Jonas. "I should've told you right away. Then we had the incident in the water and by the time my head was clear again, I didn't want to open that line of conversation. Then it felt awkward to bring it up at all, and I was going to tell you here in the cabin."

"From here on out, you have to keep me fully informed. If you know something, I want to know it too. Is there anything else you haven't told me?"

Jonas thought for a minute. "I plugged my cell phone in here yesterday and got some charge."

I took a breath to yell at him, but he put a hand up to stop me.

"But there was no signal here or between here and the lake. So, it was useless."

The phone rang again.

"Saved by the bell," I said.

44

JONAS

I picked up the phone before it had a chance to finish its first ring. "Det här är Jonas." I hit the button for the speaker-phone and a man's voice rang out, speaking in Swedish.

Gemma was walking away from the phone, but I waved her back over. She dragged a chair across the floor, its feet making a scraping sound against the wooden planks. She set it upright by the phone and dropped into the seat.

"Can you have this conversation in English?" I asked.

"Uh. I don't know," the man said. "Jag ska fråga min syster."

"He's getting his sister," I whispered to Gemma.

"I gathered that."

"Hallä," a woman's voice said into the phone.

"Hallä," I said. "Do you speak English?"

"I do."

"Thank you. I'm Jonas and I have Gemma on the line as well."

"I'm Katja," she said. "Hello."

Gemma grinned at me and gave me two enthusiastic thumbs up. "KATJA!" she mouthed.

I rolled my eyes. "Thank you for speaking to us. And I apologize for all of this."

"It is an unusual situation," Katja said, "but we're glad you're both safe. As you may know, no one is able to come get you at this moment because several of the roads leading to the property are washed out. We are expecting more rain today and tomorrow, so it could be as late as Friday before anyone can reach you."

"That's fine," I said. "We're safe and have plenty of supplies."

"Hugo might be able to find an alternate route, but I can't guarantee that."

"Where do you think we should stay for these next few days, considering weather and trail conditions?" I asked.

"We think the Forest Hut is your best option, if you are able to get there," she said. "The trail should be acceptable, but you'll have to see if the low water bridge is passible. If it's not, turn around and go back to where you are now. Do you have maps?"

"Yes, we have maps," said Gemma.

"At the Forest Hut, there is a propane-operated refrigerator in the shed along with some other emergency supplies. There should be enough food there, but bring water and some food from the Common House in case you are not able to cross the bridge."

"Do you know when the next storm will start?" I asked. The sky was only getting darker and more ominous as the day went on.

"A few hours, so you should start your journey as soon as

possible," said Katja. "Your codes of 337 and 848 will both work on that lock."

"Excellent," I said.

"Who has the 147 code?" Katja asked.

"147?"

"Yes. 147 was used to access the Treehouse yesterday."

"Were you at the treehouse?" Gemma asked me.

I shook my head. "Neither Gemma nor I have that code," I said to Katja.

There was silence on the other end of the line, then I heard the muffled noises of Katja speaking in Swedish. "Ok," said Katja. "We are removing 147 from the code bank. Please only use 337 or 848. We would also like for you to arm the Emergency Response System."

"Do you believe we're in danger?" I asked.

"We don't have any concrete reason to suspect that, but until we figure out who used that other code, we'd like you to arm the system. And Hugo will be leaving soon to investigate alternative routes to the property. Please do not open your doors for anyone other than Hugo, my father, or myself. Do you have the brochure with our photos?"

"Yes, we do!" Gemma said a little too enthusiastically into the phone.

I gave her arm a tiny pinch.

"Excellent," said Katja.

"How does the emergency system work?" Gemma asked.

"It will play a loud alert over all the alarm systems on the property. It will also ping our family headquarters, which is three kilometers from the camp area. My mother and father live there full time but have not been at home this week because of a family emergency. Hugo will try to get us back there."

"We understand," I said.

"It also texts our cell phones, but they have limited signal on the property, which is why we have the back-up system to alert camp wide."

Gemma was frowning and worry had settled into her face.

"The computer to set up the system should be in the cabinet right above the phone. There are also Personal Alert Devices in there. Please take one for each of you," said Katja. "They will turn on the alarm from remote locations and are also equipped with GPS."

Over the next few minutes Katja walked me through setting up the system. Gemma got our bags, which were still on the porch. Wind and green leaves rushed in through the door when she pulled it open. I could see that it was darker outside than it had been just a half hour earlier. Gemma dragged the bags in and locked the door behind her, which was the first time either of us had locked a door since we'd arrived.

"Which sound do I pick for the alert?" I asked.

"Your choice," said Katja. "I'll have you run a test once you have it set up."

"Ok, I have one. It's just the one called Test System."

"That's fine for the test but choose another one for the real alert. That way we know that it isn't a false alarm."

"I have the sound selected. What now?"

"Hit the button that says TESTVARNING," she said. "But know that it will be very, very loud. As soon as you hear it deploy, immediately hit TESTVARNING again to deactivate it."

"Ready?" I asked Gemma.

"Ready."

I hit the button and within two seconds the loudest alarm

I'd ever heard blared over a nearby sound horn. Gemma and I both dropped to the floor and covered our ears. I was so shocked by the sheer volume of the alarm that I'd forgotten that I also had to disengage the alert. I stood up and searched for the button, finally finding it. The noise stopped.

"I think we just terrified all the animals within 50 kilometers."

"I can adjust the volume," said Katja, "but the lower volume is for recreational purposes. For the alarm, we want it loud."

"Gemma, help me pick the alert we want."

Gemma joined me at the computer. I scrolled through the options, though most of them were Swedish phrases.

"I don't know what those are," she said. Then she grabbed my arm. "Wait! There!"

I stopped scrolling. "För bövelen. Really?"

"Yes, really."

I clicked on the link. ABBA's "Take a Chance on Me" rang out from the computer speakers.

Katja laughed. "Perfect." She guided me through arming the system and then told us about the Personal Alert Devices, which Gemma was referring to as "Panic Buttons."

"These are like something you might give to your grand-mother if she was a fall risk," Gemma whispered. She hung it around her neck with the attached lanyard. If you held the button for five seconds, apparently "Take a Chance on Me" would scream out through the Swedish Wilderness.

Katja was worried about the incoming storm and encour-aged us to get to the Forest Hut as soon as possible. We ended the call.

Gemma and I quickly dressed and found some ponchos and

rain boots in a closet. We packed water, nuts, and cookies in a backpack.

"How worried are you about all this?" Gemma asked me.

"On a scale of one to ten?"

"Sure."

"I'm a six for getting to the Forest Hut. I'm a one if we get there safely."

"What about dangerous animals?"

"I'm a four for bears, wolves, boars, and horses."

"What about owls?" she asked.

"Zero for owls."

"What about the world's most dangerous mammal?"

I didn't answer. I locked the door to the cabin and checked our route on the map. The spruce trees around us formed a twisting and vibrating wall of green as the wind burst through their branches. "Let's get going."

45

GEMMA

We kept our pace as brisk as possible as we traversed the trails to the Forest Hut. There wasn't much conversation. The wind was intensifying, and the sound of it in the leaves had gone from a whisper to a screeching hiss. It was difficult to hear each other, and we didn't want to waste the effort. We were watching for impending threats, but the forest was becoming more turbulent. Branches and brush thrust about chaotically as the storm got closer. It was useless to try to catch unusual movement with our eyes—everything was dancing.

Jonas was ahead of me, and I stayed close to him. He glanced over his shoulder every minute or so to make sure I wasn't falling behind. We'd found hiking backpacks at the Common House and traded our suitcase out for those. It made walking much easier, but the trails were still wet and difficult to navigate.

The step, after step, after step, put me back in a similar headspace from my walking journey a few years earlier. The rhythm of my feet on the ground became a meditative metronome, and I went into a kind of trance. When I hit the sweet spot, my body would go on autopilot and my mind would enter a liminal space where I was neither here nor there; I felt like I went higher, almost out of my body, but also deeper, unlocking hidden thoughts, emotions, and desires.

It was harder to zone out on a trail like this because each step held the possibility of danger and the footing was insecure. But at the same time, it was easier because I wasn't alone. I had someone looking back for me, looking out for me, and looking forward for me, as he led the way on the path.

We'd been walking for an hour when the trail suddenly headed sharply downhill.

"The bridge is ahead. We'll see if it's passible," said Jonas.

I could hear the rushing of the water in the river before I could see it. The valley was lush and dense and as the trail spiraled down, branches leaned over the path, making a tunnel of stippled light and conifer shadows.

We came to the bridge across the river. The structure was about twenty feet long and five feet wide. The walkway was formed from tightly fitted wooden planks and the railing, which was only on one side, seemed straight and strong. The water was churning and swollen from the earlier rain, but the bridge was above water and undamaged.

"Let's get across," I said. "I'm not a fan of bridges."

"Watch out for the Näcken," Jonas said.

I stopped abruptly. "Is that some kind of snake?"

"No, a naked water nymph."

"Is she friend or foe?"

"He," said Jonas, "He's handsome, but he uses his seductive violin music to lure people in to drown, so don't fall for it."

"I'm more of a cello girl, anyway," I said, holding on to Jonas's sleeve as we started to cross.

Jonas took my hand to steady me and led us across the bridge. "Vi ses, Näcken," he yelled over the din of the water.

"Did you see him?" I asked, peeking around Jonas to see if I could spy a naked fiddler on the rocky river bank.

"No, but if you call his name, supposedly you can take away his power. Don't feel like taking a chance today."

We made it across the bridge and started climbing out of the valley. The noise level in the woods had increased as the storm blew in, and I thought I heard the high moan of a violin.

"That's just branches rubbing together, right?" I asked Jonas.

Jonas didn't answer but he kept a hold of my hand and pulled me along as my feet slipped and sunk in the muddy hillside.

Thunder had been lazily rumbling in the distance for half the walk, but it was raining again. The tree canopy protected us from the first drops, but we could hear them start to hit and fall —they sounded like a swarm of razor blades slashing through the leaves.

THE FINAL APPROACH to the Forest Hut was uphill, and we were winded and weary when we crested the hill.

"Wow—this is the Forest Hut?" I asked.

Jonas checked his map again. "I think so. We're at the right spot on the map."

"I thought it was supposed to be a little hobbit hut halfway underground with moss on the roof?"

"That's what it showed in the photos," he said. "Oh."

"If that's a 'we're at the wrong place' kind of 'Oh,' I don't want to hear it."

"This is right. There are two Forest Huts. The other one is in a very different direction, and not close to the bridge. We're ok."

"Thank God. But also, they need an English consultant on their house naming."

"This one is new, and not in the brochures," said Jonas. "I think there was a note about it in my information packet. This was on the list as one of the photo shoot locations."

"I can see why."

It had taken me a moment to even *see* the house; the entire surface of the building was mirrored glass. At that moment those mirrors were reflecting trees, dark sky, rain, and occasional flashes of lightning. The cabin looked like it was part of the forest, or rather, like it *was* the forest.

"I'm calling this 'The Cube.' This is *not* a hut," I said. It was shaped like a perfect cube and was elevated about fifteen feet above the forest floor. The supports holding up each corner of the cube perfectly mimicked the trunks of the surrounding birch trees. Maybe they were actually tree trunks. I'd have to touch one to find out.

The Cube had a black metal staircase at the rear of the structure that must've led up to a door that I couldn't see from where I was standing. "Why would there not be photos of this place everywhere in their promotional materials?"

"Is that the shed?" Jonas asked, pointing off to our left.

I thought he was pointing to nothing until I noticed a smaller mirrored outbuilding nestled in among the trees. "Ok, a *shed* is a place where my Uncle Larry keeps his lawnmower and builds birdhouses. That's not a shed."

We approached the building and Jonas entered his code. The door unlocked.

"I'm doubling down on my statement that this is *not* a shed," I said.

THE INTERIOR of the outbuilding was spacious and airy. Every inch of the walls inside were covered by gleaming white tiles. In one corner stood a small refrigerator and freezer, each one operational and running quietly. Steel shelves ran along one wall and held bottled water, dry goods, oil lamps, battery operated lanterns, matches, towels, and cookware. There was a couch and table. And along the back wall stood a huge two-headed shower which called to me with its siren song.

"That settles that," said Jonas, stepping in from the rain, putting down his backpack and immediately taking off his boots. "Let's clean up."

I turned on three battery-powered lanterns so we could see what we were doing, and Jonas shut the door to keep out the rain and wind.

"I don't even care if the water's cold," I said, as Jonas reached in to turn on the tap.

He adjusted the knobs and after a few seconds he said, "It's hot." He turned the water back off so we could get undressed first. Hot water was a rare and limited resource, so we didn't want to waste a drop.

I think we were both tired, hungry, sore, and worried. And completely filthy. I didn't want to wait turns or worry about modesty, but I also didn't want to have sex in the shower. I just wanted to get warm and clean and get up to the floating cube house and see if there was a bed I could stretch out on for a long, long time.

"You ok to just shower at the same time? I'm ready for a nap."

"Yep," said Jonas. He was already stripping down.

WHEN WE WERE BOTH UNDRESSED, Jonas kept his back to me, and I kept mine to him, our shyness and fatigue overriding our attraction for the moment. He turned on the shower heads and when the water was running warm, we both stepped in.

There were wrapped bars of soap and there were solid bars for shampoo and conditioner. I unwrapped a set and put them on the bench between us. We both moaned as the water washed over us and the mud on our skin slipped off and swirled down the drain. We cleaned ourselves quickly because there was no knowing how long the water would stay warm.

The room was dimly lit with the lanterns, but we could still see each other in the light. I was rinsing off the last of the conditioner and Jonas turned to pick up the soap. Even in the semi-darkness there was no missing his impressive erection. He quickly turned his back to me again. It must have been frustrating not to be able to hide your desire when you wanted to. Jonas seemed to be ignoring it or pretending that there wasn't an elephant in the room, so to speak, so I followed his lead.

I turned off my water, opened the shower door, and reached out for some towels. The air outside the shower was chilly. Jonas turned off his shower, and I handed him one of the towels. His ass was pretty spectacular, so I wasn't sad that he was turned away from me. He wrapped the towel around his waist but kept his back to me. He put his hands on his hips and sighed.

"Having some fit problems?"

Jonas laughed a little. "A small problem. It's fine."

"Didn't seem so small from my angle."

Jonas spun around and struck a pose. It was difficult to hold in my laugh when I saw how Jonas's towel was struggling to contain his penis, which was firmly and persistently pushing out against the fabric.

I slowly reached my hand toward him, but he caught my wrist and held it away from his body. "It really is ok. Let's get dressed and get up to the hut," he said.

"The cube."

"Right, the cube."

"What are those?" I asked Jonas, pointing to a stack of folded navy-blue items on the shelf behind him.

He pulled one down. "Robes," he said, as one unfolded in his hand. It was a plush oversized robe with pockets and a hood.

"Oh yes," I said. "We're putting those on."

Jonas handed me a robe while keeping his head slightly turned. He was trying very hard to avert his eyes while I was naked. Part of me wished that he'd at least shoot me an appreciative glance, but maybe he was honoring my request to "just shower." I considered myself someone who was talented at reading people, but I was still getting mixed signals when it came to Jonas; he was nothing if not enigmatic.

Dressed and ready, we looked like time-traveling druids who liked to backpack. Our fluffy hoods were up, and we had mismatched borrowed rain boots on our feet. Hiking packs were strapped to our backs and Jonas was clutching a mesh bag that held our muddy clothes.

"Ready?" he asked.

"Good to go."

He swung open the door. Even though it was overcast, the brightness of the outdoor light was jarring to my eyes. Jonas started to walk outside, but something startled him.

"Oh shit!" Jonas shot backwards and slammed the door, bumping into me and knocking me off balance. I fell back towards the shelf and smacked my head into the edge of one before I landed on the floor with a thud.

His eyes were wide, and the color had drained from his face. He'd barely noticed that I was on the ground. "We can't go out there."

I felt like an overturned turtle on the ground as my backpack weighed me down. I managed to roll over and get back on my feet. "Thanks for the help," I said, brushing myself off and checking the back of my head for a bump. "What is it?"

Jonas pointed at the door, still shell-shocked.

"Wolves? Moose? Killer owls?" I asked.

"No," he said, shaking his head slowly. "Wild boars."

46

JONAS

"That's a twist I didn't see coming," Gemma said, as she rubbed a spot on her head. "Do you think they have ice packs here?"

Seeing the *vildsvin* had spiked my adrenaline and it took me a second to process the situation. I realized that Gemma had fallen and was possibly injured. "Shit. Are you ok?" I turned to her and ran my hands across her head in a search for bumps or blood.

Her gaze was glassy, and her eyes weren't focusing. Maybe a concussion? "Are you dizzy?" I wrapped my arms around her and pulled her toward me to prop her up in case she passed out. Still no answer from Gemma.

Suddenly her eyes focused on my face. Thank Christ. "Did you hear me?" I asked slowly and clearly.

"You asked if I was ok? I think so." She pulled herself out of my arms.

"No, I asked if you were dizzy. I think you might have a concussion."

She slapped the back of her hand against my chest, dismissively. "I don't have a concussion. Just got lost in my thoughts for a second."

"What kind of thoughts could pull you from wild boars and a head injury?"

"Sauna memories, that's what," she said, her face suddenly bright red. I felt my face get hot as well, not to mention a response in another part of my body.

"Let's make sure you're ok before you revisit any other . . . moments." I went to the freezer for an ice pack and also to hide my face from her. I couldn't believe she'd made me blush. The sauna memory was one that lingered at the back of my mind almost every minute. I tried to block the visions from my head so I could concentrate on the task at hand.

There were a few medical ice packs in the freezer. I handed one to Gemma and pulled my robe a little tighter and retied the sash. I put my hands on either side of her face and looked into her eyes again. They were clear and her gaze was steady. "You're sure you're alright?"

"I like nurse-mode Jonas," she said. "He's almost as much fun as inebriated Jonas."

That gave me pause. She'd noticed different sides of me. Times when I was willing to let my guard down, and times that I wasn't. I felt flattered that she'd seen me, but I also felt a little exposed and uncomfortable. No better way out of that feeling than to walk right into extreme danger. "I'm going to check outside. Stay very quiet, please."

Gemma gave me a thumbs up with the hand that was not holding the ice pack on her head. "I'll guard the door. I have no interest in sharing our quarters with the world's most aggressive porcine."

I wedged my toe up against the door and slowly opened it a crack. I saw the muddy forest floor and the silver trunks of birch trees. But no boars. I opened the door a bit wider to get a better view.

There they were. One large sow with brown jagged hair, long legs, and a dark snout. Two piglets followed close behind, stumbling along in the dense foliage. I closed the door and shut out the noise of the wind.

"Just a sow and her babies. I don't see any boars, which is good. They're more aggressive. But if the sow thinks we are a threat to her piglets, she can get just as violent."

"Can we eat while we wait them out?" Gemma asked.

I turned the battery-powered lanterns back on and rummaged around the shelves and backpacks. Gemma sat on the floor, and I joined her.

"Here we go," I handed her a plate and loaded it with dried sausages, some garlic crisps, and a ginger snap. "Water? Beer? Wine?"

"Water, please."

I reached to open the refrigerator door from where I was sitting. I grabbed a glass bottle of sparkling water for Gemma and a beer for myself. There was a bottle opener in a basket on the bottom shelf. I opened both drinks and handed the water to Gemma. I took a long swig of the beer. It was bright and hoppy.

"I'm sure those pigs would be intimidated to know that we're eating sausage," said Gemma.

The presence of the boars outside amped me up, but also made me weary. Our destination was so close by, but it felt too dangerous to make a run for it unless the coast was entirely clear. "Once we get to the hut—the cube—we'll be fine. It's elevated and I don't think the boars do stairs." I rested my head between my hands.

"Tired?"

"We didn't have coffee this morning."

"This morning feels far away."

"This whole week has felt like a lifetime," I said. "Not entirely in a bad way." I took another sip of my beer. It wouldn't help my fatigue but might give me just enough courage to deal with the wild pigs.

"Nothing like a few drinks to take your mind off impending doom," Gemma joked.

"That was my life philosophy for a while. In the year or two right after Anna died, I drank all the time. I was a disaster." I took another sip and tried to remember those years. I was surprised to discover that my recall was somewhat hazy. It was nice to have something going on in my life that shone a little brighter than the darkness of my past. "Now I have alcohol two or three times a month, maybe. It does make me feel more . . . human, I guess. But I don't indulge very often."

Gemma took a sip of her sparkling water, which made her hiccup. It was a delightful little sound. "I had my very own disaster period, but it didn't include much alcohol."

"Sober disaster. Yikes." I approached the door to do another animal check. I didn't see any trace of the sow or her piglets. "Could you hold the door?" I asked Gemma. "I'm going to step out further. But if I tell you to shut the door, shut it."

"I'm not leaving you out there to get trampled and impaled!"

"They don't even make the top *nine* of the world's most dangerous mammals. I'm sure I'll be fine. But do as I say."

Spots of pink popped up on Gemma's cheeks. "Yes, sir."

I helped Gemma to her feet and stationed her at the door. "Stand here with your foot against the bottom rail. Remember to shut it quickly if—"

"I've got it," she said, rolling her eyes. "I know how to handle wilderness beasts."

47

GEMMA

Jonas nodded and put his hood back up. I opened the door for him, and he walked out, surveying the landscape. He got about twenty feet away and a gentle rain fell lightly around him. He was a sight to behold. Jonas Hellgren, in nothing but a hooded bathrobe and rain boots, standing stoically in the forest, protecting me from wild boars. He turned a little toward the shed as he scanned the woods for the pigs. I could see the skin of his chest and it was dripping with rainwater. His hair was damp and falling across his eyes and his firmly set jaw made him look worried and determined. If only I could capture the moment with my phone—a post of this thirst trap would get a million likes on social media.

Suddenly, Jonas bellowed "SHUT THE DOOR!" and bolted off behind the shed where I could no longer see him.

What the hell! I flung open the door and leaped to the front step. I seemed to have zero self-preservation instinct when it came to emergency situations. "Act now, panic later" was my go-to in a crisis. So instead of shutting the door and retreating to safety, I stood out in the wind looking for Jonas or a band of killer pigs. No signs of either.

Something bumped me from behind and I came off my feet. The new headline would read:

AMERICAN WOMAN GORED TO DEATH BY SWEDISH BOAR!

Before I could orient myself, I realized I was back inside the shed, my back up against the closed door. And Jonas, his hair and face sprinkled with rainwater, was breathless and pressing against me. "I told you to shut the door," he growled in my ear.

"I wasn't going to let you get killed out there!"

"Oh yeah?" he had his palms on the door by either side of my head. "How did you plan on taking down a wild boar?"

"I didn't have it mapped out. But I wasn't going to let you die alone, at least! Are you ok?" I tried to inspect him for injuries, but he was pressing against me, making it impossible to move.

He moved his mouth toward my ear and lightly bit my earlobe. "You didn't do as I said. Do I need to punish you?" Then he bit my neck.

"Wait a second. Was there even a pig out there this time?"

"Nope. All gone." Jonas was pressing his pelvis against mine and my body was having that instant reaction again. I tried to ignore it.

"What the hell? You lied?"

"It was a test," he said as he took one of my hands in each of his and pressed them up against the door by my head. "And you failed."

"Oh yeah? What are you going to do about it?" I asked, pushing back against his pelvis with mine.

"Whatever I want," he said, kissing me roughly on the mouth and then putting his lips back on my neck.

"Is this a *Fifty Shades of Grey* moment?" I asked. "Because I might be on board, but I'm a consent kind of girl."

"I'm sorry," he said, releasing my hands. "And I thought my joke might be funny, but I may have misread the situation."

"It's just a little abrupt." If I was being honest, I didn't mind it. I was relieved that Jonas wasn't lying in a bloody heap and being mauled by an evil version of Babe. "But I'll give my consent if you ask for it."

I always thought that "smoldering" was an over-embellished word choice to describe sexy heroes. But seeing Jonas's face in that moment, I realized that no other word would suffice.

He gently pinned my hands back up against the wall. His eyes shifted in color and focus; they were brighter, and the brown and gray faded away leaving the blue and green to sparkle sharply. He was actually biting his lower lip—I didn't know that people did that in real life—but wow. That also meant that I could see his wicked tooth. There was a reason the man was a sex symbol. To have all that smolder directed at me was intense. And spectacular.

He leaned in close to my ear. "Gemma—"

". . . Yes?"

"May I keep going?"

I wanted to freeze that moment for eternity. The energy of desire that hovered around us. Jonas Hellgren waiting for me to say yes, or to say no. All the possibilities suspended there in our own personal universe. The blooming feeling that I wanted to be consumed by the man in front of me and knowing that he was hungry for me. Ravenous.

"Yes . . . you may."

HE LET GO of my hands and pulled his boots off. I bent down to remove mine and leaned against the door for balance. One boot off, then the other. I barely had my feet back on the ground before he was kissing me. He kept his lips on mine as he pushed his robe off and let it drop to the floor.

He worked my robe off my shoulders, down my arms, and over my hips. It landed at our feet. He put his hands on the sides of my neck with his fingers resting on my jaw and ears. He brushed his lips against my mouth. I moved my head forward to try to kiss him and he pulled back. Then he went in for little nips and bites of my lips before roughly kissing me and sliding his tongue over mine.

Being full-body skin-to-skin with Jonas, I should've anticipated the kind of reaction I'd have to this situation, but I was unprepared for the intensity of my response. I was wholly, fully, completely consumed with desire.

I was so aroused that I felt my wetness spread to the inside of my thighs. And all he'd done so far was kiss me. Jonas moved his hands to my ass and was moaning into my mouth.

"Ouch." Something poked the tender skin above my hip.

Jonas stopped immediately and pulled back. "You ok?"

"Something scratched me," I said, looking for the spot on my skin.

"I'm sorry," he said, holding up a packaged condom. "Must have been this."

"Where'd you get that?"

"Your backpack. When I was getting snacks."

I was both embarrassed and impressed. "So naughty."

Jonas pressed the condom into my palm, pushed his body to mine again and leaned down for another kiss. "You don't know the half of it," he said and then he spun me around.

My breasts were pressed to the door and the wood was cold against my belly. Jonas raised my hands above my head and held them against the door.

He slid one of his hands down the side of my arm, my shoulder, my ribs, my hip, and across the crease of my ass. He moved his hand between my thighs and pushed my legs apart. He slid two fingers inside me, and I easily accepted him.

He kept his fingers inside me and let go of my arms. He snaked his free hand down to my breast. He caught my nipple between the knuckles of his first and middle fingers and rolled and pinched my skin. Electric shocks shot down my body right to my center. My knees felt like they might buckle.

"I want to fuck you, Gemma," he said into my ear. His voice was rougher than usual. Deeper. I felt a rush of desire flood my body. "May I?" He was sliding his fingers in and out of me and was pushing his cock against my ass, pinning me to the wall.

"Yes," I said, barely finding enough breath to speak. I still had the condom in my fist. I held it tightly as I tried to stay upright.

"Say it," he said.

"I want you to . . . "

"To what?"

My face was burning. I felt too shy to do as he asked.

"You can say it, Gemma." He now had his fingertips

swirling between my legs, spreading my wetness into the folds of my skin. "Do you want me?"

"Yes," I gasped. "So much."

"What do you want me to do?"

There was no way out but through. Could someone die from desire? I had to say it. My voice was hoarse. "I want you to fuck me."

Still behind me, he nuzzled his face into my neck and wrapped both arms around me. He kissed my ear, the back of my head, and the side of my neck.

He reached up and plucked the condom from between my fingers. I heard the package rip open. He must have used his teeth. He shifted as he rolled it on, and then moved back up against me.

Jonas used his knee to spread my legs open even more. My hands remained against the door. He pulled my hips and ass back, bending me over. He parted my folds with his fingers and placed his tip right at my opening. He put his hand on my hip and steadied me.

I wanted him inside me. I tried to slide down on him, but he didn't let me. He was too strong, and he made me hover right above him.

"Please," I whispered.

He pushed into me. His full length, all at once. He and I both cried out at the same time. He stretched me and filled me and my body wrapped around his shaft. He slowly withdrew and then thrust into me again and lifted me off my feet. He wrapped his arms fully around me and held me like that, as if savoring the feeling. I was suspended in the air and suspended in my mind, suspended in the universe. Jonas was inside me and for that frozen moment we were fully together.

He set me down and slowly pulled out of me. "Turn around," he said, his voice deep and strong.

I turned to face him and was caught off guard. Of all the versions of Jonas I'd seen so far, I'd never encountered this one. His face was soft, vulnerable, tender, and open.

"Do I have something in my teeth?" he joked.

I lowered my eyes and couldn't even answer. I felt so attracted to him. So entranced. So connected. So attached. I'd seemingly lost my ability to put anything into words.

"You're shorter than I am," he said.

"Yep." *Yep? That's all I could manage?*

"Height difference made that a little tricky. And I want to see your face."

Jonas plucked a robe off the floor and spread it across the seat of the couch. He sat down on the robe. "Come here," he said, holding out his hand.

I moved toward him but was stymied by the mechanics of it all. If I sat across his lap, I'd have to sit *on* him, and he was still fully, fully aroused.

"Where should I sit?"

"Wherever you want."

I lowered myself toward his lap and balanced on my knees. I straddled his erection but hovered above him, making gentle contact between our bodies.

"How about this?" I asked him.

He leaned his head back and closed his eyes. "That's good," he said. "Very, very good."

"Thought you wanted to look at me."

Jonas lifted his head and opened his eyes. "I do."

"Keep looking." I lowered myself a little more, causing him, just barely, to enter me.

I raised up and then moved down again, letting him go a little deeper.

Jonas put his hands on my hips and pushed his pelvis up. I rocked my hips slowly and pushed toward him, allowing him to penetrate me.

Jonas was beautifully desperate. He was watching me, but his gaze was fuzzy, as if he were high. His lips were open, and I saw that canine tooth. God, that fucking tooth.

Jonas moved a hand between my legs and flitted his fingers across my clit. I softly pushed his hand away. "Not yet. I want to watch you come."

"God," Jonas moaned. He closed his eyes again.

I wanted to swim in the delicious heat of his desire for me. I didn't want to miss a moment. If he put his fingers on me, I'd lose my mind. I wanted to be fully present.

He tried to touch me again, but I didn't let him. I moved his hands to my breasts and held them there as I moved on him quickly and deeply. He was mine for the taking. And I was going to take him.

I watched him as he moved to the edge and over it. With his eyes closed and his mouth open, he released a primal groan. His chest heaved with quick breaths, a ruby flush swept over his neck, and he bucked his hips wildly. I felt the heat of him pulsing inside me. Something that sounded like a sob caught in his throat. He cried out again. As our bodies stilled, he let out a full sob. And another. Tears flooded his eyes and spilled out over his cheeks. He pulled his hands from my chest and covered his face.

I moved off his lap and sat beside him, pulling him towards me. Together, we went from sitting up to lying down. I rolled the condom off him and set it aside. He tried to keep his face covered but I moved his hands away.

"You're beautiful," I said.

"No . . ." he said, shaking his head. "I'm—"

"It's ok." I kissed his face, which was salty and wet. He opened his eyes, and with tears still falling, he laughed.

"I don't know what this is. Or where it's coming from."

"It doesn't matter. It's here. Let it be here."

48

JONAS

The tears were a mystery.

Gemma just waited, brushing them off every so often as they rolled down my face. I checked in with my emotional register, the best I could. They weren't tears of laughter, sadness, anger, or pain. They also weren't borne of happiness, wonder, rage, or ecstasy. I was searching, trying to find the origin, like running your tongue along your gums to find the source of a toothache . . . not there, not there, not there . . . there! They were just tears of relief. Of release. And not a sexual release, though what had just happened in my body felt magnificent.

For the first time in years, I'd been out of my mind. I let go of my obsessions, my memories, and my ghosts. I let myself exist in the exact present and I think my soul took advantage of the moment and pushed the RELEASE ALL button. I felt peaceful and still. I also felt self-absorbed.

A generous woman had just been completely vulnerable with me and let me indulge in absolute pleasure. She was minding my tears, being gentle with my body, and being more than kind with her openness, despite what an asshole I'd been over and over. I didn't deserve any of it. But holy hell, I hoped she'd keep giving it to me. And I needed to give back to her if she'd let me.

I sat up and wiped away the dampness on my cheeks. "Sorry about that."

"Why are you sorry?" Gemma asked.

"I don't know. Just seems like the right thing to say when you burst into tears after a mind-blowing orgasm."

"Mind-blowing?" Gemma gently prodded my shoulder.

"It was just a lot. This is all a lot. I know that *I'm* a lot."

"That's a lot of *a lots*."

"Should we get dressed and see if we can make it to the cube?" I asked her as I stood up, holding up one of the robes in front of myself to avoid any more "a lots" right in Gemma's face.

"Sure."

"I'd like to continue what we started here. But it must be a more comfortable atmosphere over there."

"I hope so, because I'd still like that nap," she said, slipping the other robe over her shoulders and holding it closed in front. "But no more jokes about what's looming outside."

"No more. I'm sorry."

"It worked out in the end. But I really was scared that you were injured."

"I'm realizing how much of an ass I am," I said.

"Your words, not mine."

I gently grabbed her robe with my left hand and pulled her to me. She let me bring her close, but she had her eyes down. Something was bothering her. "What's on your mind?" I asked her, while I put my right hand into her curls and softly wound her hair around my palm.

"I don't know . . ." she said.

"I think you do know. But if you don't want to talk about it, that's ok."

"It's just kind of heavy. And I've been trying to push it back, but it keeps coming up to the surface."

I stayed silent, trying to give her the space to find the direction she wanted to take.

"It might be upsetting to you. And surely there's a better time to bring it up. But I'd just like to get it out of the way . . ." She sighed, crossed her arms, and pulled her robe tighter. I took a step back to give her some space. I put my robe on. It was probably hard for her to have a serious conversation with a naked man using a robe as a loincloth. "Now I've just built it all up and I feel stupid."

"If you want to talk about it, let's talk," I said. She lifted a strand of her hair and put it in her mouth, chewing on the end of it. "If you've reached the point of eating your own hair, we'd better clear the air."

She let out a small laugh and let go of her hair. She took a deep breath. "Ok. It's just—"

I waited. I had no idea where she was going with this.

She tried again. "It's the baby."

The words "the baby" rang out and I didn't know what to do with them. What baby? Was she pregnant? Who the hell got her pregnant? I went from blissfully calm to knotted stomach and tense fists in about two seconds. So much for my self-control. "What baby?" I managed to ask in a balanced tone.

She looked at me like I was especially dense. *Your baby.*

Apparently, I *was* especially dense. What was she talking about? "My baby? What baby?"

"Your baby with Anna!" she said.

"Oh . . . my baby. Anna's pregnancy." I was still confused but at least we'd solved the mystery of what baby. And I'd be lying if I didn't admit that my stomach immediately relaxed when I realized that she wasn't talking about her own pregnancy.

"Yes, that one." She seemed somewhat exasperated.

"What about it?"

Gemma lifted her arms and then let them flop to her sides. "We've never talked about the baby. You've never said anything about it except for on the dock, after you . . ."

"After I lost my ever-loving shit?"

"Yes, since then."

"And you want to talk about the baby now? Here?" I gestured around to the shed with its shower, shelves, couch and coolers.

"No, I really don't want to. But I'd like to go into that beautiful cube over there without this hanging over us. And I need to clear the air."

"Alright. Let's clear it."

"Are you ok to talk about it?"

I'd never spoken about the baby publicly. And I'd barely ever spoken about it privately. I felt like I was on the precipice of a new life, a new world. I thought back to how at peace I'd felt just minutes before. I wanted more of that. I wanted more release and more relief. More openness. "I'll talk about it. Get your recorder. Let's get it on the record."

INTERVIEW EXCERPT

(The following is an excerpt from the interview with Jonas Hellgren, conducted by Gemma Lane, published in Profile Magazine Volume 315)

INTERVIEWER

Earlier, we spoke about the loss of your wife, Anna. You mentioned that she was pregnant.

HELLGREN

Yes, she was.

INTERVIEWER

We haven't spoken about the other loss you suffered—the loss of your unborn child.

HELLGREN

I haven't wanted to talk about it. I've never spoken about it publicly, and I don't think that many people even knew that Anna was pregnant. We'd been keeping it private for as long as we could. We wanted it to be something between just the two of us, at least for a while.

INTERVIEWER

But you're open to speaking about it now?

HELLGREN

I am. This is my season of release and renewal, I think. I hope. And I've realized that holding things in was just eating away at me . . . creating so many holes in my psyche that it was about to get to the point of being beyond repair. So, let's talk about it.

INTERVIEWER

I'm very sorry for your loss. I know that's not enough. It's just so completely devastating that I'm having trouble finding words. How did you come back from that?

HELLGREN

I don't know about the term "coming back." I didn't 'come back.' I just came around a different way. There's no coming back from that.

I didn't face it for a long time. I didn't want to think about it. Anna and I did not intend to have children; the pregnancy was unplanned. I think it took us a few months to get used to the idea. We were just starting to get comfortable with it when we—when I lost her. Lost them.

INTERVIEWER

But you've made peace with it over time?

HELLGREN

As much as I can. In Genesis it says: *In the beginning God created the heavens and the earth. Now the earth was formless and empty, darkness was over the surface of the deep, and the Spirit of God was hovering over the waters.* I read that in Hebrew, "spirit" is "ruah" which can also mean breath, air, or wind. I think about the hovering of spirit . . . how life was floating above, but not yet given to the world. Later verses talk about the breath of life in all living things.

INTERVIEWER

Are you religious?

HELLGREN

Only when it suits me.

INTERVIEWER

How did those verses help you make peace with the loss of your—

HELLGREN

My son. I searched so many works of poetry, literature, philosophy, and religion to try to make sense of it all. If something soothed me, I took it to heart. Those verses give me something to hold on to when it came to the idea of my son's soul.

He never took his first breath. He didn't even have lungs that were ready to breathe because he wasn't that far along. I like to believe that his soul stayed fluid, in flight, or hovering. If that's true, he can be anywhere. I picture him with me all the time. We couldn't be together physically in this lifetime, but souls don't need a physical form to exist. He and I are together, always.

INTERVIEWER

You've been through a lot. Heartbreak. Loss. Rebirth.

HELLGREN

You aren't without your own losses, tragedies, or road to redemption.

INTERVIEWER

I suppose so. No one is. But not everyone talks about it.

HELLGREN

I find your journey very interesting. Can we talk about you for a bit?

INTERVIEWER

I'm not the subject of the interview.

HELLGREN

You're not, but you're not a passive bystander, either. You were selected to conduct this interview because your own experiences might be in harmony with mine. And I think they were hoping you'd be able to get me to open up. I'm somewhat notorious for avoiding interviews.

INTERVIEWER

Somewhat?

HELLGREN

Ok, moderately notorious.

INTERVIEWER

Let's talk about what's next for you. What will the next year bring, do you think?

HELLGREN

I'm not ready to go there. Let me ask you a few questions.

INTERVIEWER

But I'm not—

HELLGREN

'*You're* not the subject of the interview.' I know. But *I* am, so I get to be in charge. And I want to talk about you. Let them edit it out later if they don't like it. But I bet they'll like it.

INTERVIEWER

Who is *they*?

HELLGREN

The publishing powers that be.

INTERVIEWER

Alright. Ask me something.

HELLGREN

When you took your epic walk, which you chronicled in your book, you didn't follow a map.

INTERVIEWER

Not in a traditional sense, no.

HELLGREN

How did you decide where to go? Do you think maps are unimportant?

INTERVIEWER

I think maps are essential.

HELLGREN

Then why didn't you use any?

INTERVIEWER

I used them. I used traditional maps to find my bearings, but not to plan my routes. I used a different kind of map for that.

HELLGREN

What do you mean?

INTERVIEWER

My mother used to map my monsters. I used monster maps to find my way.

HELLGREN

What are monster maps?

INTERVIEWER

I grew up in a rural area. I was an only child, and our house was on a big piece of land that included woods, grassy fields, and a creek. I loved to explore, but I was also imaginative and sometimes anxious. I would see a tree branch at dusk and think it was a stick monster who was going to click and slice through the woods and might cut my neck from behind. I'd see a dark bubble in the current of the creek and think that a water monster was about to surface and pull me under. I'd see grasses in the field part and bend with the wind, and I was sure that a three-headed serpent was slithering through the blades, about to strike if I got close.

HELLGREN

That's a lot of monsters.

INTERVIEWER

There *were* a lot. So many that I started to stay in the house because I was too scared to go out. My mother found a huge roll of paper and rolled it out on the kitchen table. She mapped our property. She drew our house, the boundaries of the forest, where the fields started and stopped, and she drew all the bends and forks of the creek as it moved through our land. Then she put the monsters on the map. She labeled them and added them to the legend. She told me that they only existed in specific places, and every place other than those was safe. I hung the map on my wall with thumbtacks and looked at it every night before I fell asleep. I memorized it. And after that, I could go out walking. I could climb the trees again and swim in the river. I just avoided those specific places where the monsters lived. By mapping them, she took away their power and opened the rest of the world to me.

HELLGREN

How did this help you on your walking journey?

INTERVIEWER

I drew my own map. I'd been dealing with some personal demons. So, I put them on a map. I found physical places for psychic fears. The nursing home where my dad died. The gas station where my fiancé and I broke up after a big argument in my car. The cemetery where we had a marker for my mother. And, unfortunately, my home, which was my family home that I used to share with my parents. Those were the places I had to escape. I just went anywhere but there.

HELLGREN

That left you with a lot of places to go.

INTERVIEWER

Yes, but it was an evolving map. If I was somewhere and felt uncomfortable, or the terrain was tricky, or people weren't welcoming, I'd mark it on my map and go in a different direction. I eventually made my way back home, and the monsters weren't there anymore. I made a new map. That's how I keep moving forward.

HELLGREN

I think this is all more interesting than any of my stories. Can we make *you* the subject of this interview?

INTERVIEWER

I'm afraid that's not in the contract. Though if acting doesn't work out for you, maybe you could go into journalism.

49

GEMMA

I turned off the recorder. Jonas and I sat in silence.

"That was a lot," I said.

"Another *a lot* to add to the list."

"Do you feel like we've lived about five lifetimes in this shed?"

"Let's get out of here," said Jonas.

"We're still in robes."

"Who cares. Let's just put our boots on. It's a short distance—"

"Unless there are boars."

We pulled on our boots, tied our robes, and got our bags ready. The rain outside was coming down steadily, but nothing like the night before. We found some ponchos and put them on, but I suspected they wouldn't help that much.

Jonas went out the door first. "If it's clear, let's make a run for it."

Jonas walked out into the storm. He circled the shed and came back around. "All clear."

We weaved through the trees and made it to the metal stairs.

The cube was almost as high up as the treehouse. Jonas made me go first and he stayed close behind me as I made my way up. I was out of breath by the time we got to the top, but Jonas seemed fine. The door was mirrored and only the hinges and handle gave it away. There was a keypad and Jonas quickly entered his code. A red light turned green. We opened the door and went inside, dripping water all over the mat by the door. Jonas shut the door firmly behind us. After a few seconds the door automatically bolted, but Jonas secured the chain lock as well.

He bent over and put his hands on his knees. I noticed that he was panting after all. Maybe he'd been holding his breath. "I'm really glad to be in here," he said. "Christ." He slid down the door into a resting squat.

I took off my boots and my poncho. My robe wasn't too wet.

The cube was the simplest of the cabins we'd been in, but also the most elegant. "Well. Wow."

Jonas rubbed some of the water out of his hair and stood back up. "Nice."

"How big do you think this is?" I asked Jonas. "Fifteen feet?"

"It's a four-by-four-by-four cube."

"Four meters?"

"Yes."

"So, fifteen feet?"

"Around thirteen. I can't believe your country still uses the imperial system."

"God save the Queen." The room was spare and light, despite the gloominess outside. "This has electricity!" There was an architectural light fixture hanging high above our heads that created a soft glow in the room. The walls were covered in beautiful creamy blonde plywood. Cutouts were made for several square windows of different sizes and at different heights. Half the roof was glass, the other half was also covered in the plywood.

Right by the entrance there was a vestibule with a door that led to a small dry closet. There was an open area beyond that which held two sleek leather chairs looking very Swedish in their lines and shapes. There was a small table between the chairs. The final feature of the room was a double bed, which was tucked into a nook. With walls on three sides of the mattress, it created a hideaway cozy spot for rest. Or other activities. "This takes minimalism to a new level," I said.

"I guess that's why there are so many supplies in the shed."

We both took off our robes and our boots, dimmed the overhead light with a switch on the wall, and got into bed. There was one large down comforter and cream-colored linen sheets. We were both naked, but too tired for it to matter.

The sound of rain on the glass ceiling quickly lulled me to sleep. When I woke, probably hours later, it was dark out and Jonas was passed out by my side. It was still raining, but more softly. The bed felt comfortable, cozy, and safe. I let sleep pull me back under.

50

GEMMA

When I opened my eyes the next time, it was dark beyond the windows, but the overhead light cast a gentle warm light into the room. Jonas was sitting in one of the chairs with a book in his hands. At his feet a blanket was spread out across the wood floor and upon that was a platter with meats, cheeses, bread, and chocolates. A few bottles of water and beer rested next to the food.

"Where did you get all of this?" I asked as I worked my way over to the edge of the bed.

"Good morning," said Jonas.

"Is it morning?" I had no idea what time it was, but Jonas had a watch.

"A few minutes past midnight. So technically, yes." Jonas closed his book. "I brought a few things over from the shed."

"I'm alarmed that I didn't hear you."

"The rain is like a white noise machine. And you were really out."

I suddenly had the urge to eat all of the food set out on the blanket. "I'm starving."

"Let's eat."

"Maybe I should put some clothes on first."

"No need. But suit yourself."

I TRIED to savor the food, but I ate quickly. I drank one beer and Jonas was finishing his third as we relaxed into the chairs. "These are more comfortable than they look," I said, running my fingers along the soft leather on the arm of the chair.

"That's what most people say about me."

"That doesn't make any sense," I said.

"Must have gotten lost in translation," said Jonas. "Or it could be the beer."

The rain fell loudly on the glass portion of the roof, but there was no thunder or lightning.

"Do you think it's our last night out here?" I asked.

"Maybe. Probably."

"I don't know how to feel about that."

"I'm trying not to think about it," he said.

"Are you looking forward to going home?"

Jonas laughed ruefully. "What do you think?"

"I don't know. Maybe you have a hamster to go home to? Or a goldfish?"

"No pets. Though I wouldn't mind a cat. Haven't felt up to the responsibility of caring for another living being. I haven't done a great job with just myself."

Jonas was wearing a charcoal-colored sweater and lighter gray pants, rolled up a few times. His feet were bare. "You have really nice feet."

Jonas glanced down at his toes. "Thanks. I worked hard on them."

"You're obnoxiously handsome. You know that, right?"

He moved his lips into a wicked half-smile and let a little hair fall across his forehead. He raised an eyebrow and turned toward me, giving me what I realized was a very sexy and very rehearsed expression.

"You are NOT allowed to use that face on me!"

"What are you going to do about it?" he asked.

"You know I'm good at punishing you. Don't push me."

"That's exactly why I'm pushing," he said as he extended a leg and poked me with those lovely toes. "But actually, I think it's my turn to be in charge. You've had your way with me several times and I'm starting to feel taken advantage of."

"I'll never give up control," I said.

"Let's play for it."

He was still throwing his movie star smolder at me. It was not a level playing field when an experienced actor was using his face as a weapon against a mere mortal.

"What game do you have in mind?"

He went to the bag by the door and pulled out a deck of cards, another item he must have collected from the shed. "You choose. What can you play?"

"Old Maid? Crazy Eights?"

"Might be too complicated for me. One round of War, winner takes all?"

"Wow, a real card shark."

Jonas smoothly shuffled the cards overhand, then flipped them so quickly into a riffle shuffle that they were all a blur. He finished by bridging the cards and then set the deck in front of me. His hands moved like those of a master magician. "You want to deal?"

"Shit. I take it back. You can deal."

Jonas dealt the cards swiftly, each one landing perfectly on top of the piles in front of us.

"Have you just spent these last years in hiding learning card tricks?" I asked. "How are you so good at that?"

He shrugged as he dealt the final card. "We could've played a game of pool, but this cabin is lacking a table."

"I suck at pool," I said. "But I would've accepted darts, air hockey, axe throwing, or skee-ball."

"What kind of taverns are you frequenting? Don't you have regular billiard halls?"

"I'm still confused about what billiards is. Are. Whatever," I said. "But there are cool bars where you can play all those games. But not at the same time. They have special lanes to throw the axes so no one gets hurt."

"Let's just stick to cards," said Jonas as he turned over his first card, a five of hearts.

HALFWAY THROUGH OUR stacks of cards I was feeling confident. Jonas had a lot of threes, fours, and fives, and I was rich in eights, tens, and Jacks.

"This isn't fair," said Jonas, as my nine of spades took his two of diamonds.

"Blame the shuffler," I said. "Though, where are all the face cards?"

My question was quickly answered over our next few turns: they were in Jonas's hand. He won the next few battles with a king, a queen, an ace, another queen, another ace. I hadn't been counting, but his pile was alarmingly fat. We had six cards left and both turned over sevens. We stacked up our two extra cards for war and both played twos. I felt nervous, mostly because I wasn't exactly sure what prize we were playing for.

"Last two cards," said Jonas. We put our cards down. "On the count of three?" He started counting. "One—"

I felt a vibration move through the floor of the cabin. "Did you feel that?"

Jonas had stopped counting. "I did."

We waited to see if it happened again. One second, two seconds, three seconds... *thump, thump, thump, thump.* "Is someone on the stairs?"

"Shit." Jonas jumped up and crossed the room to stand by the door. He held his hand against it.

"Feel anything?"

He shook his head and waited another ten seconds. "I'm going to open it with the chain on. Stay back there."

My stomach dropped and my hands trembled. Jonas opened the door slowly, peered out, and closed it again.

"No one there, at least on the top platform. I'm going to explore a little further. Can I have your flashlight and one of the panic buttons?"

Shit. I got both items for him. "I don't want you to go out there."

"It should be fine. But if you hear an obnoxiously loud ABBA song, keep the door locked and the chain on. I'll knock two slow and three fast when I'm back." He grabbed my face and kissed me roughly. "And this time, do NOT keep the door open or come out. I will not be playing any jokes." His expression was grave. I nodded. He put his hand on the door handle. "The moment I'm out, put the chain on." He slipped out the door. I shut it quickly and slid the chain into place. Then I waited.

51

JONAS

It was darker than dark outside. With the heavy clouds, no light from the moon or stars, and zero artificial light other than Gemma's flashlight, it was unnervingly black. I couldn't make out the trees and it felt like I was surrounded by thousands of invisible eyes. I wished I had one of Gemma's monster maps. Something was out there that shouldn't be there. I just couldn't see it.

Whatever it was, it wasn't on the stairs, and it wasn't within the range of the flashlight's beam. Rain was still falling, and it pattered against the trees, the cube, and the forest floor, so there was no way I'd hear something walking about.

I considered going deeper into the woods, but what if something *was* out there, and I found it? I was barefoot (that was an oversight) and armed with a flashlight and a panic button. Fuck it. I ran back up the stairs like I was being chased by a demon. Two slow knocks and three fast on the door. Gemma opened it slightly but still had the chain on. I was relieved to see that she was taking the situation seriously.

She let me in and quickly shut the door behind me. She

reengaged the chain and the automatic bolt locked after a few seconds. She pulled me into a hug, seemingly unbothered by the dampness of my clothes and hair.

"That was scary," she said. "Maybe don't go out there again."

"I'm fine to stay in here," I said, as I closed my arms around her and let my pulse return to its normal rhythm. She had on wool socks, soft cotton bottoms, an Air Supply t-shirt, and a black open sweater. She should've been plenty warm, but she was trembling. I tried to get her mind off of whatever danger might have been lurking outside. "We need to finish our game so I can crush you properly."

She glanced over at the cards on the floor as if trying to decide if she'd allow herself to be distracted. "What does the winner get again?"

"Total control."

"Of?"

"Whatever they like."

She laughed and glanced around the room. "This is a pretty small domain. Not that much to control."

"Then you won't mind losing. Because you're going down."

We returned to our game and flipped our final cards over. I was pretty sure that I could pull off a victory even if I didn't win that last battle, but I won it anyway, 10 to 2. I let out a whoop and Gemma rolled her eyes.

"Congrats, Hellgren. Does this mean you're in control of cleaning up our dinner mess?"

"I've got it. You relax in the chair and drink some water. I'll be right with you." Winning the game made my plans for the evening easier, but I would've had my way no matter what the outcome was. Gemma had been very generous with me, and I was quite overdue for returning the favor.

She leaned back in the chair, stretched out her legs, and closed her eyes. Her hair fell in gentle waves over the headrest, like a dark waterfall suspended in motion. She laced her fingers together and placed her hands on her stomach. Her eyelashes were long and rested on her cheeks. Her upper lip had a delectable dip in the center that I wanted to run my tongue across. But first things first. I stacked the platter and empty bottles in the corner by the door. I folded the blanket, capturing any crumbs that may have fallen. I didn't want to risk going outside if I didn't have to. Shaking out the blanket would have to wait until daytime.

I dimmed the light so it barely cast a light down on us like a waning crescent moon. I sat on the floor at Gemma's feet and put my hands on her knees, letting her know I was there. "Tired?"

"A little," she said. "You'd think I'd be awake all night after all that sleep, but—" she yawned.

"You only slept for about three hours total. You probably have a lot more to catch up on."

"Only three? Felt like longer."

Maybe she was too tired for what I had in store for her. I didn't want to pressure her. "You ready for bed?"

"It's not up to me."

"Who is it up to?"

"The person owho won the game. As I understood the rules, he's totally in charge now." Gemma opened her eyes, and they glinted in the low light. *Perfect.*

"Close your eyes again," I told her. "And keep them closed, please." She closed her eyes. I got comfortable on the floor and sat in between her legs, with a foot on either side of me. Through her thick socks, and one foot at a time, I slowly rubbed her toes, the soles of her feet, her heels, and the top of each foot. I took my time, kneading with my fingertips to work out her tension, her aches, her worries.

I pulled off her left sock, and then her right. I lightly scratched the skin of her feet and ankles with my fingernails and she let out a sweet sigh. I repeated the rubbing, kneading, and scratching up her shins, calves, knees, and lower thighs. That was as far as I could reach, given the restriction of the bottoms she was wearing.

"Doing ok?" I asked her.

"More than ok."

My next move was a big one. I ran my hands up her legs and reached into the waistband of her bottoms. She kept her eyes closed and didn't move. I pulled on the fabric a little, and then pulled some more. She lifted her hips slightly, allowing me to pull them past her hips, her ass, and down to her ankles. I waited. No protest from Gemma. I slipped the waistband over her feet and tossed the pants aside, leaving Gemma clad only in her t-shirt, sweater, and a pair of green underwear that had a rainbow and a pot of gold on the front. "Are you into leprechauns?" I asked, lightly touching the rainbow between her legs.

"I have a weakness for mischievous men, if that's what you're asking."

My view from the floor was spectacular. Gemma's long legs were soft and full. I indulged in her skin by running my hands up and down the length of her thighs. I moved up to my knees and lifted her shirt a little so I could kiss her belly.

Gemma responded with a murmur of pleasure.

I debated taking off all her clothes, but she looked so warm and comfortable that I decided to leave her be and just focus on the lower half of her body, which was more than enough with which to entertain myself.

I lowered myself into a sitting position and settled in again between her thighs. I crossed my legs and made myself comfortable. I ran both index fingers along the edges of her underwear and traced the lines they made across her skin. Her waist, her hips, the sensitive skin of her innermost thighs. I pushed her legs further apart and continued to move my fingers along the edges. She squirmed a little and pushed herself slightly closer to me.

I ran my fingertips along the center of her underwear, and she inhaled sharply. I leaned forward and hooked the edge of the green fabric with my fingers. I paused for a few seconds, and then shifted her underwear to one side, fully exposing her. This was the best part. Watching her. Waiting. Making her wait. She tried to close her legs a little, but I pushed them back open, even more so than they were before.

"Don't move your legs," I said gently. She moaned a little but kept her legs open. I decided to narrate what I was doing. "I'm looking at you. Between your legs. It's dark but I can see the folds of your skin." She made a sweet low sound in her throat.

"I'm going to touch you, just slightly, to see if you're wet." I touched my finger to her opening and then pulled back. "You're so wet already. I barely touched you and I could feel it. What's it like if I go a little deeper?" Gemma's breathing was quick and audible and she arched her back ever so slightly. I touched her with two fingers, swirling them around in her wetness and pushing into her just a bit.

"God," she sighed. "Do that again."

"This?" I said as I pushed my fingers deeper still.

"Yes. Please," she said.

"You sound a little breathless. Do you like that?"

"I like that."

"What I'm really wondering," I said, running my fingers up the inside of her thighs, teasing her, "is what you taste like."

Gemma fully whimpered at that, and she grabbed the ends of her sweater and balled the fabric into her fists.

"Let me just take a little taste." I hovered over her, breathing onto her skin, making her wonder where I might strike. I decided to put my tongue where my fingers had been, pushing fully into her. Losing all inhibition, Gemma cried out loudly. I pulled back again. "I wonder what it tastes like up here." I spread her folds apart with my hand, stretching her skin taut. Her scent was floral and musky and perfect.

I flicked her clit with my tongue, and she writhed in the chair. Another light flick across her soft skin, then another. Then I let my tongue linger and swirl while closing in on her with my lips. She was moving her pelvis into my mouth and saying my name. I loved it. Every second of it. I put my fingers back inside her and my fingers and mouth worked together to play the instrument of her body. She moved and I moved, and all her muscles tensed. She threw back her head and I felt her spasm around my hand and mouth. I kept soft pressure on her until she rode the wave out, out, out to sea and then opened her fists and tried to close her legs. I let her close them a bit, but I stayed between her legs and rested my face on her thigh.

"Can I open my eyes?" she asked me.

"Yes."

I looked up and saw Gemma. Really saw her. Her cheeks

were bight pink and her lips were wet and full. A section of her hair fell in a soft wave over her face, making her look a little wild and undone. I felt transformed under her gaze. It was like I was the most perfect being that she'd ever seen. And there, in the darkness of the cabin and the woods and the stormy night, I let myself believe her.

She startled me by scooting off the chair and joining me on the floor. She pulled me down and put her mouth on mine. My stomach felt flighty, and my chest felt dizzy. She unzipped my trousers and put her hand down the front of my underwear.

"Wait a minute," I said, putting my hand on hers. "I thought I was in charge." She didn't say anything. She just stroked me slowly, and then faster. I had no will to stop her. I felt my fullness and heat grow and push and God, was she going to make me come that fast? Yes. Yes, she was. I grabbed her hair and put my mouth back on hers, sucking on her bottom lip as a rough-edged climax swept over me and I lost control. I made a ridiculous sound, giving up any pretense of coolness. She seemed to like it, groaning along with me, and pulling me closer.

"So much for being in charge," I said. Gemma kissed me again and pulled her hand out of my trousers.

"Have a towel in your goody bag over there?"

I found a napkin and helped her clean up. We drank some water, used the dry closet, and turned off the light. We climbed back into bed, curled up, and fell asleep in tandem, the rhythm of our breath synchronized in the darkest hours of the night.

5 2

———

JONAS

At some point, in the middle of the night . . . or middle of the morning, or middle of whenever, I didn't care, it was dark out, and Gemma was asleep—I woke up with her in my arms. I was behind her, and my arm rested on her hip and my hand was settled on the soft skin of her belly. I was in that state between dream and waking. Her body was comfortable in mine; she was both new and familiar. I felt excited and calm, stimulated and peaceful, wakeful, and lazy—all those dichotomies of attraction mixed into a beautiful potion of togetherness. I also felt ridiculous and like the most brilliant man in the world to have gotten myself into the position I was in. I'd only known of Gemma's existence for a week and there I was with this punch-drunk feeling blooming in my gut, moving up to my chest and out through my mouth . . . *don't say it, don't say it, don't say it, Jonas—she's asleep, it's ok, you can say it—I'm going to say it,* "I love you," I whispered into her hair.

Gemma stirred and leaned back into me. She turned her head. *Oh shit oh shit oh shit.* "Jonas?"

I played dead, played possum, played *I'm Jonas and I have a problem with talking in my sleep so don't pay any attention to it.* I tried to keep my breathing even and deep to feign sleep. Maybe she didn't hear me after all.

Gemma wrapped her hand around mine and lifted it to her lips. I tried to keep my arm as dead weight, but she caught me off guard. My arm was half dead and half alive as she kissed the palm of my hand. "Thank you," she said, and then she wrapped my arm tightly around her chest and snuggled in closer to me.

Thank you? Close to the worst-case scenario as far as "I love you" replies went. But I didn't say it to her face. I said it to her hair in the middle of the night. I hadn't wanted her to hear it. There was a good chance she thought I was actually talking in my sleep. "Thank you" was a fair response, given the situation. Why did I say that out loud? God, why was falling for someone always so excruciating?

"GOOD MORNING," Gemma said, sitting up in bed, bright eyed and rosy-cheeked. She was wearing the same Air Supply shirt that she'd fallen asleep in, the one with the blazing red orange sun with someone parasailing across it. She was wearing a different cardigan on top. This one was red and white striped. On her bottom half, she only had underwear on. No St. Patrick's day theme this time, but there were lots of rainbows across a yellow background on soft boy-shorts. The cabin was quiet. The rain had stopped, but the light coming through the windows was dreary.

"All dressed up, I see," I said as I reached out my hand and let it rest on her bare thigh.

"I dress to impress."

"Now and Forever."

Gemma cocked her head to the side in a gesture of mild confusion.

"Your shirt. It's like the album cover from *Now and Forever.*"

Her jaw slightly dropped. "You like Air Supply?"

"I didn't say that."

"You do!"

I grabbed her and pulled her to me. "Hold me as close as love will allow—"

"I knew it!" she said, digging her fingertips into my ribs in an attempt to tickle me. I grabbed both of her hands and kissed her chest and neck as she squirmed in the bed.

"Speaking of love," she said, between gasps of laughter.

"Were we speaking of love?"

"*You* were, via Australia's top Soft Rock band."

"If you say so," I lifted her t-shirt to see what else I could find to kiss.

"You said something to me last night."

I froze, panic seizing my chest. "What did I say?" I was going to play dumb and see where this went. Maybe she was talking about something else. I rested my head on her stomach, unwilling to look her in the eye.

Gemma paused. She ran her fingers through my hair, igniting a sensory explosion throughout my body, starting with my scalp and shooting all the way down to my toes. "It was in the middle of the night. You said it into my ear."

Play it cool, Jonas. I lifted my head to resume kissing the skin over her ribs. Maybe this would distract her. "I don't remember." Great. Now I was a liar. I was usually proud of my honesty, even telling the truth when it hurt. But now? Liar, liar, pants on fire.

"You don't?"

I'd try not to lie directly again. I took a different route. "What did you hear?" I was really hoping that she'd back out now. Just say that she didn't remember. What would I do if she called me out on this? I was such a stupid asshole.

"Well . . ."

I risked a glance at her face. She was chewing on a strand of curls again. Not a good sign. Maybe I could change the subject. "Are you hungry?" I said, at the same time that Gemma said,

"You said that you loved me."

"Oh," we both said. Silence loomed heavily in the air of the cabin.

"Did I?" I said, while at the same time Gemma said, "A bit."

Another silence fell between us.

"I've been told that I talk in my sleep," I said. Lie number two.

"Hm," she said. "I didn't mean to embarrass you. I'm sorry."

"You have nothing to be sorry for," I said, sitting up and lowering her shirt. "Should we find you some food? I have to pee."

"I guess so," she said, rolling away from me.

I'd screwed that one up. But not only was I not ready to say "I love you" to her in the cold light of day, I was barely willing to let myself believe it. Not because it wasn't true . . . I just wasn't sure I was ready for everything that came with being in love. I needed some time to get used to the fit of that feeling again, like a wool sweater that you'd shrunk a little, and you had to put it on, stretch it out, and wait for it to mold to your body the way it used to.

I rushed to the dry closet, grabbing a water bottle and my

toothbrush and toothpaste on the way. I was in there much longer than peeing and brushing my teeth really took, but I was nervous to face Gemma. We were old enough that playing games felt like a waste of time. I needed to be honest with her and with myself, but Jesus, I was scared.

I came out to the living area and Gemma had clothes laid out for me. Jeans, underwear, a wheat-colored Henley, socks, and boots. I was thankful for the diversion. "Are you my new fashion advisor?"

"I thought you'd look good in that," she said. "And the sooner you're dressed the sooner we can eat."

"You're not wearing any bottoms."

"I'll just wait here and keep the home fires burning while you hunt down some food for us."

I got dressed while she openly watched me. I felt admired, and that made me feel proud and shy at the same time. I was used to people looking at me, thinking I was handsome, or whatever, but Gemma's gaze had a different weight. An importance.

"This might not be the time, but I may as well bring it up now," she said.

Shit. Was this the "I love you" thing again?

"This might be our last morning here. I assume someone could be here any minute to get us."

"Maybe," I said, zipping up my jeans.

"Any thoughts on where we go from here? You and I?"

I exhaled loudly and ran my hands through my hair to buy me some time. I picked up the shirt Gemma had put out and slipped it over my head. "What do you think?" I asked her. Maybe she could take the lead on this. Because what were my thoughts? My thoughts were that I wanted to take Gemma to my home, lock her in, and never let her leave. I didn't want to share her with my fans, the photographers, or anyone, other than maybe my parents . . . in a year or so. I wanted her all to myself and I wanted her day after day after day. The thought of her going back to America and me never seeing her again was horrifying. Unacceptable. I was a selfish and greedy bastard. I slipped on my boots and tied the laces.

"Well, I like being around you," she said. Her eyes were lowered, and she was wringing her hands. She was nervous. "And I know we could just let things develop organically, but I live like, 5000 miles away, which is even more in kilometers, and I want to see you again, but I don't know what you want and if we can do that and . . . I'm rambling. Save me here."

My heart felt like it had jumped into my throat. This was it. This was the moment. Gemma was so generous and brave. She was looking at me sweetly and with a level of trust no one had put in me for years. I couldn't even admit to my late-night whisper and there she was, putting herself fully out there, neck on the line, open for me to love her, or to crush her heart to pieces.

What did I want to say? I wanted to say: *You're coming home with me. I'm not going to let you out of my sight. We'll have your things sent over. You're mine. Forever.*

But what came out of my mouth? "The logistics would be tricky." *Did I just use the word* logistics? *What the fuck.*

"Ok," she said. "But do you feel like you—"

"I'll have a lot going on," I said, interrupting her. "Publicity for the movie, a book tour. I don't think any kind of relationship would stand a chance."

Gemma's face mirrored what my stomach felt. Her skin was the brightest red, tears had formed in her eyes, and her nostrils flared. She pivoted so she was facing the window. I felt nauseous. I stood there like the idiot I was, dumbfounded into silence by my own stupidity. I waited to see what she'd do next. Even then, I was putting it all on her. Never had a man been more of a loser than I was at that moment.

Gemma was laughing. Sharp, rough, barking laughs. Each one felt like a punch in the gut. She turned back to me. "You're a liar."

I felt like I'd been slapped. And completely exposed. "What?"

"You're a total liar. Not to mention a coward." She spit the words at me, each syllable cutting and brutal. "You know exactly what you said to me last night." She walked over to her bag, shoving her shoulder into mine as she passed by. "And you know what the worst part is? You meant it. I don't know why I know you as well as I do, but," she spun around to face me again, one shoe in her hand. She poked me, hard, in the chest along with each word that she spoke, "I. Know. You."

Gemma pivoted and stomped toward the door. Where was she going?

"I *know* that you like me," she said. "I *know* that you want me." She put her hand on the door handle. "And I know that last night, what you said, that in that moment, you meant it." She looked at the shoe in her hand and then threw it at me, narrowly missing my head. She unlatched the chain lock. "You're a coward and a liar, Jonas. Why I'm falling in love with an asshole like you is beyond me. But I am," she said. She opened the door and stepped outside.

Falling in love? An icy and burning vice grabbed my stomach and twisted, hard. Where *was* she going with no pants, no shoes, and no panic button?

"Do NOT follow me!" she yelled as she ran down the stairs, nearly slipping on the wet metal steps.

"Don't go!" I tried to yell, but my voice was caught under the wet blanket of my emotions and almost nothing came out.

"Stay away from me. You're a fucking nightmare. Shut the door!"

I stood at the top of the stairs, dizzy and horrified, watching my heart run away from me and it was all my fault. All of it.

"GO. BACK. IN. AND SHUT THE DOOR!" Gemma demanded. Stunned and numb, I did as she said. I went inside. I shut the door. I slid down to the floor as the bolt automatically locked. I was an absolute fool.

TIME WENT BY. I don't know how much. Fifteen minutes? A half-hour? I'd remained on the floor, pitifully devastated. Gemma had to come back. Literally had to. All her stuff was in the cabin with me. She must've been in the shed. I hoped she was enjoying a long hot shower. I wanted to give her time and privacy, but if she wasn't back in five minutes I was going after her. And I was going to tell her the truth. I didn't deserve her forgiveness or grace, but I couldn't leave this place without her knowing the truth. Well, she *knew* the truth, but she deserved to hear it from me.

A soft vibration shook the cabin, and relief flooded me as I heard Gemma's footsteps on the stairs. She was making her way up slowly. I stood up and quickly checked my reflection in the bathroom mirror—my hair was going three directions at once, my lips were chapped, my nose was red, and my eyes were bloodshot; not my best look. I ate a disgusting little pebble of toothpaste right before she knocked on the door just in case there was the slightest chance in hell that she'd let me kiss her again.

I opened the door.

The woman who stood there was not Gemma. She was tall with shocking blonde hair and a grin that looked like it was cut from a terrible Halloween costume and pasted onto her face. Her lips curled in a twist and her stark teeth were lined up like mini blocks of ice.

"Freja?"

53

GEMMA

I was so angry that I had no tears. Rage had cleared out all my senses like a hit of emotional wasabi. If it weren't so awful, I could've laughed. Jonas was pitiful with his obvious feelings and his even more obvious insecurities. Maybe I should've been nicer. More patient. Probably should have. But I was tired of playing nice, taking it slow, being the careful one.

I saw what I wanted. I wanted Jonas Hellgren. The night before, I'd opened my eyes just a little when Jonas was between my legs. I saw it then, on his face. Not just desire and attraction, but affection. He wanted me. All of me. I felt it in his touch. It came through his fingertips and his tongue. And when he'd whispered it to me in the darkness it rang through to my soul like a pure truth. It surprised me, and I stupidly said, "thank you," when I just wanted to say "I love you" right back to his beautiful face. I pretty much bombed any possibility of us, though. Maybe it was for the best.

I made my way to the shed, which was a painful and awkward journey in my bare feet. I stepped on needles, pinecones, and branches that had fallen in the storm. I wouldn't go farther than the shed . . . it was hard to complete a proper storming off when you were half naked and had nowhere to go. I'd find some food, take a shower, and maybe calm down.

I entered my code into the door of the shed and the green light came on. I propped the door open with a jug of water. It was dark in there and the natural light from the open door made it easier to see everything. Just hours before, Jonas and I had been *together* in this shed. And now it felt like we were worlds apart.

I searched the refrigerator to see what was available for breakfast. There were some eggs, but I didn't feel like starting a fire or figuring out the propane stove. Was that smoked salmon?

Everything went sideways. Just like the day before, when Jonas had grabbed me during his "running from the boars" farce, my feet were off the ground, and I was held by some very strong arms. But these were too strong. They were hurting me. It felt like they were crushing my ribs. Why would Jonas hurt me? "Put me down!" I tried to yell, but he'd knocked the wind out of me. A meaty hand covered my mouth and part of my nose, and I couldn't catch my breath. That wasn't Jonas's hand.

Sheer terror sliced through me, and I started to kick and bite. I kicked over an entire shelf of canned goods and drew blood from my attacker's hand.

"Scheisse!" he yelled, dropping me from his grip and dumping me on the ground, face first.

I'd never seen knockout stars before, like all the characters did in cartoons when they've suffered a blow, but I saw stars that time. Gold and white sparks bloomed in front of my eyes as I tried to lift myself from the ground. All my limbs seemed fine, but my face was burning. I gingerly touched my nose—wow that hurt—and my hand came away covered with blood. My beloved t-shirt was ruined for sure. If only I'd been wearing my *True Blood* shirt, I could've had bonus style points for the real blood added to the fabric.

"Why did you do that?" boomed a voice from above me. A voice that sounded familiar. I blinked to try to clear my vision and saw a tall man with broad shoulders and blindingly white teeth looming over me.

"Derek?"

Derek Drach was holding his hand like he'd just suffered a mortal wound. "You bit me!"

"You grabbed me and nearly smothered me to death!" Also, where the hell was Jonas? Could he not hear all of this? And why had I not taken a panic button with me?

"I was trying to help you!"

"Help me with what?" Why did men think that nearly killing me was somehow helping me?

"I was saving you from Hellgren," Derek said in a self-important tone, while crossing his arms and raising his chin. He was like a caricature of a dense Disney hero, which was doubly bad.

I chortled. Which made me sound like a donkey, but screw it. "What the hell are you talking about?"

"Freja said that he'd kidnapped you and was holding you hostage. I'm taking you out of here."

"Freja's a liar, then. No one has kidnapped me or taken me hostage, though you just tried to. I'm fine. Leave me alone." I needed to get back to the cube, but Derek was blocking the door.

"She said you'd say that," he said.

"Like I said, she's a liar." I walked toward him and tried to push by, hoping that my confidence would convince him. But he blocked my path with his stupid barrel chest.

"I heard you screaming at him. You're not going back up there."

"He hurt my feelings, ok? It was a lover's quarrel. Come with me and talk to him. You'll see."

"No way. He has a gun."

"Says who?" This was getting worse by the moment and my nose was still bleeding all over the place.

"Freja said he had guns. I'm not going up there. I only have a knife."

My insides went cold. "Where's Freja?"

"On her way."

I had a feeling that Freja could be even more dangerous than Derek. And if I couldn't let Jonas know that they were down here, I didn't like my chances two against one.

"Derek." I was going to try to make one last appeal to the single brain cell that Derek seemed to possess. "Jonas does not have a gun or a weapon of any kind. He doesn't even have an extra pair of socks. We got stuck out here and I'm very glad you've come to help! But we are not in danger. Not me, not you, not Jonas."

Derek furrowed his brow and chewed on his lower lip. He was thinking it over. That could take a while. Suddenly he grabbed me and threw me over his shoulder like a sack of potatoes. "I don't want to hurt you," he said, "and I'm sorry about your nose. But Freja said you'd say that. I have to get you out of here." He trotted off down the sloppy, muddy trail as I dripped blood down the back of his shirt.

54

JONAS

Freja pushed past me and slammed the door.

"Jonas." She took stock of the cabin. "Nice place. Not as great as it looks from the outside, but whatever."

Freja's hair was matted, and she had dark circles under her eyes. She was dressed all in black, but her boots and pants were splattered in mud. There were fresh cuts on her hands and neck. She was also holding an axe.

"What the hell happened to you?" I asked her. "Are you alright?"

"I've been sleeping in an outhouse during these storms," she growled, "while you've been fucking around in luxury with your little Cinderella." She turned around and walked toward the bed. Something was off. Something was wrong. It was then that I noticed the zip ties poking out of her back pocket. Something was very wrong.

Freja was pulling off the bed covers and throwing them on the floor. Was she looking for Gemma? I reached to the bag near my feet and pulled out a panic button by its lanyard. She spun around and I hid the device behind my back and then slid it into my back pocket before she had a chance to notice.

"Is this your love nest?" Freja asked, her eyes narrowed.

"My what?"

"Did you fuck her?"

"Excuse me?" I said, trying to back up toward the door. I hoped to God that Gemma was safely locked in the shed.

"I wasn't good enough for you, but she has what it takes?"

"Shut your mouth, Freja."

"You're coming with me."

I laughed. "The hell I am. Fuck off.

Freja raised the axe a little and glared at me.

"What, are you going to chop me into pieces? I'd like to see you try." I wasn't quite as secure as I sounded, but I was going with it.

Freja raised the axe a little higher, but then lowered it. "I don't have to. You'll come with me."

"Get out." I opened the door and walked out onto the platform. No sign of Gemma. I heard a beep and then static, as if someone had a two-way radio. I turned to see Freja with a transceiver in her hand. "How's the bitch?" Freja spat into the radio. She let go of her button and I heard the beep of the responder. "Uh," said a male voice. "Not great . . . there's a lot of blood." Who was that? What was he talking about? How could everything shift so fast? Where was Gemma?

"Stay away from me!"

I knew that voice. I'd heard that voice scream the same thing at me just an hour earlier. But this time, it was laced with fear. Gemma's voice was coming through Freja's radio. It was slightly garbled, and loud static crackled in the background, but it was Gemma.

I rushed Freja, knocking her into a wall. "What have you done?" I roared at her. "Where is she?"

Freja looked calmly wired; like she was just about to lose it in an unhinged, bloodbath kind of way. "I'll take you to her," she said. "Just put these on and we'll be on our way." She pulled the zip-ties out of her pocket and held them in the air. They protruded from her fist like a demented bouquet.

"Have you lost your mind?"

"Don't come. Fine with me. I'll let Derek have his way with her. But you don't know where she is. I do. And I won't take you until you put these on."

"Derek?" Derek fucking Drach. If I'd had the power of pyrokinesis, the forest would've been burning.

MY MIND WAS SPINNING. I couldn't think of a way out of this other than to let Freja put the zip-ties on me. I could over-power her if she didn't swing that axe at the last second. But she was right—I didn't know where Gemma was. Every second I hesitated was an extra second that Gemma was in danger. Even if I hit the panic button now, there was no guarantee I'd be able to find Gemma on my own. I had to go with Freja.

"Fine," I said, seething. I stretched out my arms in front of me and offered her my wrists.

"Behind your back, asshole," said Freja. "How stupid do you think I am?"

Just stupid enough to fall for it. I put my hands behind my back and tried to keep my wrists as far apart as possible, but Freja tightened the ties pretty well.

We walked down the stairs and past the shed, where the door stood open. Items had tumbled from the shelves and were scattered on the floor, as if a fight had taken place. Was that blood on the floor? I tried not to panic. If anyone had hurt Gemma, I'd kill them with my bare hands.

It just took a second to realize that *I'd* been the one to hurt her. If I'd just been honest with her, and vulnerable, she'd probably be safely locked in the cabin. I didn't know how I'd forgive myself, but I'd figure that out *after* I found her.

55

GEMMA

Derek hopped and hobbled down the trail with me over his left shoulder and a small backpack over his right. I punched and kicked but he seemed to be made of industrial grade rubber, and every blow bounced right off. Once in a while he'd yell, "Stop hitting me! I'm helping you!"

I recognized the trail as the one Jonas and I had taken from the Common House. Derek was coming to the part of the trail that included a steep hill down to the low water bridge. Surely the water had washed out the bridge. If I could stop Derek, maybe Jonas could catch up and find me. He had to be looking for me now.

Something on Derek beeped and he came to a halt. He tried to reach his pocket but couldn't do it while holding on to me, so he slid me off his shoulder and I landed on a mossy slab of forest floor. "Don't move," he ordered.

I was dizzy from my head hanging down and I put my head between my legs and tried to take a few deep breaths. Though my nose had stopped bleeding, I was covered in blood and must have been a horrifying sight. Derek pulled out a walkie-talkie. A woman's voice sliced through the speaker he held in his hand.

"How's the bitch?" The woman asked.

"Uh . . . not great. There's a lot of blood," replied Derek into his walkie-talkie.

Was I the bitch? How rude. Had to be Freja. Derek's eyes were wide, and his face was pale. I guess I looked about as bad as I felt. He reached his hand out to me. "Stay away from me!" I yelled at him.

"I'm trying to help you!" he huffed. I wondered if he really believed that. "Do you want to walk, or should I carry you?" he asked.

"I can walk. But my ankle is sore, so maybe I could hold on to you?" My ankle was fine, but my new plan was to walk as slowly as possible and to try to play into Derek's "Knight in Shining Armor" complex. Derek held out his arm like he was my father walking me down the aisle.

"We just have to get down the hill," he said. "Freja said to wait for her at the bridge." We started to move at a snail's pace, with me holding on to him and faking a limp. He tried to prop me up and we were definitely the world's worst three-legged race team.

"When did you last see the bridge?"

"Yesterday," he said. "We almost couldn't get across."

"Did you see the Näcken?"

"Is that a snake?"

"It's some kind of creature that can lure you to your death. We need to be careful."

Derek took this at face value and squinted his eyes at the trail ahead of us. We walked for about five minutes until we came to a large rock. I remembered it from my walk in—its surface was dotted with sparkling mica and its edges were rounded, making it an ideal place to sit and rest. I knew the river was just around the next corner and I could hear the water raging. "Can we wait here for Freja?" I asked Derek. "It's safer here than right next to the water. And she'll come down this way, right?" He nodded and pulled out his radio again. He clicked on the button to speak. "We're waiting on a big rock close to the river. Are you headed this direction?"

"On our way. Should be there soon," said Freja over the radio.

She said "our." Did that mean Jonas was with her? And what was her plan when we all met up at the bridge? Drowning me? I wouldn't put it past her. I started to shiver, and a few pains shot through my stomach. Hunger pangs, I hoped. Derek pulled a rain jacket from his backpack and laid it across my bare lap. He offered me a bottle of water and a candy bar. I ate the entire bar in two mouthfuls and drank half the water. "Thanks."

"I don't have anything to clean off the blood," he said.

"He really didn't hurt me, you know," I said.

"But he kidnapped you."

"If he wanted to kidnap me, why would he bring me to a place where everyone is scheduled to arrive within days?"

"Then why . . ." Derek glanced up the hill, maybe anticipating the arrival of Freja.

"Did she pay you?"

"No!"

"Then why are you here?"

Derek's shoulders slumped, as if something weighty he'd been holding at bay had finally landed on him. "I wanted to help her," he said. "And help you?"

"Are you and Freja together?" I asked, trying to keep the conversation going.

"I think so. Some of the time. I want to be together," he said, though his sentence seemed to end with a question mark rather than a period.

"And does she seem . . . stable? To you?"

Derek squatted next to me, his gaze at his feet. "She did. Until she didn't."

"When did she change?"

"Last few weeks.

"Does Freja have any weapons?"

"No," he said. "Unless you count the axe."

56

JONAS

I couldn't hit the panic button until I saw Gemma. I wasn't willing to risk Freja running off, though it sounded like Gemma and Derek might be by the river. Freja and I had started the descent into the river valley and our feet were slipping and sticking in the thick mud.

"Why are you doing this?" I asked Freja.

"You should be thanking me."

"How so?"

"I'm saving you from that wretched American."

"I don't need saving."

"You don't know what you need," she said, swinging the axe as she walked. She'd almost grazed my shin with it a few times, so I was trying to stay a few paces back.

She'd obviously had some kind of break with reality, and out on the trail was not the place I was going to crack the case of what had gone wrong for her. I just needed to try to get everyone out of this situation unharmed.

We rounded a corner and what I saw ripped my heart right out of my chest.

"Oh my god." I was dizzy and almost lost my footing on the sloppy trail. Gemma was sitting on a rock about five meters away. Derek was squatting beside her. Her face, chin, and chest were covered in blood. So many scenarios flooded my brain: Had she been shot? Cut? Punched? It took every ounce of willpower I had to not shove Freja out of the way, run down the hill and rip Derek's jugular out with my teeth. The primary things stopping me were the axe and the fact that Derek was strong and not hindered by zip-ties.

"I'm ok," Gemma called out when she saw me.

"You're not ok!"

"You should see the other owl!"

"Aren't you two cute," snapped Freja. "Jonas, go ahead and tell your princess what you told me back at the cabin."

Gemma couldn't take her eyes off Freja's axe. "Chekov's gun, in the flesh," she joked, but her face betrayed her fear.

"What are you talking about?"

"That you can't wait to get out of here and away from her. That she's a diversion at best."

Gemma's face went white, and Derek tilted his head in confusion.

"I didn't say that."

"Tell her!" Freja swung the axe wildly at a tree, whacking into the trunk with a sickening crack.

"I thought you said that Hellgren was hurting her," Derek said glumly.

"Oh, he's hurt her," said Freja. "Has he done anything to hurt you, Princess?" Freja asked Gemma. Gemma opened her mouth to speak but paused before any words came out. "Thought so," said Freja. "You're a real heartbreaker, aren't you Hellgren."

Derek's face was crumpling, and I couldn't tell if it was from anger or despair. I took a step back, just in case.

Freja managed to get the axe unstuck from the tree and she casually swung it as she took a few steps toward Gemma. Derek stood up and put himself between the two women.

"Let me guess," said Freja. "He made you feel beautiful. He told you some sad stories. Gave you some great orgasms. But won't commit to anything. Sound about right?"

Gemma, probably not wanting to be at eye level with the axe hanging from Freja's hand, stood up. Aside from her face, she appeared uninjured. She put her hands on her hips. *Don't say anything, Gemma,* I willed her with my mind. *Don't poke the bear.*

"What's with the axe?" Gemma asked Freja.

Freja looked at the tool in her hand like she was seeing it for the first time. "There were some trees down on the trails. Had this just in case."

"Can you put it down?" Gemma asked.

Freja considered the request, seeming almost normal for a second, at least as normal as Freja ever did. But then a shadow crossed her face, and her wild eyes were back. "I don't take orders from American sluts," said Freja. Then she spat at Gemma's feet.

Oh, Christ almighty. Judging by the expression on Gemma's face, Freja had just activated the "fight" in Gemma's "fight or flight" response. Gemma was smiling, and the blood that covered her face gave the whole scene a sinister vibe.

"Is that so?" Gemma said, taking a step toward Freja. Derek was frozen, and I was still standing on the hill feeling neutered and powerless.

There was a face-off as Freja, Derek, and Gemma stood in a

tense triangle. Suddenly Gemma yelled, "Watch out!" and pointed in my direction. Freja and Derek whipped their heads around, probably assuming I was coming at them. Nope. I was still standing stupidly on the hill. Gemma took advantage of the distraction and grabbed the axe from Freja. In some kind of superhero move honed in the odd taverns of America, Gemma threw the axe into the woods like Thor throwing Mjolnir. It did not return to her, however, but it did impressively wedge itself in the slim trunk of a birch tree.

Freja took a moment to process her empty hand and the sight of the axe now stuck in a tree and out of reach. Derek's shoulders relaxed and he took a huge breath and released it loudly.

It was now or never. "Gemma, take a chance on me?"

"What?"

"Take a chance on me." I saw the light of recognition in her eyes. She covered her ears and I held down the button of the panic button in my back pocket.

A second passed. And then another. Did it not work? *Shit, shit, shit.*

Then it worked. Never had I loved ABBA so much. The song screamed out through the trees, across the valley, and over the river. Gemma had her ears covered, but my tied hands wouldn't let me cover mine. The intense volume of the alarm pounded my eardrums. Derek jumped, and Freja dove into the bushes, screaming and smashing her palms against her ears.

I tried to get to Gemma but slid on the mud, lost my balance, and face planted into a thick puddle. I pulled myself up but couldn't wipe my eyes. I couldn't see much through the slop stuck to my face, but I could make out Derek running my way with something in his hand—a knife? Was this how I was going to go out? Stabbed by a B-grade German actor right in front of the woman I loved?

Derek grabbed my arms. I heard Freja yelling again, but she sounded closer. I realized that Derek was sawing at my ties, trying to free me. The song had moved into the second verse. We were the stars of a very demented musical. My hands were suddenly free, and my arms slumped in relief. My shoulders and hands were numb, and I felt useless and lame while I waited for the blood to return to my limbs. I was able to wipe the goop from my eyes just in time to see Freja running toward Gemma at full speed.

57

GEMMA

The volume of the emergency alert made my whole body throb. I couldn't see any siren horns, but it sounded like we were surrounded by them. Everything seemed to be happening in slow motion. Jonas was on the ground, covered in mud, but in a plot twist, Derek had turned into a *good* Disney prince and freed Jonas's hands.

I had a two-second moment of relief until I saw that Freja was running at me.

Instinct forced me to jump and run, and I sprinted down the hill as fast as my bare feet would allow. Wearing no pants in the woods was a real liability. Everything was sharp, scratchy, and stabbing, and by the time I'd run down two switchbacks, my legs resembled a cat's scratching post.

Freja was chasing me, but she tripped and tumbled over some roots and hit the ground. She rolled and spun, a jumble of long limbs and blonde hair; she was a Swedish tumbleweed. Then she was back on her feet and moving forward again.

Jonas was behind Freja, and Derek was behind Jonas. The four of us were running toward a raging river while ABBA rang out all around us. Why *I* was the carrot in this bunny race was beyond me. I ran down the final switchback, somehow still on my feet. My bare toes were able to grip the muddy ground while the others, wearing thick shoes, were falling, getting up, and falling again. It was like a mashup of *The Three Stooges* and *The Shining*.

I'd reached the bridge, which was barely visible. The river was swollen, and the water was violently rushing over the walkway planks of the bridge. I had to stop. I turned around. Freja was about six feet from me, looking like a rabid hyena ready to pounce.

Freja had her hands out as if she wanted to tackle me—don't ask me why—but was calculating her move. One wrong push and we'd both go into the water. Jonas was trying to get to Freja to pull her back, but the same peril threatened him. If he pushed Freja, she'd push me, and all three of us would be the Näcken's next conquest. Derek, using his giant arms for good instead of evil, was holding Jonas back, maybe saving us all.

Just beyond my motley crew of followers, something caught my eye. As new rays of sunshine began to pierce through the gloom of the forest and warm the air, three angels slowly rose from the mist among the trees. They were behind Derek, Jonas, and Freja. One to my left, one straight ahead of me, and one to my right. I was the only one facing their direction, and the only one to see them rise from the ground as if they were growing straight from the earth itself. They were blonde angels. With crossbows?

As the forest creatures came into focus, I realized they weren't tree nymphs or a host of angels; they were the Sandström family. My heart thrummed at the idea of rescue. Bjorn was to my left, quickly moving in with a crossbow pointed at

Derek. Hugo was in the center, also armed with a bow. And Katja, on my right and weaponless, was crouching and moving through the brush, closing in on the scene. They were a wilderness SWAT team. I tried to keep my face neutral to not give away what I was seeing. The alarm and the river were so loud that no one else could hear them approaching.

In a choreographed formation, more beautiful than any dance I'd ever seen, the three Sandströms began to move. They progressed swiftly and gracefully, each of them weaving between tree trunks and sidestepping branches with ease. The men had lowered their weapons but kept their gazes sharp as they drew closer. Then they paused, and made eye contact with each other, and I saw Katja give the slightest nod. Like a three-headed mythical creature, they moved as one, suddenly swirling and swooping and then they were upon us.

Bjorn had Derek incapacitated in a headlock, Hugo had Freja on her belly on the ground, and once again, someone had grabbed me, but this time it was a woman's arms that pulled me up into the air. Katja swept me off my feet and ran up the trail with me with such ease you'd have thought she was carrying a kitten and not a full-grown woman. She left Jonas in her dust and, only because I knew he was safe, I didn't completely mind. Let him worry about me a little longer. It served him right.

Katja reached the spot where I'd been sitting earlier, and she sat me gently on the cool surface of the rock. She produced a shiny silver space blanket from a pocket in her vest and had it wrapped around me in a second. She entered a code on a hand-held remote-control device and the alarm stopped. Sweet silence filled the air.

She turned on her own walkie-talkie and barked instructions into the transceiver. Kneeling in front of me to study my face, she put her thumbs on my nose and pressed gently. She took my pulse and gave me a small bottle of water. Did she have some kind of magic vest related to Mary Poppins's bag?

"We have more medical supplies at the house. I'll take you there on my ATV. Do you have any pain anywhere?"

I opened my mouth to speak but had trouble finding words.

"Have you hit your head?" The magic vest produced a pen light. "Follow the light with your eyes." I did as she said, and my words came back to me.

"My nose hurts. And my legs and feet." I opened the blanket to inspect my lower limbs. They were scraped and a little bloody, but nothing catastrophic. "But otherwise, I think I'm ok."

Jonas came flying around the bend in the trail, muddy and frantic, sporting an intense Arnold Schwarzenegger *Predator* vibe. Katja held out her arm and ordered, "Halt!" Jonas obeyed and came to a sliding stop. He was panting and appeared to be on the edge of panic. "She's ok," Katja said. "Sit." She pointed at a spot on the rock next to me. Jonas sat and Katja pulled out another foil blanket.

"She has a magic vest," I whispered to Jonas.

He wiped at his face with a shiny silver wing of his blanket. It only resulted in him smearing mud around. "You're ok," he said.

"I'm ok."

Katja handed each of us a small disposable towelette. I used mine to wipe off some blood, and Jonas rubbed his eyes, removing some of the mud caked in his lashes and eyebrows.

"I'm so sorry," Jonas began, but I interrupted him.

"I know. I know you are. Let's just get out of here."

"I'm not letting you go," he said.

Katja put her hands on her hips and stared down at Jonas with a stern expression. Jonas glanced up at her and tried again.

"I mean, what I should've said before and that I need to say now, is that I want to be with you. I don't know how it will all work, but I'm not letting you go."

"What about the *logistics*?" I asked, bumping his shoulder with mine. "I hear they could be tricky."

"I'm such an asshole. I'm so sorry."

Katja nodded as if she approved of that admission. "I need to get Gemma to the house," she said. "Jonas, Hugo will bring you back to the house once Freja and the German are handed over to authorities. Go back to him and my father."

"I can carry Gemma," he said.

"*I* can carry her," replied Katja, "if she needs that. Can you walk, Gemma?"

"How far?"

"Just up the hill. Our ATVs are there."

I stood up to test my feet, but my head felt spacy, and my knees started to buckle. Jonas and Katja both lunged for me, catching me before I fell.

Jonas pulled me up into his arms. "*I'll* take her to the vehicle, and *you* take her from there."

In an adorable showdown of Swedish wills, Katja and Jonas scowled at each other for a few seconds. "Fine," said Katja, spinning on her feet and beginning the march up the hill.

"Thank god," Jonas said, close to my ear. "She was definitely considering kicking my ass."

58

GEMMA

Katja drove slowly along the access road as the vehicle bumped over gravel, dirt, and mud. I had my own seat behind her and had a harness across my chest and a heavy helmet over my head and face. She had told me to hold on to the handles on either side of my seat. "No letting go. If you need me to stop, pinch my arm."

She'd said that the ride would take about fifteen minutes which meant that I was moments away from food, water, and shelter. My adrenaline had fizzled out, so my body felt liquid and leaded, ready to collapse. Katja extended her arm and pointed her finger. I saw a house. A real, regular, normal, spectacularly ordinary home. Complete with a front porch where a tall silver-haired woman stood in blue jeans and a patterned wool sweater. Her arms were crossed, and she was leaning forward like her body was anticipating our arrival.

Katja stopped and turned off the engine. I pulled my helmet off, hoping I hadn't gotten any blood on the inside padding. "Who's that?" I asked her. Katja hopped off the vehicle in a fluid motion and held out her hands for me to hold as I slid off the seat.

"That's Agnes. My mother."

Her mother. Her mother who was waiting for her daughter, son, and husband to return home. A woman whose entire family had raced into unknown peril. A mother whose face was soft and lined and shining with relief to see Katja crossing the path and walking to the porch. I stopped. I didn't know if I could go another step. Agnes's face flushed with worry, and she pointed to me, alerting Katja, who doubled back and held my arm. "You alright?" she asked me.

I was, and I wasn't. I was mixed up, shaken about, and inside out. "Can I hug your mom?" I asked her in the voice of a lost child. Katja raised her eyebrows and looked at her mother, trying to figure out what ailed me and why I'd stopped so suddenly. Probably realizing this was an emotional wound rather than physical, she put her arm around me.

"Of course."

My feet started working again and I hobbled quickly in the direction of Agnes.

"Hon vill krama dig!" Katja called out to her mother, probably warning her that the American lady was coming in for a landing. Agnes stepped forward and held out her arms and a gentle smile slid onto her face like a sunrise.

I picked up my speed and Katja had to jog to keep up with me. I either looked like a toddler taking manic first steps and trying to cross from one parent to the other without smashing my head on the coffee table, or like a last finisher in an Ironman, straggling across the finish line where I was sure to collapse in a frazzled heap.

Agnes, arms still outstretched, stepped off the porch. I

made it to her and Katja let go of me, which allowed me to fall into Agnes's waiting arms. I put my head on Agnes's chest and wrapped my arms around her back, squeezing her into a tight hug. I started to cry. To bawl. My shoulders shook with sobs as I pressed into the softness of her sweater and her scent of cinnamon, vanilla, and woodsmoke.

Agnes murmured gentle words, all in Swedish, so I had no idea what she was saying, but that didn't matter. They were a mother's words, which meant I was safe.

59

———

JONAS

It had been a long afternoon. After sending Gemma off with Katja, I reunited with Bjorn and Hugo who were escorting Derek and Freja up the hill. Derek was beside himself, chattering on in German while Bjorn stoically ignored him. Freja was eerily calm and silent. She trudged up the hill with a steady robotic gait, her eyes fixed on an invisible spot in the distance.

We made it to a gravel road and waited for the eventual arrival of two police officers. After a round of questioning with me serving as Derek's translator, custody of Freja and Derek was transferred to the police and the Sandströms and I began our journey to the family house. I was glad for their help, and I was relieved that Gemma was safe, but I wasn't looking forward to an evening full of more people. I craved the solitude of forest cabins where Gemma and I could sleep for days, undisturbed.

We pulled up to the house, which appeared modest and warm. It was a two-story home with brick-red wooden siding and white window frames that encased the wavy bright panes of old glass. A welcoming porch ran along the front of the house, and the golden blonde wood of the door gleamed in the low light of the late day sun.

I was covered in dry mud and there was no way I could enter the house without dumping dirt everywhere. Hugo must've read my mind.

"There's a gardener's hut along the back where you can shower and change. We've had all your belongings gathered from the cabins and those are in the main house, but Ms. Lane chose some clothing for you. Those items are in the hut along with towels and soap. Just come up to the house when you're finished."

An older woman came out to the porch and raised a hand in greeting. She welcomed Hugo with a hug and Bjorn with a kiss on the cheek. "There's food waiting for you when you're ready," she called to me. I waved back to indicate understanding and as I walked to the hut, I felt a curious warmth rolling gently in my stomach. It may have been . . . gladness? It was a feeling with which I used to be intimately acquainted, but we'd been estranged for years. Perhaps this was a reunion.

The shower was a warm and watery christening. I let the spray rain down on me until my skin was pink and splotchy and the last traces of mud swirled down the drain. I toweled off my hair and made use of the light robe hanging by the shower door. My pile of clothes was neatly folded and waiting on a bench. I saw underwear, socks, jeans, a white t-shirt, a sweater jacket, and sneakers. I recognized everything but the shirt—I didn't pack anything like that. I got my pants and socks on and unfolded the shirt. *That little shit.* This was no plain t-shirt. It was an oversized Air Supply concert shirt, probably from 1984. It featured an awkward photo of the duo, decked out in their eighties garb, singing passionately into their microphones. The sweater she'd chosen for me was an open one, with no zipper or buttons. I had no choice.

I STOOD at the front door of the house. My pulse was jumping along at a brisk pace and my palm left a damp imprint on the brass handle. Five second inhale. Five second exhale. I arranged my face into what felt like a pleasant expression and opened the door. The wood floor of the foyer was rich and warm, and I pulled off my shoes and placed them on the shelf by the door. Voices came from my left along with the sounds of dining: spoons clanking against bowls, chair legs scraping on floorboards, and the kind of laughter sparked by inside jokes and family teasing.

"Jonas!" called Hugo warmly. He had a beer bottle in one hand, and he put his free arm around me as he walked me into the dining room. The whole family was around the table, but no Gemma. There were two empty chairs. The matriarch noticed my concern.

"She has already eaten and she's bathing now. Come sit and you can see her when she's finished."

A kettle of soup sat on the table aside a round loaf of bread that had been torn in half. There was a beautiful green salad along with a plate of sliced fish and a bowl of olives. The aroma of the meal awakened my hunger, but I didn't know if I could eat until I saw Gemma with my own eyes.

Katja ripped off a hunk of bread and picked up a few cheese slices. She reached out and offered me the food. "Take this and go check on her. Then come back and eat. Room's at the top of the stairs, on your right."

"Thank you," I said as I stuffed the bread in my mouth and took the stairs two at a time.

I opened the door to the bedroom and found the room simple and inviting. The walls, bed, and rugs were all the shade of warm cream, and a light green wooden rocking chair sat in the corner. I heard the movement of water from the adjoining bathroom. The door was ajar, but I did not enter. "Gemma?"

"I'm in here. Come in."

She was submerged in a white soaking tub grounded by four ornate silver feet. Bubbles covered the surface of the water so only her head and shoulders were visible.

"That looks nice," I said, pulling over a stool to the side of the tub. I found myself unable to make eye contact with her. How, after all that had happened, could I feel shy around this woman?

"I had to shower first. Otherwise, this bathwater would've turned to sludge."

I kept my eyes pointed at my feet and concentrated on the grey canvas and white laces of my shoes.

"Jonas, look at me."

I did as she asked. Her nose was a little swollen and she had faint half-moon bruises under each eye, but she was as beautiful as ever. Her hair was dark and damp and the ends of her curls floated lazily in the bubbles.

"Nice shirt, by the way," she said. I laughed but it came out sounding like a grunt I'd make after a sudden gas pain. "What's wrong?" she asked, extending a bubbly arm, and poking my shoulder with one dripping finger.

I was looming there like a petulant, lovesick teenager. I recognized the mood because I'd been wearing it like a hair shirt for eight years. Time to wake up, grow up, man up.

Gemma was waiting with clear eyes. She was present and close, but she wasn't going to do this for me. I scoured my mind for the right conversational entry ramp. Tearful apology? Beg for forgiveness? Pledge eternal loyalty? All valid options. I decided to go with the cold hard truth.

"So," I started, my voice wobbling. Since when did my voice ever fail me? This was new.

"So," she echoed.

"Here's where I stand." I cleared my throat. Gemma waited. "I'm an insecure, imperfect man." Gemma's eyes held a sparkle of withheld laughter. "It has been correctly established that I'm a coward and a liar. But no more!" I said, with a rowdy punching gesture of my elbow and fist. Gemma flicked a bubble at me, and it landed on the tip of my nose. I wiped it away.

"Gemma Lane, I'm in love with you. You're too good for me. But if you'll have me, I'd like to ask you to be my—" I searched for the word, "—companion. Today, tomorrow, and all the tomorrows you can stand." I glanced at her face. A soft smile danced on her lips and latent tears made her eyes glisten. "And I'm so desperately sorry . . ." I began, but Gemma interrupted me with a bubbly kiss.

"I know you're sorry," she said. "And so am I. Let's mark this moment as the beginning of our next chapter, and we can turn the page on what happened before."

"I'd like that," I said as my stomach contributed to the conversation with an aggressive rumbling growl.

"You should get some food. I'll get dressed and meet you down there."

"I might prefer you undressed," I said, testing the waters for flirtation.

"That's later tonight," she said, before leaning back in the bath and closing her eyes.

The soapy froth in the tub was fading away and I could see the outline of Gemma's curves coming into focus. Perhaps the bubbles had transferred over to my chest, as a light, airy, popping sensation was brewing. The feeling had the distinct fingerprint of that elusive white whale of emotions—hope.

60

GEMMA

I slowly descended the stairs, savoring the feeling of safety and satisfaction that came after a nice meal, a hot bath, and after narrowly escaping death and dismemberment. I heard voices coming from the living room at the back of the house. The conversation was all in Swedish and I let the jumpy cadence of the words wash over me.

When I entered the room, the conversation stopped, and all eyes turned to me. Jonas and Katja were sitting in wooden chairs on either side of the fireplace where a small fire crackled and glowed. They both hopped up when I entered the room; maybe there would be another standoff over who got to carry me! Bjorn was stretched out on a couch and Hugo sat cross-legged on the floor, sipping something out of a mug. Agnes was nestled into one side of a loveseat and smiled when she saw me.

"I thought I'd come and say hello before I turn in for the night," I said. Katja beat Jonas to the punch in translating my words for Bjorn, Hugo, and Agnes, who were not fluent in English. I sat next to Agnes, who seemed delighted and put her arm around me. Katja brought me some tea and Jonas collected some cookies from the kitchen to offer as a before-bed snack. The conversation moved between Swedish and English, and I grew drowsy as the events of the day settled into my bones. I needed to go to bed before I fell asleep on Agnes's shoulder, which wasn't entirely objectionable.

I took advantage of the time to watch Jonas. Swedish Jonas. His stubble was just about to cross the finish line into beard territory. It was dark under his lip and across his jaw but had a nice dusting of silver at his chin. A few times, a smile lingered on his face and once, in reaction to something Bjorn had said, he threw back his head and laughed. It was an open, free laugh, the sound reminding me of a bubbling brook rushing over stones—liquid, vibrant, and beautiful. He'd changed out of the cardigan jacket I left out for him, but he looked so charming walking into the bathroom in that Air Supply shirt that I didn't regret my wardrobe decisions. He'd opted for a black turtleneck sweater that no American man would've been able to pull off, but on *him*, it was so sexy that I found myself imagining ripping it off. Among other things. Jonas was textbook gorgeous, but now that I knew him, he truly felt like the Sexiest Man Alive.

I made the slightest move to stand, and Jonas was on his feet and crossing the room to me. He held out his elbow so I could hook my arm into his.

"I think we're going to retire for the evening," he said, like he was a Count, and I was his Countess.

"Could you translate for me?" I asked him. He nodded and squeezed my arm.

"I want to thank all of you. For everything," I started. "This last week has changed my life, and it would never have happened if it weren't for your beautiful resort, or for your bravery and generosity." I stopped to give Jonas a moment to relay my speech in Swedish. "Part of my heart will live on this land forever, and with you. Thank you so much." Jonas completed my message and the Sandströms all stood. I felt a little embarrassed because it sounded like I was giving an acceptance speech—I should've started with, 'I'd like to thank the Academy."

Maybe Jonas's translation was better than the original; they lined up to hug me goodnight and my eyes grew hot with tears. Despite the trouble I'd caused, they had rescued me, fed me, bathed me, and were sending me off to bed with affection. I felt alive and of the world in a way that I had not felt in a long, long time.

JONAS TUTTED like a worried nanny as he attempted to tuck me into bed. "Will that blanket be enough? Do you have water? Can I get you anything out of your bag?"

"Jonas," I said. "I don't need anything else. Except you. Get in here."

He straightened the covers and turned out the light. "I'm going to open the curtains. You can see the moon from this window, and I think it might be full tonight."

"Jonas."

"I might go down and see about a nightcap." He was standing by the side of the bed, holding my hand. He wasn't making eye contact with me. "You need to get some sleep and I'm feeling restless. I don't want to keep you awake."

"A nightcap?"

He patted my hand, leaned in to kiss my forehead, and then headed toward the door. "I'll be back up in a bit. Get some sleep."

"Jonas Alexander Hellgren," I said as sternly as I could manage. He stopped walking but didn't turn around. "Take off your clothes and get into this bed. Right. Now."

Jonas turned so he was facing me. He crossed his arms in front of his body, grabbed the hem of his sweater, and lifted it over his head. The sight of his bare chest, even though the room was dark and he was more shadow than light, sent a thrill through my body. He used his heel to slide off one shoe, then the other. Socks and pants came off next. He stood by the bed in only his underwear.

"Go ahead and take those off too," I told him. "It'll save us a step later."

"I want you to be able to sleep," he said, his fingers resting on the waistband. "And I don't want to make it about me, and I really fucked up back at the cube—"

"We're moving forward," I said, interrupting him. "That was our deal. Now get in here."

He tugged a little on his underwear but then he stopped. "You're not naked under there. You have a nightgown on!"

"Then do something about it."

He paused again, and then jumped out of his underwear and leapt into bed like a little boy pretending that the floor had suddenly turned to lava. He swept the blankets up over his body and gave a full-body shiver next to me in the bed. "I'm here."

61

GEMMA

We were facing each other with Jonas on his right side and I on my left. He reached his arm across me and pressed his hand onto the small of my back in a way that felt possessive and sexy as hell. "Are you sure you want me here?" he said. "I can't trust myself to just fall asleep. I'm—distracted—by you."

"I'm not quite ready for sleep either," I said, running my hand through his hair and over his scalp. He closed his eyes and let out a satisfied murmur.

"You're sure? I can try to—" he said, his eyes still closed. With our bodies so close, I could feel his erection growing and pushing into my belly.

"How about we don't talk for a few minutes."

My hand was still on his head, and I slid it down his jaw. I kissed him. Once. Twice. Then a third time. Short, soft kisses on his lips. He received them but did not push into me. He was letting me take the lead. I moved in for another kiss, this time opening my mouth, hoping to find his tongue. He opened to meet me, and we slowly tasted each other. Jonas moaned as I kissed him, and his vibrations warmed my lips.

I pushed my pelvis into him which brought out another noise in Jonas. I wanted him. I didn't want just a kiss or a touch or an orgasm. I wanted Jonas Hellgren. I wanted him to be part of my body, part of my heart, part of my life. And at that moment I wanted him inside me like I'd never wanted anything else, ever before.

I kissed him more roughly and bit his lower lip. Jonas growled. I rolled onto my back and pulled Jonas on top of me, his weight resting on his forearms. He was breathing heavily, and he pulsed his pelvis against me as if trying to hold back animal instincts.

"Is this ok? You're sure?"

Instead of answering, I reached my hand between his legs and swirled my fingertips across his thigh, over his balls, up his shaft, around the head, and back down where I grasped the hot width of him in my fist and gently squeezed.

Jonas's breath hitched. "Christ. Ok, you're sure," he said.

I opened my legs wider and wrapped them around his waist. I lifted my face to meet his and kissed him again.

"I need to get a condom," he said against my lips, the words muffled.

"They're in my bag. In the bathroom." Jonas started to lift off me. "But my period is due to start any day. Any minute really. So, if you wanted to just—" I had no idea how he would take that suggestion, but I was desperate to feel the pure heat of his bare skin inside me.

Jonas was still, and then he moved closer to me again. "Gemma," he said, and my name in his throat, his mouth, spoken with the air from his lungs, hit me like an angelic note from Gabriel's trumpet.

He kissed me firmly with hard lips and a bossy tongue, letting me know that he was taking over. He moved his hand to my pussy and slid one finger along my folds, gently opening me as he moved down. He swirled his fingertip at my opening and then moved it softly back up to my clit.

I grabbed at his ass and tried to press him into me. "I want you inside me."

"Not yet." He rested his lips on my neck, kissed my collar bone, and then with his tongue he left a wet trail down my chest, across each nipple, down past my belly button, finally landing between my legs. He nibbled at me with his lips and every few seconds he took a swipe with his tongue, which made me quiver and open. He pushed my legs wide with his elbows and with the fingers of both hands he spread my skin and left me completely vulnerable to the whims of his mouth.

Jonas flicked his tongue at my opening before pushing in once, twice, and another time. I lifted toward him as he fucked me with his mouth, his hands still holding me open. He placed his forefingers on either side of my clit and slid them up and down as his tongue danced across the tip. Pressure built and a slick flood of desire melted out of me. I covered my face and whimpered as I held on to the last seconds of control.

Jonas suddenly stopped and pulled completely away from me. I cried out in protest as he kneeled over my legs and took in the sight. "God. You're beautiful." He touched me again, with one finger, and glided it easily into me. "Now we're ready."

In a flash of movement, he was back on top of me, his face at mine. He pinned my legs open with his and closed his mouth over my lips. I felt his tip play at my entrance for a second, and then Jonas slid inside me. He felt perfect. He thrust in, pulled back, pushed in again, all while keeping his mouth on mine. Our breath became one, just the same as our bodies, and it felt like a communion of hearts.

He lifted slightly and wiggled a hand between us and began to stroke me again. I was already so close, and that put me over the edge. I grabbed his hair and pulled his face down to my neck. He moved faster and harder with his hand and his cock and I lost my place in the space time continuum. As I came, my pussy gripped him in a tight spasm. He leaned back and brought my body up to his until he was kneeling, and I was straddling his lap. He thrusted wildly and I held on and rode the waves of his passion as he climaxed inside me, filling me, filling me, filling me.

I rested my head on his shoulder and kissed his neck as we both tried to catch our breath. Sweat lubricated the skin of our chests and thighs. Everything between us was slippery, hot, and easy.

"That was nice," Jonas said, when he found his voice.

I laughed, my stomach moving against his. "I was going for better than nice."

"Sorry," he said. "English isn't my native language."

"May I kiss you?" I asked.

"I don't know. That's pretty intimate."

I lightly bit the stubbled skin on his jaw and then kissed him. Everything fit. Everything felt perfect and lovely and warm. He felt like home.

"I FEEL like we should clean up a little," he said.

"How do we get off the bed without leaving—" I tried to

figure out how to get out of the position gracefully. I was still on his lap. One wrong move, and we'd need to change the sheets.

"I've got this." Jonas lifted me up as he scooted over toward the side of the bed on his knees. Then he leaned back and unfolded his legs as he held on to me.

"A little more practice and we'll be ready for Cirque du Soleil." I giggled as he awkwardly maneuvered us to the edge of the mattress.

"Got it!" He slid me off his lap and my feet landed gently on the floor. I ran to the bathroom and sat down on the toilet as Jonas stepped in behind me and started the water for the shower.

It was in that ordinary moment that I realized we might really have a chance. A chance to be friends, lovers, companions, partners. A chance to try this life thing together.

Jonas had the water temperature where he wanted it. He held the shower door open for me like a naked butler. "You even look cute on the toilet."

"I'll put that on my business card."

CLEAN, dry, and mess free, we were settled back in bed. We were quiet as we let the bed hold us up and the blankets cover us in soft warmth. Jonas was right—the moon was full, and it sent a cold splash of light across the room. There were so many stars and I felt like the light of each one of them was a kiss from the universe, sprinkling us with love.

"You awake?" asked Jonas. We were both on our backs and holding hands, our fingers interlaced.

"I am."

"You can hear me?"

"Yes," I laughed. "I can hear you."

"Loud and clear?"

"10-4, good buddy."

"I love you, Gemma," said Jonas. His words hung in the air. I pictured them dancing in the darkness of the room, mingling with the light of the moon and the stars. He squeezed my hand. "Just wanted to make sure you heard me this time."

"I hear you," I said, rolling over to snuggle up to his side. "And I love you right back."

62

———

JONAS

When I woke up, Gemma was beside me, lost in sleep. Her hair was scattered across the pillow and the auburn curls against the white linen backdrop were like a piece of modern art. I had slept. All night. No dreams, no nightmares, no restless waking. Just a heavy glorious sleep. I felt so intensely awake yet so fully peaceful that I lay still and lingered in the paradox of it all.

Smells of food cooking wafted up the stairs from the kitchen. Was there any greater comfort, knowing that a meal was being prepared for you while you luxuriated in a comfortable bed? I heard voices, mostly familiar now, but it seemed like more than just the family. I'd wait in bed until Gemma woke up, no matter if she slept another hour or another day.

"Rava?" Gemma shot into a sitting position and blinked at the morning light. So much for another hour. "Do you hear that?" she asked me.

"Hear what?"

"Voices."

"Yes, I hear them." I patted at her hair which was tangled and beyond curly, probably from the late-night shower.

She flopped out of bed and stood swaying and naked in the bright light of the window.

"Where are you going?"

"I swear I heard Rava. Come with me." Gemma dug through her bag, searching for clothes.

"Are you sure you don't want to come back to bed?" I wasn't sure she even heard me. She was on a mission. I got out of bed, brushed my teeth, and then tossed on some clothes while Gemma took her turn in the bathroom.

A minute later, Gemma rushed through the bathroom door. "Let's go!" This was too much energy for the morning. She clomped down the stairs and disappeared from my view. I heard a delighted yelp and came down to find Gemma hugging a woman with tight black curls, jeans, and a white sweater. Rava, I assumed. She wasn't the only *Profile* employee crowding into the Sandström kitchen that morning.

"Carl," I said, as Carl Berg moved toward me to shake my hand.

"Very happy to see you safe and sound," said Carl as he vigorously pumped my hand and patted me on the shoulder. Bouncing behind him, waiting to get a hug from Gemma, was Kristina. When Gemma and Rava stepped back from each other, Kristina grabbed Gemma.

"Oh my god, I'm so glad to see you! We couldn't find you and then we thought you were ok, but then you weren't ok and OH MY GOD!" screeched Kristina.

Agnes was at the stove and Hugo was getting plates out of the cupboard.

"I was prepared to search the wilderness for you," said Rava, her voice husky and strong. "But thank god it didn't come to that." She hugged Gemma again. "Don't do that to me ever again." Rava was giving me the side eye and I could see the moment when Gemma realized that Rava had never met me, and most certainly didn't know that Gemma and I were on … friendly terms, so to speak.

"Rava, this is Jonas Hellgren," said Gemma, putting a hand on my arm while she made the introduction. Rava raised an eyebrow when she saw Gemma's hand but was professional and polite when she greeted me.

"It's nice to meet you," she said.

"Likewise."

Gemma hovered for a moment, obviously contemplating which way to go with it. A look of resolve crossed her face. She stepped in front of me, put her hands on my face, and kissed me with her sweet, perfect lips. She lingered for a few seconds, probably for show, but I wasn't going to argue with it. "Could you get us some coffee?" she asked me.

"My pleasure," I replied, squeezing her shoulder before I walked away to find some mugs. Rava and Kristina's mouths were open and their eyes wide. Carl, however, was unfazed. He had a smug, fatherly smile on his face and as I passed, he nodded and raised his coffee cup, as if offering a congratulatory toast.

PEOPLE MOVED in and out of the kitchen and dining room, collecting servings of boiled eggs, cinnamon buns, muesli, and sandwiches. After we ate, Carl and I relocated to the front porch with our coffees.

"What's next?" I asked him. "Are the roads clear for travel?"

"They're pretty good, though a few back roads are still washed out. But we'll get you out of here today."

"I have mixed feelings about leaving," I said.

"I thought you might." Carl took a sip of his coffee as steam rose from his mug and cut into the chill of the morning air. "If it works for you and Ms. Lane, we've reserved a suite for both of you at Ett Hem in Stockholm."

"A suite to share?"

"That option is available if you'd both like to do that. Rava will be staying in Sweden for several more days, but we've booked her a separate room."

"What's Ett Hem?" I heard Gemma ask from behind me.

Carl stepped aside to make room for Gemma on the porch. "It's a lovely hotel. And we thought you and Jonas might want to finish the interview without some of the extra stress of—"

"Running for our lives?" she asked.

"Exactly."

"That sounds good to me!" she said brightly. "Speaking of, does anyone have an update on Freja and Derek?"

"Derek has been released," said Carl, "and Freja has been admitted into a facility not far from here. I assume she will be there for at least a few weeks. It's suspected that she's had some personal trouble lately, but that also she may have been having an adverse reaction to a prescription medication."

"That's awful," said Gemma, sounding legitimately concerned.

"It is," said Carl. "I just hope she's able to recover. She's always been eccentric but not dangerous. Rest assured that we've assigned a different photographer to the piece."

The sound of tires on gravel crackled in the distance. An

SUV appeared as it turned into the driveway leading up to the house. "Who's this?" I asked.

Carl checked his watch. "That should be your driver."

The car stopped and the gravel dust settled to the ground. After about twenty seconds the driver's side door opened and out stepped Alfred.

"Alfred!" cried Gemma as she ran up to the man and collected him into a hug. His cheeks turned red, and he patted at her back. I had mixed feelings about that guy. The passenger side door opened, and a woman got out. She was about 60, and very short. She stood next to Alfred, and he put his arm around her.

"I'm Sofia," she said in accented English, putting a hand out to Gemma. "Alfred is my husband. And he's very, very sorry." Alfred looked like he'd gladly be swallowed by a sinkhole if the opportunity arose. Sofia elbowed Alfred in the ribs.

"I'm very, very sorry," he said.

Gemma laughed in a big, loud, American way, with her mouth open and eyes shining. She hugged Sofia and then hugged Alfred again. "I'm grateful to Alfred for getting us safely to this resort," Gemma said. "My life has changed in a thousand ways, and none of it would've been possible without him." She turned toward me. "Isn't that right, Jonas?"

"Right indeed." I'd decided to go with the flow.

OVER THE NEXT HOUR, our belongings were loaded into the car, and we said our goodbyes to the Sandström family. Gemma had collected email addresses and phone numbers, along with a mailing address for Agnes. "It will be good practice as I learn Swedish," Gemma told her. Katja hugged Gemma and shook my hand, though still looked at me a little suspiciously as if this whole week had been my plan to begin with.

Rava, Carl, and Kristina left in their own car with promises to reunite at the hotel later that evening. Alfred and Sofia got back into the SUV and waited patiently while Gemma and I said our final goodbyes.

"I'm not sure I want to leave," she said. "It feels like we're leaving a whole world behind."

"We can always come back," I told her, pulling her into an embrace. "But let's finish this interview. With electricity and indoor plumbing." Gemma laughed and wiped a tiny tear from the surface of her cheek. A gust of wind whirled through her hair, whipping her curls into the air.

"Andiamo, amore mio," she said.

"Andiamo, tesoro."

EPILOGUE

GEMMA

Five Months Later

"You're sure that's not an ocean?" asked Jonas, looking out over Lake Michigan.

"Just a freshwater lake. A big one. Some might even say a great lake."

"But it's so large. I can't see anything but water out there."

"Taste it if you don't believe me."

"I'm not going to taste the lake. Besides, it's frozen here on the shore."

"Then you'll have to take my word for it."

Jonas and I walked on the beach, which was a mixture of sand and rocks covered by patchy snow.

"You have a mini ocean just kilometers from your home," said Jonas. "I like this."

It was Jonas's first visit to my hometown since we'd met, and he'd wanted to stop by the lake when he saw it out of the window of the car. "But let's go to your place."

It was a ten-minute drive to my house, and I was nervous as

we turned into the long gravel driveway. I put the car in park and Jonas quickly jumped out. He had my door open for me as soon as I'd turned off the engine. I climbed out from the driver's seat and he kissed me, his lips already chilly from the January air. While he collected his bags, I tried to come to terms with the reality of Jonas Hellgren in my front yard.

"You're an anatopism," I told him.

He cocked his head to one side. "Is that a cousin of the platypus?"

"It's like an anachronism, but with place instead of time." I was used to Jonas in Sweden. Or in London, where we'd spent a few weeks in November. Or even in New York City, where we'd met up over Christmas while he did some work. But Jonas at my house was going to take some getting used to.

He smiled, and his eyes sparkled and shone. "I've missed you. Let's go inside."

I UNLOCKED the front door and opened it for Jonas, who lingered at the threshold.

"May I come in?" he asked.

"Shit. Did you get turned into a vampire since I last saw you?"

He bit his lip on purpose, displaying his sharp incisor. Butterflies launched in my stomach.

"You may enter."

Jonas leapt through the door and kicked it shut with his foot while grabbing me in a tight embrace. "I don't like being away from you," he said in between kisses on my neck. "It's been too long."

"It's been two weeks!"

"Like I said, too long." He kissed me on the mouth but then pulled away with a gasp. "Shit. I'm sorry." He bent to remove his shoes.

"I promise that wearing shoes in the house isn't as big of a deal here as it is in Sweden."

"I hear your words, but I don't understand them," he said.

"Fine." I unlaced my boots and tossed them by the door.

Jonas stood in the living room and waited for instructions.

"I'll give you the tour," I said. As I showed him through the house, I tried to imagine what it looked like through his eyes. Small? Modest? Messy? He held his arms behind his back and walked slowly through the rooms, as if he was in a museum. He studied the art on the walls, lightly touched the arm of a chair, closed his eyes as he stood in my bedroom.

He caught sight of the spider plant soaking up the last few rays of sunlight in my bedroom window. He pinched one of the leaves and gently moved it up and down, as if shaking someone's hand. "The man of the house. Nice to meet you, Louis. I've heard a lot about you."

We finished the tour in the kitchen where Jonas sat at the table and ran his hands along the wooden top. "It's beautiful, Gemma."

"What's beautiful? The table?"

"Well, yes, the table. But I mean all of it. Your house. It's so warm. Comfortable. Unique. It's just lovely. I'm glad to be here." He reached up and pulled me into his lap. He kissed me gently, his lips now warm and soft. I always felt a little shy after I hadn't seen Jonas for a while, but his kisses brought me right back into him; into us. He felt familiar all over again and I wanted to take him back to the bedroom where we could really remember each other. I was discovering that long-distance relationships were frustrating, but the sex upon reuniting was always spectacular.

"Now we need to go back outside," he said as he pulled away from the embrace.

"Why would we do that?" I kissed him again, the bedroom still on my mind.

"I'd like to see where the monsters were. Can you show me?"

"Now? It'll be dark soon. And did you notice that it's a wee bit chilly out there?"

"I'm Swedish," he said, like that should alleviate all my concerns.

I thought about it for a few moments. "If I take you outside, can we go to bed when we get back?"

"We can go to bed, and stay in bed," he said, and he kissed me again.

We bundled up and put our shoes back on. "If we'd just left them on in the first place, we could've saved several minutes," I told him.

"Nonsense."

OUTSIDE, the sky was navy blue and violet with streaks of orange and pink. "It's gorgeous here," he said, taking a deep breath of the twilight air.

First up was the field, where I used to worry about coming upon slithering serpents. It was now a barren patch with short, dried grass and snowy dirt as its main features. "My neighbor mows it for me at the end of fall, so it isn't much to look at right now," I said.

"No monsters here."

"None. Let's walk to the creek." We held hands as we walked, and even though our gloves prevented our skin from touching, I felt an electricity pass between us. "That's the creek down there," I said, pointing to a grove of trees downhill from where we stood. Our boots crunched across the icy ground as we stepped over rocks and roots. The creek was frozen and quiet, and we stood quietly in the valley, listening to the wind move through the trees.

"Any monsters here?" Jonas asked.

"Monster-free."

"We're making quick work of this. One more stop."

"If we walk along the creek, the woods will get thicker," I said. "I'll take you to where I used to build forts in the summers."

"THERE'S something I wanted to tell you," said Jonas. We worked our way across my property. "And I thought it might be better in person."

"That doesn't sound good."

"No, it's fine. It is. It's just . . . weird."

"You aren't allowed to give me any bad news at my own house, so tread carefully, Hellgren."

"I had lunch with Freja last Saturday," he blurted out, like he'd been holding on to a heavy secret.

"You did?"

Jonas studied my face as if searching for a clue about my feelings on the subject. "Yes. We were both in Stockholm and she texted and asked if I'd like to meet. I was already at my hotel restaurant, and she was a few blocks away, so I said it was okay. She showed up a few minutes later and we had lunch, and it was fine . . . she was much more balanced, as you know, and she'd wanted to apologize in person, and I should've asked you first, maybe, if you felt alright about it, but it was such short notice and—"

It was fun watching Jonas run at the mouth and wring his hands, but I decided to put him out of his misery. "I already know about your lunch with Freja," I said. His mouth fell open a little and he seemed confused.

"What do you mean?"

"I mean I know because Freja texted me and asked me if it was okay with me."

"Freja texted you?"

"She did."

Jonas stared at me with a blank expression on his face.

"She sent me a letter about a week ago. Actually, she wrote it a month ago, but she sent it to Rava for approval. Rava held on to it for a few weeks and then decided to send it on."

"Wow," said Jonas.

"So, as you know, she's doing a lot better. And she's making amends. I texted her after I read the letter, and now we text from time to time."

"You text with Freja?"

"Yep. Like I said, I'm not a grudge holder."

"But you didn't tell me!"

"Thought it would be better in person," I said. Jonas huffed out a laugh that turned into a puff of steam and floated off in the cold air.

"I can't really argue with that reasoning."

"I guess this would also be a good time to tell you that I had Derek out to the house last week. He was in Detroit for work and made the drive over. We had a nice time—"

"Derek Drach was at your house?" Jonas's eyes flashed and I could've sworn that I saw his chest puff up under his winter coat.

"Yes. What's wrong?"

"Nothing's wrong. I'm just surprised. He was kind to you?"

"More or less. He did get a little handsy at one point—" Jonas moved to interject, but I couldn't let him suffer much longer. "I'm just kidding, but it was fun to see your reaction."

"God, Gemma, you're awful," Jonas said, reaching out to grab me, but I took off running and made him chase me through the woods.

I didn't get very far before Jonas caught up and captured me, bringing me close as he tried to wrap his arms around the bundled-up version of me. My lips were numb, but I kissed him anyway.

"I don't have a flashlight. We need to get back soon."

"Gemma Lane! I thought you never left home without one."

"I'm getting lazy in my old age. I didn't bring condoms, either."

"We're totally unprepared."

We were deep in the grove of trees, and something rustled about twenty feet away. It was getting darker, and it was hard to make out shapes among the tree trunks. An owl hooted.

"Uh-oh," said Jonas.

"Don't worry. We only have benevolent owls in my woods. Not those assassins you breed in the North."

"I doubt the rodent population feels the benevolence of which you speak."

The sound came again, but louder. Jonas stepped in front of me, putting himself between me and the noise. Then the sounds of rushing, rumbling, stumbling whirled around us, and Jonas backed us up, trying to get away from what felt like a stampede of ghosts. Something large loomed in front of us, its shape taking form in the forest.

"You weren't kidding about the monsters," Jonas said in a whisper so slight I could barely hear it.

My eyes adjusted and the creature came into focus. A buck stood before us, close enough that I could see hot breath steaming from its nostrils. A flash of movement behind the stag caught my eye. I hadn't noticed her before, but a doe stood a few feet back, sniffing the night air. Up close, the deer seemed enormous. Neither Jonas nor I moved or made a sound. The doe flitted off deeper into the wood, and after a moment the male followed. The sounds of their feet on the forest floor faded away, leaving us with just the sound of bare branches creaking in the wind.

"The world's third most dangerous mammal is intense," Jonas said. "I'm definitely going to map that monster for the both of us."

"Jonas?"

Jonas turned to face me. His nose and cheeks were bright from the cold. "Think we're done out here?"

"Come on up to the house." I hooked my arm through his and we walked up the hill and against the wind to the home that was warmly waiting.

ACKNOWLEDGMENTS

In the summer of 2023, my ten-year-old son asked me to tell him one of my lifelong dreams. "To write and publish a book," I said. He considered my answer for a moment and asked, "Then why haven't you done it?" I had no reply. Why hadn't I?

In September of that year, I sat down and started writing. Two months later, I'd written this novel, but I still had to publish it.

Thank you to everyone who helped this book, and my dream, become a reality.

Special thanks to my husband David, who never doubted me, always encouraged me, and helped make this book the best it could be. To Terra for cheering me on from the very first sentence and for reading the manuscript again and again so I'd get it right. I couldn't have done it without you! To Laura-Rose for your edits and for asking important questions and making me push harder. To Cara for saving the cover, bringing a new level of fun and beauty to the book, and for championing me whole-heartedly. To Jen and Katie for being so excited about the book and offering enthusiastic and hilarious feedback. To Jonathan for reading early drafts and telling me that "every scene is vivid and radiant with emotion" and that it was more fun to read than *Reaganland*! To Jennie for keeping an eye out for signs from the universe and being my sounding board. And to the rest of my friends and family who have been so gracious with their words of support for me and my book.

I wouldn't have predicted that my first novel would be a romance, but now that it's written, I wouldn't have it any other way. Romance readers are voracious, kind, curious, and supportive, and I'm excited to put this book out for them. I had so much fun writing about love and all the twists and turns that come with it.

My next life dream: Write and publish LOTS of books.

Megan Moores is a writer, reader, and caretaker of many creatures. She holds degrees in Creative Writing and Teaching from the University of of Arkansas, and especially loves reading Romance, Nordic Noir, Police Procedurals, and Southern Gothic novels. She currently lives in Indiana with her husband, four children, four cats, two fish, and one giant Labrador Retriever.

meganmoores.com
https://meganmoores.substack.com